Joss Wood loves books, c[...] the wild places of South[...] She's a wife and a mom[...] bossed around by two cat[...] size of a small cow. After a career in local economic development and business, Joss writes full-time from her home in KwaZulu-Natal, South Africa.

https://josswoodbooks.com

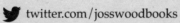

🐦 twitter.com/josswoodbooks
f facebook.com/josswoodbooks
📷 instagram.com/josswoodbooks

CONFESSIONS OF A CHRISTMASHOLIC

JOSS WOOD

One More Chapter
a division of HarperCollins*Publishers* Ltd
1 London Bridge Street
London SE1 9GF
www.harpercollins.co.uk
HarperCollins*Publishers*
Macken House, 39/40 Mayor Street Upper,
Dublin 1, D01 C9W8, Ireland

This paperback edition 2023

2

First published in Great Britain in ebook format
by HarperCollins*Publishers* 2023
Copyright © Joss Wood 2023
Joss Wood asserts the moral right to be identified
as the author of this work

A catalogue record of this book is available from the British Library

ISBN: 978-0-00-865557-0

Printed and bound in the UK using 100% Renewable Electricity
by CPI Group (UK) Ltd

Katherine Garbera, thanks for being on the other side of a Whatsapp message, five days a week. I'm not sure how I lucked out on getting you as a writing partner, but I'm so grateful I did!

Chapter One

'I love you, you love meeeeee…'

Sutton Alsop couldn't remember the next line to the song she'd sing to her younger half-siblings and wrinkled her nose. Given she'd belted it out about a million times, it should be burned on her mental hard drive. Maybe if she tried again. 'I love you, you love me…'

Nope, nothing. She couldn't retrieve it. But if one's brain only had space for x amount of data, she didn't mind sending the song to her mental recycle bin. God bless the purple dinosaur, but if she never heard it again, it would be too soon.

Fascinated by the fluffy snowflakes, snow wasn't big in Africa, Sutton tried to capture one on her tongue but her aim, thanks to numerous shots of tequila – four? Maybe five? – she missed and the snowflake drifted past and fell to the ground, where it instantly melted. Aw…bye, beautiful snowflake.

Sutton adjusted the straps of her bulging backpack. It seemed a lot heavier now she was drunk than when she was sober. Her boots had also acquired steel soles and her coat was lined with lead. God, she was tired. Cold, drunk, tired and broke...she'd hit the trifecta. No, a trifecta in a horse race was three, and a superfecta was four selections. Huh, so she *had* learned something from her ramblin', gamblin' stepdad. Either way, she was four for four.

Where was Jason's uncle's house? It felt like she'd been walking for hours, and miles. All she wanted was a bed, even a couch would do, and a tall glass of water to dilute the felony juice swishing in her stomach. Free booze was always dangerous, she *knew* two shots were her limit. Bad girl.

Sutton squinted at the steep hill and saw blazing lights in the distance. Was that a landing strip for a spaceship or laser show? Either would be cool. She peered through the trees, and it took her a while to realise it was just a house covered in Christmas lights. No, covered was the wrong word, smothered was better. Damn, she was pretty sure the place could be seen from space.

It was totally Conningworth's Christmas House, no doubt about it! Earlier in the pub, there'd been a lively discussion about the highly decorated house. According to the locals, Mr Christmas, the owner of the year-round Christmas shop in town, had finally finished decorating his house for the holidays a few days before – roughly a month before Christmas! – and it was, so they said, his best display yet. Sutton winced, relieved she didn't have to foot the bill for his electric consumption. But hey, at least the whole town would get to enjoy the Vegas-like display without breaking the bank themselves.

She could easily imagine Mr Christmas, he'd be a little fusty and a lot musty. Aged somewhere between sixty and dead, he'd smell of peppermints and old books, his faded corduroy trousers held up by suspenders, leather patches on the elbows of his ancient tweed jacket. Wire-rimmed spectacles, slightly battered but well-loved, held together with tape would sit midway down his long nose. And those eyebrows of his? Oh, they would be awesome! All scratchy and white and bushy, resembling puffed-up, utterly terrified caterpillars.

She'd passed his quaint, old-world but closed Christmas shop earlier, its bow-fronted display windows puke-pretty. Sutton didn't do Christmas, but she did do money. So in the morning she'd see if Mr Christmas, maybe, had a job for her at his little store during what had to be his busiest time of the year. Sutton hoped she wouldn't have to know any Christmas facts or sing carols to land the job. Christmas wasn't that big a deal in the Alsop house, or any kind of deal, and she and Layla usually found a bar and got hammered. They routinely spent Christmas day on a beach nursing their hangovers.

Layla, best friend. Betrayer? No, she wouldn't think of Layla right now. If she did, her tears would freeze on her face.

'This little light of mine,' Sutton sang, trudging up the hill to the Christmas house. Somewhere along this road was the house she'd occupy – squatting was such an ugly word – until Christmas Eve. She loved her friend, Jason, she really did. She loved Jason's uncle for being a ship's entertainer and for him being in the Caribbean for most of December, more.

'I'm going let it shi-*i*-ine.'

That song was a Christmas carol, right? Or was it a hymn? No, 'Hallelujah' was a hymn… 'Now I've heard there was a secret chord…'

Nope, Leonard Cohen's brilliant classic didn't mention Christmas. And if it didn't have Christmas in it, then it couldn't be a carol, right? Right. God, this hill! How steep was it, a thousand and twenty degrees? Everest steep? *Jeez.* Sutton stumbled over a rock and weaved on her feet, her backpack going one way and her body the other. Whoo boy!

Sutton closed one eye and scowled at the dim glow of the nearest streetlight, thinking it did a crappy job of illuminating the road ahead.

When the world stopped shifting under her feet, she started walking again, her attention caught by her breath mixing with the cold air. She puffed hard, entranced by the silver light shooting out from her mouth, fairies dancing on a light beam. Man, she was soooo pissed.

Feeling hot, Sutton undid the buttons of her heavy coat and yanked her beanie off her head. She shoved it into her coat pocket, pulled her gloves off with her teeth and pushed her fingertips into her hot cheeks. How could her skin be so cold when she felt like her inner thermostat was turned to hell high? And how much further did she have to walk?

Her calf muscles wanted to quit, and her back threatened to go into a spasm.

Think about something else, Alsop. How did she distract her siblings when they were fractious? She'd sing to them, or play word games, Simon Says or I Spy, or musical cushions.

'Jack and Jill went up a hill...'

Was that really the best she could do? She decided on a tongue twister, her brothers loved those, the grosser the better. Damn, she missed those little buggars!

'If a dog chews shoes, whose shoes does he choose?' was what she meant to say but it came out sounding like *dogshooshooshoochoo.*

Maybe she had tequila tongue. She needed to check, *immediately*! Stopping halfway up the hill and bending forward to keep her pack balanced, Sutton pushed out her tongue and tried to grab it with her index finger and thumb. After several attempts, she managed to snag it and stood there for a minute, trying to remember why she was gripping her tongue, afraid to let it go.

Maybe she had sudden onset Alzheimer's. That would be bad. Very bad.

A dog barked in the distance, and Sutton yanked in her tongue. Unfortunately, her coordination skills were a little off and she snapped her teeth too soon. She howled in agony when her incisor caught the edge of her tongue. Sutton yelped and slapped her hand over her mouth, dancing on the spot, her yelping muffled by her hand.

Owowohshitowowow...

Sutton tasted blood and swiped her hand over her tongue. *Ugh.* Unlike earlier in the pub, she was *not* having any fun out here. She should've stayed in the Wailing Ghost…wrong. The Ghostly Wail? More wrong. Anyway, she should've stayed in the pub, but they'd called last shout and she had to leave. The very cute bartender – after every tequila, his resemblance to Tom Holland grew stronger – flirted with her, constantly refilling her shot glass and handing her slices of lemon. It would've been rude to refuse. He said something about him being the pub owner's son and he'd comp her the drinks. He also offered to take her home and show her a good time, naked.

Sadly, while she knew her way around a tequila, she'd forgotten how to navigate one-night stands. Plus, she was plastered, and come on, she wasn't exactly a spring chicken anymore. Tiptoeing upstairs, trying not to disturb sleeping parents? Pass.

Onwards, Alsop! Sutton looked around to orientate herself – right, she was going up the hill! She lifted one heavier-than-before foot, then another. The cutie bartender – Harry? Gary? – was, at most, nineteen or twenty, just a little younger than her youngest brother, Brynn. Had he been older, with his own place, she might've considered it. Not for the sex but because, God, there was little she wouldn't give to snuggle down into a pair of muscled arms, to lay her head against a wide chest, to hear a rough and growly voice tell her everything was okay. She hadn't had that for so long…no, she'd never had it. She'd rested her head on a

6

couple of chests but, come morning, they were usually gone. Or she was.

Her lovers weren't good at sticking around. And neither was she. As she knew, the thinnest strands of love or affection could quickly thicken to ropes and chains. She'd been tied down as a teenager and a young adult and she didn't like being unable to move.

A gust of wind, sneaking under the coat of her collar, sent chills down Sutton's neck. A head-to-toe shiver racked her body. She looked down and frowned. Why was her coat open and why wasn't she wearing any gloves? Jamming her hands into the pockets of her too-thin puffer jacket, she bent her head, her footsteps echoing on the quiet country lane.

God, it was so quiet. Serial killer quiet.

Killers didn't live in Conningworth, an isolated and very lovely town in the Lake District. She hoped. But someone with serial killer-ish tendencies could easily fly under the radar here. He, or she, could live as a teacher or a church elder, or a shopkeeper, with no one suspecting they kept eyeballs in jars in the garden shed. Or that their massive train set stood in front of a door to a secret room that held a hospital bed and eyeball-removing instruments. Right, now she was scaring herself. Sutton's eyes darted from one side of the road to the other, looking for shadows behind the snowbanks, listening for a heavy breather. But all she could hear was her own laboured pants. Lugging herself up this goddamn-it-to-hell steep hill had her sounding like a hippo with emphysema. She needed to get fit.

But fitness fell way down on her priority list. Waaay down. Housing and feeding herself occupied the top spots.

The road levelled out and Sutton released a thankful sigh. It was also a lot brighter up here, thanks to the light pouring from the Christmas-house-from-Vegas a hundred yards away. Where was Jason's uncle's place? She narrowed her eyes and trudged on, taking in the spectacle.

It looked like a light factory had vomited its contents all over the building and the lawn. *Dear God*. Sutton stopped, taking in the dizzyingly festive house. Underneath the twinkling lights was a standard two-storied house with a slate roof, and what she thought was a painted black, or maybe navy blue, front door and cottage pane windows. When stripped of its cascade of lights, it would be just another reasonably sized country house in a small, rural English village.

But thousands of fairy lights adorned the roofline, window frames and the edges of the gutters, and Sutton lifted her hand to shade her eyes. Honestly, it was enough to cause an epileptic to fit.

The front garden was even worse than the house. Multicoloured string lights illuminated the neatly trimmed hedges and encircled mature trees. The trunks and branches of a few trees were wrapped in warm white lights, acceptable, while others boasted an eye-blistering medley of red, green, blue and yellow hues. Red and white light-up candy canes, interspersed with neon snowmen and reindeer, lined the path to the front door. Two brightly decorated Christmas trees sat in matching bright red pots on either side of the door. And if that wasn't enough, a ten-foot-high inflatable Santa, looking a little grotesque and utterly creepy, squatted on the lawn, like it was about to take a…

You're drunk, Sutton, there's no need to be vulgar. Keep it tidy, chicken.

Sutton blinked. A man – a rather dishy one – landed a dropkick on Santa's temple. Then another one. Seriously? Tequila wasn't her friend, but it never made her hallucinate before. Thinking she might forget this in the morning, Sutton opened her phone and started filming Conningworth's equivalent to John Wick. It would be a fun clip to put online. Maybe it would go viral and gain her more followers. Like, more than the twenty she had at the moment. A great-looking guy beating the crap out of a fake Santa…good for a couple of likes, right?

His fist rocketed into Santa's stomach, his knee into his kidney. The man, mid to late thirties, with shoulders as wide as Canada – she was a huge fan of tight, long-sleeved T-shirts and straight-legged track pants – looked to be in his mid-thirties, maybe a little older but he was fit. Properly fit…muscly, brawny and ripped. Unlike her: she was skinny unfit. And despite landing some massive blows, the guy wasn't even breathing heavily.

Unlike Sutton. After walking up *that* hill, she needed an oxygen tank and, possibly, a defibrillator.

'I fucking hate Christmas and I hate Kate's Christmas Shop! I fucking hate Christmas decorations and I fucking hate December!'

Preach it, brother.

He landed a series of kicks on Santa's hip, one after another while standing on one leg – how did he do that? – and Sutton envied him his balance. How was hers? She lifted her right foot two inches off the ground, and she wobbled, her pack swaying as the world tilted. She dropped her foot, the world stabilised itself and she gripped the straps of her backpack. *No sharp and sudden movements, Alsop.*

But she did envy him for having a convenient punching bag. And she didn't blame him for kicking the crap out of Santa, as he'd yet to drop his shit-eating smirk. She cocked her head to the side. The inflatable was huge, but he wasn't going down. Hot and Cross looked like he could do with some help.

She could kick. And punch. Okay, not well, she had ramen-noodle arms, but it was the thought that counted, right? She could be his Hot Guy's wingwoman, his backup plan, someone to help inflict a little more pain.

Santa was going *down*, baby.

'Hey, do you need some help?' she called, allowing her pack to drop to the grassy pavement.

He whipped around, as fast as the wind, immediately lifting his fists and bouncing on his toes. She raised her hands and stepped onto the path. 'Whoa, Rocky, I'm on your side. I can help you beat up Santa.'

'What?' he demanded, hoisting up the sleeves of his T-shirt to reveal very nice, muscled forearms. His forehead glistened with sweat, there were damp patches on his shirt, under his arms and spreading over his chest, and she figured he'd been at it for a while.

Not fair. He could've waited for her. She'd had a crappy day, a crappy month. She needed an outlet for her frustration too. 'Can I have a go?'

'Who the hell are you and where did you come from?'

'I'm a resident of the world and a traveller of its lands,' she grandly declared. She was also a little – or massively – drunk and didn't want to explain she was about to sneak into one of his neighbours' houses – what number was this house and where was Sunshine Cottage? – to misappropriate a bed. Not her finest moment, but she was out of options. She gestured to the inflatable. 'Lemme have a go.'

'Are you pissed?' he demanded, frowning. In the light coming from the godawful decorations, she saw thick, dark eyebrows pull down. That was quite a scowl. She couldn't see him clearly and wished she could: she suspected his face matched his rather spectacular body. She needed to know if it did, but she couldn't see from where she stood on the wet road. And there was no way she could punch Santa from here. She needed to hit the fat old bastard. Hell, she needed to smack *someone*. Pretty much anyone would do.

Sutton's genius plan to reach Hot Guy and Santa faster was to take a shortcut by cutting across the lawn. She veered off the road and onto the path and came to an impenetrable wall of neon candy canes and snowmen. Undeterred, Sutton plunged into the candy cane, reindeer and snowmen maze, determined to find a way through.

Crap, why were there sneaky electrical cables lying around? Whoops! Her feet got tangled in the cables, and suddenly her body was on the move while her feet struggled to catch up.

Out of the corner of her eye, Sutton noticed a couple of snowmen and candy canes taking flight. Hot Guy shouted what she thought might be a warning. *Too little, too late, dude!* She heard his filthy curse as the brick path rose to French kiss her face.

Ah, *man*. This would hurt.

And then all the lights went out.

———

Right, *shit.*

Gus Langston dropped to his knees and cast a glance at his now dark house. He didn't need to be an electrician to realise he'd blown a fuse or five.

He pulled his phone from his pocket, activated the torch and pointed it at the girl who'd, somehow, ended up faceplanting on his grass. Had she passed out? Hurt herself? Did he need to call an ambulance?

He heard a soft giggle, then another, and he released a long sigh. Right, if she was laughing then she was fine. He placed a hand on her shoulder and helped her roll over, keeping the torch angled so it wasn't shining into her eyes, deep brown or black. She wasn't as young as he initially thought. The fine lines next to her eyes suggested she was in her mid-to-late twenties, older than most backpackers who came through his adventure tour company. Straight nose, a wide mouth, and a scrape on her cheek where she'd caught the edge of the paving. That was going to hurt when she sobered up.

'Hello, Rocky,' she murmured, in a surprisingly deep voice for so little a person. She couldn't be more than five two or three, although most of her height was in her legs. He glanced at her heavy-looking backpack, surprised she'd lugged it up the hill. She winced and raised her hand to her cheek.

He held up two fingers. 'How many fingers can you see?'

'Six hundred and fifty-two. But don't worry, I couldn't count before I did those tequila shots.' He kept his fingers up and she released an exasperated sigh. 'Two.'

'Are you hurt? Legs? Arms? Did you hit your head?'

She did a snow angel movement, then rolled her head from side to side and up and down. 'Nope, all good.' She looked okay, and her pupils weren't dilated so she wasn't concussed. But he'd give her a minute or two to get her bearings.

'What happened to Vegas?' she asked, turning her head to look at the dark house. Gus balanced on his toes and rested his arm on his thigh.

'You ploughed through the decorations, got tangled up, then tripped and ripped the electrics apart. The fuses blew.'

Her eyes widened in distress. 'I killed your lights? I'm so, so sorry. I mean, I thought about suggesting you take most of them down, because you should stick to white.

13

White is classier, you know. And neon snowmen? The reindeer *and* candy canes? Stick to a theme, I say!'

Excellent, a dissertation on the design. Just what he needed. 'Are you done?' he asked.

'No…well, yes, I suppose so. But I didn't mean to destroy everything.' She lurched up and waved her hands in the air, suddenly agitated. Her accent, distinctively South African, deepened. 'Are they expensive? Do I have to replace them? I don't have any money, so that might be a problem. But do you take IOU's?'

She didn't have any money. Why not? And why was she on this road and where was she going? Moira closed the BnB at the Hall during winter, and she wasn't expecting visitors. If she was, she would've told him. The only other house on this road was Sunshine Cottage, and the boys were only due back tomorrow. If a friend used their place, they usually asked him to do a meet and greet. And, again, they would've sent him an email or a message.

She looked around at the carnage. Admittedly, it was impressive. Santa was rapidly deflating, a couple of snowmen, three reindeer and the candy canes lay on their sides. From what he could see, a couple were broken.

She moaned. 'Oh, it looks like a Christmas hating spree killer targeted your place.' That wasn't a bad description actually. 'I'm so sorry, I just wanted to punch Santa. I'll pay you back—'

'Relax, you blew a fuse or two, you didn't set the place on fire.'

She bit her lip and settled down. Her being on this road,

and carrying a backpack, in the middle of a cold night, made no sense at all. And having no money – even less.

Gus looked at her heart-shaped face and pale skin, her slight but still curvy body, and knew, from a place deep inside him, she was going to be trouble. He had a soldier's instinct for recognising it, and he'd learned, in hard places in foreign lands, to listen to his gut.

Trouble. In capital, bold and six-foot-high letters.

An owl hooted, breaking the still, cold night. He needed to get inside, and so did the sexy stranger He'd make her coffee, sober her up and then he'd find out why she was walking on a dark country road. He held out his hand for her to take but she looked at it and shook her head.

'Life is a bitch,' she declared. Yep, so he'd heard and experienced – in high definition and technicolour. 'I've had more than most to deal with, Rocky.'

Oh, God, she was feeling sorry for herself. Because he'd dealt with more than a few drunks in his time, had been one often enough, he knew the best way to get her moving on was to let her get it out of her system. 'Tell me five bad things that have happened to you in five sentences. And quickly, because it's cold.'

'I was four when my dad left, ten when my stepdad left my mum and me, leaving me to help her raise my much younger brothers. I looked after them, cooked for them, got them to school on time and made sure they did their homework and showered.'

Bad, but not terrible. He was a product of foster and group homes and knew that not everyone was raised easy.

'I had to work to put myself through university, though lots of people do that... So is that a bad thing? Maybe not.' She wrinkled her nose in a way he found quite adorable. *Stop, Langston. She's drunk, and she's vulnerable.*

'That's two. Three more.'

'My best friend was supposed to be on this trip with me, but she backed out, so I'm travelling alone.'

'That's a brave thing to do.' Still nothing too awful so far.

Her face crumpled. 'But then she asked to borrow the bulk of my travelling money, she said she would pay it back in five days.' A tear rolled down her cheek, over her scrape. 'She still hasn't paid me back and I'm broke. And I drank too many tequilas tonight at the pub, HarryGary comped me them.'

Larry was the son of the pub owner, Ian, and Ian would not appreciate him giving away free booze. It was Larry's favourite way to pick up girls, but it hadn't worked on her. He was, for a reason which he didn't want to examine right now, extremely glad about that.

But borrowing money and not repaying it was a shitty thing to do. And bloody dangerous. The older he got, the more people sucked. And they'd sucked plenty before.

'Where were you going tonight...what's your name, by the way?' He doubted she'd remember his name in the morning, but thought he'd give it a shot. 'I'm Gus Langston.'

'Sutton.' Her dark eyes met his, and within them he saw fear and a certain amount of panic. His protective instincts rose, and he fought the urge to take her in his arms and tell her everything would be all right. Kate always said he was a 'fixer', that he had a White Knight complex. At times like this, he suspected she was right. The urge to protect, to shield, was strong.

Was that what pushed Kate away? Caused her to do what she did? Who the hell knew? He'd never get an answer to his questions.

He stood up, gripped her small wrist, and hauled her up, far too easily – the woman needed to eat a few hamburgers! – to her feet.

'So, where were you going tonight?' Had she taken a wrong turn and found herself lost?

'Can't tell you.' She shook her head and her hair, a tumble of blonde and honey, fell out of the messy bun on top of her head. She made a zipping, throw-the-key-away gesture and Gus sighed. He didn't have much patience – almost zero late at night after a full day's work. December was also his least favourite month of the year, one he gritted his teeth through.

He sighed and rubbed the back of his neck. He was now very cold, and he couldn't leave her out here, not until he knew where she was headed. 'Sutton...you *need* to tell me.'

'Can't.' He recognised the stubborn light in her eyes, as he saw it in Rosie, his oldest, more often than he liked. Dammit! What the fuck should he do? Dust her off and send her down the road, to God knows where? Not an option. Call the police and get them to take her in? She'd spend the night in a cell, but she'd be warm and safe for the night.

'The thing is,' she said, on a huge gulp, 'being drunk and disorderly, standing on someone's lawn after destroying their house isn't me! I'm an occupational therapist, I have a degree! In my pack is a folder filled with letters of recommendation to show my prospective employers – I want to get a job in the UK working as an OT, did I tell you that? – how wonderful I am! And I am wonderful! I'm sensible and stable! I shouldn't be broke, drunk, or homeless! I'm nearly twenty-nine years old, dammit!'

He lifted her hand to touch her bright hair, wanting to reassure her, but dropped it before he made contact. She looked so young, so vulnerable and his heart rolled over. Stupid bloody thing.

Get with the program, Langston! She's drunk and maudlin, and, judging by her blue lips, on her way to freezing. He needed to get her inside where it was warm. He aimed his phone to light the path leading to his front door. 'Come inside. No, leave your backpack, I'll get it later.'

More shaking of her head, and she wobbled back and forth. 'No! Someone might steal it! Everything I own is in my pack!'

A fox was more likely to piss on it than it being stolen, but he didn't want to argue with her. He walked over to the pack and hoisted it up and over his shoulder. 'Inside,' he ordered her.

'' Kay.' She looked at the path and swayed. She took a step, then another and stopped. 'The world is spinning,' she told him, her dark eyes even bigger than before. 'I don't like it.'

Yep, too much tequila. The wind lifted the hem of his shirt and its icy fingers danced across his bare stomach. He was tired, pissed off and he needed to change some fuses to get the lights on in his house. He didn't have time to wait for her to stumble and weave her way to his front door.

Bending his knees, he curled his forearm under her butt and lifted her, quickly and easily, up and over his shoulder. He ignored her *'oof'* and strode towards the front door, making quick work of the distance.

Sutton didn't seem remotely fazed at being lugged around.

'Pretty star! And that one has an angel!' Sutton said as he passed between the potted Christmas trees. She reached out to grab the angel on top of the tree on his right, gipped it and the tree came straight out of the pot. *Fuuuuccckkkk.* He ran two businesses and was trying to raise twins as a single dad. He was at his limit for chaos.

Gus opened the front door and dumped Sutton, her backpack, the decorated Christmas tree, it's lights dangling, and its soil onto the carpet in the hall.

Fun times.

Chapter Two

'Is she dead?'

No, but she wants to be.

A finger pulled up her eyelid, and a sharp light hit her eyeball and drilled into her brain. God. *Ow.* Sutton squeezed her eyes shut, her stomach roiling as spiteful gnomes played dodgeball with her brain.

Pain whistled through her, accompanied by a pushing sensation on her upper arm. She lifted her other eyelid a fraction of an inch, and frowned at the toy syringe pressing into her bicep.

'Do we need to draw some blood?'

The voice sounded like one of the Munchkins from *Charlie and the Chocolate Factory*. Sutton was happy to let them proceed, provided they brought her an IV drip of rehydration fluid and morphine to chase away her hangover.

A soda packed full of sugar and caffeine, followed by a

full English breakfast, might also do the trick. Tequila, *you bitch. You aren't my friend, and you didn't make me look cool.*

'I need to hear her breathe.' A little hand snuck under the hem of her sweater and Sutton yanked in her stomach as something cold and plastic touched her lower ribs. Through the slit of her eyes, she saw a golden-haired moppet, three or four, bending over her, the buds of a toy stethoscope in her ears.

Navy blue eyes, the colour of old-fashioned ink, met hers, both concerned and frustrated. 'You've got to breathe in and out,' she bossily informed Sutton. 'How do I know if you are dead or not?'

She was dead. She had to be. Why else would two cherubs, a girl and a boy, be checking her over? Someone had to check people were really dead when they arrived at the pearly gates, right? If not, there would be mass confusion and possibly, overcrowding. Could heaven get overcrowded? Was there a heaven? What happened when you died?

Had she passed over? Where was she?

'The bump on her cheek is a bit blue.' A small finger drilling into her cheek accompanied the pronouncement by the boy cherub. Pain ricocheted from her cheekbone and exploded in her head.

'Owowowow!' Okay, not dead then. She just wished she was.

'She lives.'

This voice was much deeper and darker, like rich

chocolate over brushed steel. Nice. Sutton opened her eyes a little wider, turned her head – painful – and looked past the little boy in a navy sweatshirt into the eyes of the man who had beaten the crap out of Santa last night. Dark hair, not brown but not black, a shade between the two. Another pair of deep blue eyes, as dark as the little girl's, a long nose with two distinct bumps on the ridge and a sexy, sexy mouth.

His thick stubble showed flecks of grey. It was a nice face, attached to a spectacular and, very obviously, fit body. He wore dark jeans, and another thin, long-sleeved T-shirt, this one dark green. Big feet, in battered hiking boots, rested on the coffee table between them. He held a large travel mug in one hand.

The smell of excellent coffee wafted over to her, and Sutton considered mugging him for it. But that would require her to move, and she wasn't up to that yet. She wouldn't be for a few hours. Or days.

Possibly years.

She was warm and this long couch was comfortable. The munchkins could carry on examining her while she was unconscious. Sutton sighed and felt herself sliding off into sleep.

'Oh no you don't,' Deep Voice said, and Sutton felt a big hand on her shoulder shaking her awake. When she finally obeyed his command to wake up, she blinked up at him, thinking his would be a very nice face to wake up to every morning.

'Sutton! You need to wake up and we need to talk.'

She didn't want to. She tried to shake her head. 'So tired.'

'Hungover, you mean,' he shot back, his expression, and his tone, irate. 'You rocked up on my lawn drunk, and stumbled through my Christmas decorations, which you said were tacky.'

That didn't sound like her. She was usually more diplomatic than that. 'I'm sure I didn't,' she weakly protested.

'You said it looked like someone vomited Christmas lights over my house and lawn. And that Vegas called, and they wanted some of their lights back.' *Ugh*. Sutton grimaced. But...*yeah*. In *vino veritas*, or tequila truth.

'I'm so sorry, and so embarrassed.' Sutton bit down on her bottom lip, wishing she had the energy, and the courage, to have this conversation with him sitting up. But that was more than she could manage right now. Apparently, she could slam back tequilas like a '70s rock star, but she couldn't handle her hangover like one.

'Felix and Rosie, go and get your coats, hats and gloves, we're late for school.'

The girl Cherub yanked her stethoscope out of her ears and dropped the buds on Sutton's chest, and boy Cherub let go of her arm. Had he been trying to take her pulse? Or maybe he'd been preparing to open a vein.

Sutton, thinking she might die if she moved her head, moved her eyes and looked up. He – God, what was his name? – picked up a bottle of water from the coffee table and cracked the lid. A broad, strong hand appeared, gripped her elbow and hauled her upright. Her brain bounced off her skull, and Sutton released a low moan.

He pushed the water bottle into her hand and Sutton raised it to her lips, drinking deeply. When she was done, she sent him a tepid smile. 'Thanks, from me and my organs. Look, um, I'm sure you told me, but I can't remember your name.' In fairness, there was a lot she didn't remember about last night.

'Langston, Gus.'

She rested the cool water bottle against her aching head. 'Thank you, Langston, Gus. Did I do anything else last night?'

'Apart from destroying three neon candy canes, two snowmen and one of my potted Christmas trees, and blowing the electrics? No.' She tried to make sense of his words. She'd destroyed them – how? She didn't remember anything after she decided to help him beat up the reason for the season and fell over. She freely admitted she was drunk – far drunker than she normally allowed herself to be – but she didn't think she'd consumed enough to pass out.

'You tripped, fell and smacked your cheek on the path. You came around, and we spoke for about ten minutes, do you remember any of that?'

She grimaced and shook her head. She knew she could be a chatty drunk, so she hoped she didn't indulge in any verbal diarrhoea.

'You couldn't walk in a straight line, so I picked you up and tossed you over my shoulder. You reached for the star on one of the potted Christmas trees and somehow managed to pull it, decorations and all, out of its container. I brought you inside, in the dark, because fuses blew when you tripped over the electric cables.'

She bit her bottom lip. 'Anything else?' She pushed the words over her thick tongue.

'You sang lullabies and kept assuring me everything would be all right.'

The blood drained from her head. Dots appeared in front of her eyes, and she swayed. A hard, strong hand on her shoulder kept her from toppling sideways.

Trying to ignore the heat from his hand, she stared down at her fingers tapping her dirt-stained jeans. When she was younger and looking after her siblings, on those nights when times were tight, her mum was short of work and they were in danger of being evicted she recalled the songs her real dad sang to her before he left, trying to find comfort and strength in the few memories she had of him. Thinking of him, singing those lullabies, comforted and reassured her. She, in turn, sang them to her younger brothers when they felt scared, or when they picked up on her or her mum's stress.

Talking about kids...

'The twins are yours?' she asked. She already knew the answer. They both looked like him, although the girl had lighter hair and a rosebud mouth.

'Yeah. They're four,' he replied curtly. 'Felix and Rosie.'

Cute names. Very English. 'I'm Sutton.'

'You told me last night. Sutton Alsop, born in Cape

Town, almost twenty-nine years old.' Did he have to loom over her?

'So I got myself tangled up in the electrical cables, stumbled and tripped, cracked my cheek on a piece of paving, wrecked a Christmas tree, blew the fuses to your house and passed out on your couch. Anything else?'

'I think that covers it.'

She dimly, somewhere back in the fog of last night, remembered him cursing a blue streak. 'You swear pretty well.'

And creatively. If only she could remember some of his more colourful phrases. They might come in handy one day.

'It's amazing what you can learn in the army,' he drily replied.

Sutton cocked her head and tried to nod, but stopped before her chin hit her chest because…*ow*. Yes, she could see him as a soldier, he had the don't-fuck-with-me-or-I'll-fuck-you-right-up vibe down to a tee. Man, he was breathtakingly, panty-meltingly good-looking.

She felt battered and more than a little blue, her head was on the point of exploding and she'd been an absolute muppet, but she wouldn't mind seeing this man naked. He'd be glorious…

Sutton fought the urge to lie down again. Nauseous and dizzy, she leaned forward and rested her forearms on her knees. Out of the corner of her eye, she saw his long legs and big feet. He was taller than she'd thought, maybe six-three or six-four. A good foot taller than her.

Where was Mrs Hot Guy? Was she out of town? Were they divorced and it was his week to have the kids?

He raked his hand through his hair and threw an impatient glance at his watch. 'Twins! We're leaving!' he bellowed.

Sutton clutched her head. Fu-fudging-*fuck*. Was he trying to kill her? She swallowed her moan. Every sound was amplified and even the clatter of tiny feet in the hall hurt her bruised brain. God, she felt rough.

'Dad, I can't find my shoes!' Male Cherub, or baby devil, shouted.

'Daddy, my ribbon is falling out of my hair. I need to kiss Pepper. Felix, where's Pig?'

'I let him out. He told me he needed to go pee.'

Sutton heard Gus's deep groan and saw him tip his head up to the ceiling and close his eyes. Dark, stubby eyelashes lay against his skin. 'Daddy's going to yell at you,' Rosie told her brother, sounding gleeful. 'Daddy, Pig is in the garden.'

'*Fuck.*'

Sutton's eyes shot up at his just audible curse. He slapped his hands on his hips. 'Felix, how many times have I told you not to let him out? Am I just talking to myself?' he demanded, his raised voice taking on a hard edge.

Felix popped his head around the door, his expression angelic. 'We've got a cake sale at school today,' he said, in an obvious ploy to change the subject. 'Can I have some money?'

'Pepper, give me a kiss!' Rose shouted.

'This house is a shitshow this morning. To be fair, it's a shitshow most mornings.' Hot Guy – Gus – slipped his phone into the back pocket of his dark jeans and snagged a set of car keys out of the shallow dish on the coffee table. The dish also held a half-eaten tennis ball, a pair of kid's sunglasses and a plastic medicine spoon, as well as a gas bill. Sutton counted about five pounds in coins in there as well.

'I'm taking the kids to kindergarten,' Gus told her, his voice low and determined. 'I'll be about forty minutes. I want you out by the time I get back.'

His statement was not unexpected. After all, she'd been drunk, and definitely disorderly, on his lawn the night before. She was lucky he'd brought her inside and allowed her to sleep on his sofa. He could've woken her up and sent her on her way. She might've ended up sleeping in a hedgerow and dealing with hypothermia this morning.

Or adjusting to being dead.

Sutton nodded her head. Fair enough. 'Yeah, I'll get out of your hair.'

He opened his mouth to say something, shut it quickly and nodded. Picking up a leather and sheepskin bomber jacket from the back of the chair he'd occupied, he strode into the hall, calmly issuing orders.

'No, you *can't* kiss Pig goodbye, Rosie, he's outside. I'll deal with him when I get back.'

'Is the lady going to be here when we get home from school, Dad?'

He stood on the other side of the wide-open French

doors and his eyes slammed into hers. Sutton felt pinned to her seat by the intensity of his hard blue gaze. 'She most certainly will *not*. If she is, she'll be in more trouble than she already is.' Gus scowled at her. 'Don't piss me off further by stealing anything.'

Huh! She managed a what-the-hell scowl. She was broke, in a stupidly tight spot, but she wasn't a thief. Sutton considered defending herself but decided she didn't have the energy. She simply prayed Jason's uncle's house, the house she had planned on temporarily, secretly, occupying for the next three weeks, was a lot further down the road from this one, preferably out of sight.

She had no intention of running into Hot Guy and his Cherubs again.

The front door opened, and Gus ushered his kids outside. The door slammed shut and Sutton cocked her head, waiting to hear his car reversing down the drive before pushing herself off the couch. Every muscle screamed in protest and a million fire ants started snacking on her brain. She wouldn't go looking for cash or steal the silver, but she *would* raid a bathroom cabinet for aspirin.

Feeling the room spin, she decided to lie down for five more minutes.

After making sure that the twins were safely buckled into their car seats, Gus reversed down his driveway, his mind on the blonde on his couch.

He had a *blonde* on his *couch*. For the first time in three years, he'd had another woman who wasn't his wife in his house.

Gus had no idea how to feel about that.

Because he kept an eye on Will and Eli's house, he crawled past their too-sweet, too-charming cottage, not noticing anything amiss. There was minimal crime in this part of the country, but he'd seen enough of the crappier side of life to know that an empty house, even in a rural setting, was an attractive prospect for thieves or squatters.

His neighbours would be back today, and Gus let out a sigh of relief. When Will and Eli were home, he had a fraction more freedom than he usually did, as the boys were always happy to have the kids over.

It also meant he could go down to the pub or go into Kestell for a hook-up without asking Moira to babysit. Kate had been dead for a few years, but it still felt tacky to ask her mum to babysit his kids when he wanted some naked action.

He did it, but it wasn't something he enjoyed.

Gus swung his SUV into the High Street, crawling along behind the other cars heading for the kids' school on the outskirts of the village. The twins spent the bulk of the day there, and he normally collected them around five, unless he had to keep the shop open for a bus full of tourists.

Kate's Christmas Shop was his shop, open all year round. It did a fair trade in summer when you couldn't move for tourists in the Lake District, but many people, locals and tourists alike, flocked to the shop in December.

They spent more at this time of the year too, carried away by the festive spirit and charmed by the free hot cocoa and shortbread biscuits he provided.

He came to the intersection, and looked left, as he always did. *Kate's Christmas Shop.* The sign was old fashioned, curly red writing on a white shingles board, as was the shop with its two bay windows, a fat, highly decorated Christmas tree in each. The premises for his adventure tour company were right next door, and he moved between the two businesses through an interconnecting door in the storerooms. For most of the year, he and his guides provided adventure activities for the tourists. Rock climbing, hiking, kayaking and SUP-ing for groups and individuals. But in December, when only the hardiest outdoor adventurers wanted to be out on the fells in the wind, rain and snow, the indoor climbing wall picked up but adventure business slowed down, and he switched his attention to Kate's Christmas Shop.

It had been Kate's idea to open the year-round shop, and she'd planned it, as she had planned everything, with meticulous detail. She'd been a week away from opening when she died in a car accident outside Manchester – she'd been on a buying trip, acquiring the last of her stock so that she could be ready for the grand opening the following Saturday. Nobody in the village could believe it when they heard that their beloved Katie skidded off the road and hit a barrier. The twins were a year old when she died, and he was left with two babies and two businesses to run.

And a broken heart. And, although no one else knew it, a broken marriage.

He heard the twins arguing about something and decided it wasn't vociferous or ugly enough for him to intervene. Pulling off, he lifted his hand to wave at Jim, who ran their village shop, and smiled at old Miss Porter's dachshund trying to keep up with her long-legged stride.

Conningworth, this tiny village situated between his beloved fells and the always lovely Lake Conningworth – yeah, his wife's family once owned *everything* around here – was home and had been since he met Kate, the Baroness of Conningworth.

'Daddy, why was that lady on our couch? And why did she have an owie on her cheek?' Rosie asked.

And he was back full circle to the blonde on the couch.

'She fell over last night, baby, and hurt her face.'

Man, that was the understatement of the century. One moment she was standing there, the next minute she was ploughing through his decorations, twisting cables around her legs and face-planting. It all happened within a few seconds and although he started sprinting as soon as she started to topple, he was too far away to stop her from injuring herself.

If she hadn't been as pissed as a frog, she might've done more damage.

He knew nothing more about her than he did last night. He found the folder she mentioned in her backpack and flicked through the thick wad of letters of recommendations – all extolling her virtues – and certified copies of her degree and qualifications, and her latest, very sad, bank statement. A rummage through her over-the-shoulder fanny pack turned up her passport, an old lip gloss and five pounds. He didn't like going through her stuff, but he needed to know whom he was dealing with. He hadn't found any red flags.

But he still didn't know what she was doing on his lane, in his quiet village on a freezing night. He instructed his onboard computer to call his mother-in-law. Was she still his mother-in-law if Kate was dead? Did it matter? Not to him.

Moira answered and the twins squealed, hearing their beloved nan's voice. Moira was a great granny and Gus was grateful for her support these past few years. Yeah, she still thought, as did the village, that his and Kate's relationship was the love story of the century, but that was okay. He'd been blindsided by the events surrounding her death and still didn't know the truth about her, or their marriage. The one thing he was sure of was that Kate loved Christmas, and his getting involved in the village's Christmas festivities was his way to hang onto something he admired about Kate. It was his way to keep the anger, and resentment, from overwhelming him.

'Can you talk, Moira?'

'Absolutely, darling. I'm having a lovely lie-in. It's the best thing about not having any guests.'

To keep Conningworth Hall standing, Moira – helped by Kate before her death – turned the manor house into a B&B and a venue for events. The hall hosted weddings and corporate team events, and his company frequently provided teambuilding challenges.

Moira's statement indirectly answered his question. The blonde on his couch hadn't been making her way up to the hall. But he thought he should make sure. 'So you didn't get a call to take in a stray guest last night?'

'No.'

Right. So where the hell had Sutton been going? The lane led nowhere…

'I really enjoyed the pictures of the Christmas lights on your house, Gus,' Moira said, with laughter in her voice. 'The twins did a fine job directing operations.'

'Didn't it look great, granny?' Rosie said. 'What was the big word you used, Daddy?'

Gus looked into the rearview mirror to see his daughter wrinkling her nose. 'I said it looked flamboyant, baby,' he murmured. Sutton was right when she said that it looked like someone vomited Christmas on it, but that's what happened when you gave Rosie a free hand to decorate – or to tell him where to place the lights. Felix, being a boy, spent most of the time kicking around a soccer ball and playing with the animals.

Moira laughed. 'I thought it looked wonderful,' she lied.

Gus knew she'd prefer to see it lit and decorated the way Kate did it every year, according to the detailed list in her Christmas file. Kate was a great planner and list maker. He still ran Kate's Christmas store according to her detailed checklists.

'How are the preparations for the Christmas market coming along?'

Organising the Christmas market was something else he'd inherited from Kate, with the so-called help of a fairly useless village committee. The Christmas shop also had a stall at the market and at some point, he had to think about what he was going to sell, and who was going to run it. Or maybe he should just close the shop for the day. 'Yeah, good.'

Because what else could he say?

How had Kate done it all – had she been superhuman? She'd juggled a million balls and managed to make it look effortless. The only ball she let drop was their marriage... and he'd only realised it the day she died.

'You need to think about a Christmas tree for home,' Moira said. 'I saw a wonderful one on my walk yesterday that would be perfect for your hallway. I can ask Ben to cut it down for you.'

The twins erupted at the idea of a Christmas tree, as she knew they would. Gus narrowed his eyes at his phone and sighed. He'd got away with not having a Christmas tree at home last year – he'd told the twins that Moira needed them to share hers – but he wouldn't be so lucky this year. Or he'd be nagged to death.

It was impossible to explain that Christmas existed outside of his house: everything, from the lights on his house to the Christmas market and everything else Christmas-related, was a part of his life out *there*. Yes, he did it to keep a connection to Kate, to remind himself that his wife wasn't just a…he hauled in a breath and pulled his anger back.

That she wasn't all bad, that she was hardworking, energetic and charismatic, and he wanted to keep Kate's love for this town, and Christmas, alive. But his house was *his*. It was where he cried and raged, and punched walls and questioned himself over and over again. Bringing Christmas inside was like letting her back in…God, it was hard enough keeping photographs of her up for the kids, having to look into her face, stabbing himself with the reminder of what she did.

But his kids deserved a Christmas tree, they deserved a fabulous Christmas. He just didn't know if he could give it to them.

He saw the gates of the twins' school and steered his SUV into the drop-off zone. He told Moira he'd talk to her later and left the car, walking around the bonnet. He saw a couple of mums, dressed in their workout gear – short leather jackets over tight leggings – and wished he had the time to go for a run. He felt their eyes on his arse as he leaned forward to unclip the twins' harnesses. Yep, one word of encouragement and they'd be popping into Kate's Christmas Shop on some pretext or another.

Gus didn't have time to waste but, more importantly, he didn't shit on his own doorstep. And he didn't screw married woman. It was his line in the sand…he'd rather go without or date himself. Felix hopped down by himself and pulled his backpack onto his back. Gus knew that his stubborn son wanted to do it himself and would ask if he needed help. Rosie, on the other hand, tumbled into his arms and he held her for a moment, inhaling her little girl smell.

They all used the same shampoo and soap, the same toiletries but Rosie still smelled girly, sweeter somehow. He placed a kiss on her hair and placed her on her feet.

'I'll see you guys later,' he said, placing his hand on Felix's head.

Rosie placed one hand on her hip and her eyes met his. 'Daddy, don't fight with the lady with an owie, okay?'

He looked at his daughter, who was dressed in black and white tights, yellow rain boots, and her summer short dungarees over a Hello Kitty sweatshirt. She'd dressed herself and Gus winced. But she was warm and that was all that mattered. There were some hills he wasn't prepared to die on. His daughter's fashion sense was one of them.

He watched his kids half-walk, half-run into their small school, grateful they were happy. Two out of three wasn't bad.

Chapter Three

Ten blissfully quiet minutes later, Sutton, still on the couch, turned her head to take in the details of the living room. The bones of the room were good; it was a large space with another set of French doors leading onto what she thought might be a patio and, from there, a large garden. The couch on which she lay was wide, and deep, and the cushion under her head plump. The two deep chairs opposite her were covered in a bold floral fabric. Behind the chairs was a modern credenza, every inch covered in silver-framed photographs, many were of the dark-haired, blue-eyed man and his curly-haired, angelic-looking bride.

So he *was* married. Divorced people didn't display wedding photos. Sutton sat up and wondered where his wife was...why hadn't she seen her this morning. Was she at the gym, or on a business trip? Was she away looking after a sick parent?

Cute kids, by the way. But more than many handfuls. She was glad they weren't hers to raise. She'd done her fair share of wiping snotty noses and packing lunches, supervising bathtimes and reading bedtime stories, talking to teachers and refereeing childish arguments. She might be broke and homeless, but at least she only had to look after herself.

Sutton noticed her phone on the coffee table, and she swiped her thumb over the screen, her heart rate increasing when she saw she had messages. She opened the app and her heart fell when she saw a couple of messages from Alex, the oldest of her three siblings. Her brother was studying aviation engineering in the US – he'd been awarded scholarships to study in the US, the brainiac – but he was also more sensitive and thoughtful than the two younger boys. Seeing that it was a reasonable time in Boston, she initiated a video call, and his lovely face appeared on her small screen. Damn, the little boy whose nose she'd wiped was now a man.

'What the hell happened to your face?' he asked, frowning.

She touched her cheek. 'Would you believe I got drunk, fell over and hurt myself?'

His eyebrows shot up. 'You?' She understood his disbelief. She was the good girl, the one who never got into trouble while she lived at home and, well, if things happened when she left home, then she didn't tell them about her escapades.

They caught up for a couple of minutes, but Sutton

40

quickly saw something was bugging her brother. 'What's up, Alex?'

He rubbed the back of his neck, uncomfortable. 'I could never get anything past you, Sutt. Mum, yes, but you? Never.'

Well, she did spend far more time with her brothers than her mum did. Their mum worked two jobs, sometimes three and when she did have some nights free, she tended to spend them with her girlfriends, telling Sutton she needed 'me' time. That Sutton might need a break from looking after three boys never crossed her mind.

'I haven't been home for three years, Sutt, and I want to get home for Christmas. There's a special on flights from New York to Cape Town—' God, she knew what was coming and her heart plummeted. 'I can put some money toward the flight, but—'

But he didn't have enough. And she couldn't help him. Not this time. A cold hand gripped her heart and squeezed. 'Ah, *bud*—'

She didn't need to finish her sentence, and resignation crossed his face. He was so used to being disappointed, used to not getting what he needed. 'Mum?' she asked.

Alex lifted one shoulder. 'I asked, but she said no. She went on to give me a ten-minute lecture about how much she'd sacrificed being a single mother, how this was her time, and that she expected us to stand on our own two feet.'

Shit. Sutton pushed her fingers into her forehead, red-hot anger washing over her. Their mum didn't make big bucks, but she could put *something* into the pot. If they all did, maybe Alex could come home. But, because Layla cleaned her out, she couldn't help her brother get home. 'Al, I'm so sorry. I would help you if I could, but I'm properly skint at the moment. When I land my new job, I promise I'll pay for a ticket for you to visit me in London.'

He managed a low, still-sad smile. 'Mum's expecting you to pay for hers first.'

She loved her mum, and appreciated how hard she worked and how difficult it was for her to raise four kids as a single parent, but her brothers came first. They always would.

'No worries, I'll be fine. But you need coffee and to find your self-respect, big sis,' he told her, with a teasing grin. 'And I need to go. I need to hit the books.'

She waved a listless hand. 'I love you, kiddo, be safe. And I'm not kidding about the UK visit.'

She recognised his I'll-believe-it-when-it-happens look. Hell, she'd probably taught it to the boy.

Sutton disconnected the call and placed her face in her hands. Guilt rolled over her, hot and acidic. She wasn't his mum, but she *was* his older sister, the person he turned to time and time again. He'd been such a good kid, sensitive and mature, and he helped her out by not being as overly demanding as Brynn, or as wild as Jamie. He just got on with whatever was expected of him, and he never, ever asked for anything. It killed her that she couldn't help him.

And, God, what was wrong with her mother? Why couldn't she see that being a mum didn't end when her kids turned eighteen? Her kids still needed her, but she was on her own mission. She'd fed and clothed them, and that was where her responsibilities to them ended. Her brothers were expected to sort themselves out, and they did, with a little help from their big sister, financial and otherwise, over the years.

She shouldn't be in the UK, why was she on this trip? She was no better than her mum, putting herself front and centre and saying to hell with everyone else. If she'd stayed in Cape Town, she could've helped pay for Alex's ticket home. He was so far away, and being away for so long was hard. She shouldn't be on a six-month holiday, she should've stayed home, employed and financially stable. But a part of her, the selfish, hard part of her, understood her mum's need to be free, and unencumbered. Her mum had her at seventeen, and birthed three more kids before she was thirty-three. Her mum hadn't had a life, but then neither had Sutton. She'd given up so much in her teens and early twenties, dating, partying and being a kid, to look after her brothers. She overdosed on responsibility as a kid, and her needs – emotional and financial – came last. These days, she was only responsible for herself, and she goddamn loved the freedom.

The difference between her and her mum was that she was only their sister, not their mum. But she still experienced a healthy dose of guilt for not doing enough, being enough, and giving enough. This trip was the one thing she'd promised herself, her reward for years and years of hard work.

She and Layla had started saving for this trip when they were twelve years old, and they'd discussed what they'd do and where they'd go every month for sixteen years. As per their plan, Sutton spent the first three months travelling around Europe – alone, because a month before they were due to leave, Layla told her she couldn't, after promising her she could take time away from her businesses. Layla was due to fly in on the 24th and spend Christmas and New Year with her in London. Their accommodation was already booked and paid for, and she'd bought two Oyster cards and a pass to visit all the city's main tourist attractions. But those plans, like their friendship, were up in the air.

What had Layla been thinking? How could she do this to her? Why did she think it was okay to put her in such an untenable situation? And, because Layla was ghosting her, her questions remained unanswered. If she had the money Layla borrowed she wouldn't be lying on a stranger's couch, trying to gather her courage to squat in a friend's uncle's vacant house. Sutton placed her forearm over her eyes and blinked back tears.

Where did they go from here? Even if Layla repaid her— and that was looking less and less likely – would they be able to repair their now bent-almost-broken relationship? Could trust be restored? Layla knew Sutton needed the borrowed money, but she'd ignored her increasingly frantic pleas. She'd hung her out to dry. How? *Why?*

They'd been friends since they were five. They'd studied together and partied together. They knew where their skeletons were buried. Layla'd seen the best and worst of the Alsop family and was her sister in everything but name.

Thinking about Layla made her heart ache – this was worse than any betrayal or breakup with any man – so she sat up, a million gongs sounding in her head at the same time. God, she felt dreadful. And she desperately needed to use the bathroom. When her dizziness abated, she stood up slowly – she'd aged a hundred years in a few hours thanks to her one-night stand with tequila – and used the back of the couch to keep her balance. There was nice art on the walls, and more photos on the mantelpiece above the fireplace, including one of Santa's ass-kicker looking serious in a smart uniform. Despite his feather-decorated beret, he still radiated an I'm-a-scary-badass vibe.

Sutton crossed the hall, narrowly avoiding tripping over a scooter, and found a bathroom neatly hidden under the stairs. After washing her hands, she reluctantly lifted her head to look at her reflection in the small mirror above the basin. Her loud groan bounced off the walls. The bruise on her cheek was pansy violet, edged in red, and mascara streaks slashed through the blue rings under her eyes. Her hair desperately needed a cut. Luckily, she was a natural blonde, so she didn't need highlights. On a good day, she was girl-next-door attractive. Today wasn't, in any way, a good day.

Sutton dried her hands on a hand towel and walked back into the hall. The next door down led to a spacious kitchen and open-plan dining and living area leading out onto a glass-walled conservatory, the floor of which was covered in car tracks, Barbie dolls and building blocks. A loud woof drilled into her head and the mournful whine made her ears bleed. It looked cold outside, the clouds hung low in the sky, and, judging by the beds she saw in the hall, and the chewed-up pull rope lying on the carpet, dogs were allowed inside. She hadn't owned a dog growing up – *four kids were enough mouths to feed, thank you very much!* – and Sutton loved animals.

A big paw scratched at the kitchen door, and she couldn't resist the pitiful whine, so Sutton walked between the island and the kitchen cabinets and opened the back door. A streak of blueish-black fur brushed past her, splattering mud.

Oh, bugger! She'd let a mud-streaked, soaking wet dog of indeterminate breed but of great heft into the house. Where was a bucket, a mop, and cloths? Sutton felt a small wet nose sniffing at her sock-covered foot. She looked down and saw a little black and white pig, its stomach nearly brushing the tiled floor.

A monster dog *and* a pig. *Right.*

Sutton shivered and closed the kitchen door. But where had the dog gone? Dog – Sasquatch? Who could tell? She looked across to the living-slash-playroom and didn't see it in there. Grimacing, she checked the dog beds in the hall and found them empty. She walked back into the more formal reception room. Praying she wasn't right, she peeked over the back of the deep, expensive cream-coloured couch. The creature rested its shaggy head on the cushion she'd used earlier, and wet, brown patches bloomed on the cream upholstery.

The dog – if something the size of a small cow could be called a dog – lifted its head at her and smirked. The pig placed its hooves on the cushion next to the dog's head and tried to defy gravity by attempting to climb onto the couch to join his friend.

'*Off!*'

The dog yawned and closed its eyes, blatantly ignoring her. The pig batted its eyelashes and Sutton shook her head, knowing she needed to ignore the desperate plea in its eyes.

'No,' she said, lifting her hand. 'Hell, *no*. I've done enough. I've blown fuses, wrecked his garden, broken Christmas decorations, destroyed a Christmas tree and now I've allowed his dog to dirty his couch.'

Sutton attempted to tug the dog off the couch, but it wasn't going anywhere. Her head pounding, she turned her back on the hard-done-by pig and walked out of the room. She'd write Gus another IOU for the bill to get his couch cleaned. Damn, she was racking up debt like there was no tomorrow.

It was time to leave before she did more damage. Her hiking boots, no longer waterproof, stood by her backpack by the door and her puffer jacket hung on a hook next to the heavy front door. She sat down on the chair next to the hall table and pulled on her right boot. It was time to get out of here. Jason's uncle's house had to be close.

Sutton was about to pull the laces on her boots tighter to tie them when the landline next to her released a blare, causing her to jump. She knocked her elbow on the wall and released a sharp curse. *Ow, that hurt! Jeez!*

The ringing phone stopped, thank God. Blessed silence filled the hall and her brain pulled back from her skull, just a little. She was about to bend over when the phone rang again. She eyed it with trepidation. There was no answering machine so should she answer the call?

The phone stopped, but immediately rang again. Sutton picked up the receiver, mostly to stop her head from exploding.

'I'm calling from Shipman Distributors, about your order,' a brusque female voice informed her. 'I know it's early, but it's the busy season and you did tell me to call at any time to update you about your order. I dialled the cell number I was given but it routed my call to this number.'

'My order?' Sutton asked, wondering if she could ask the caller to speak more slowly. And more softly. Foghorns would envy her ability to transmit sound.

'Your specialised order of Christmas decorations. This is the Christmas Shop, right?'

'Uh—'

'Anyway, you can expect the delivery tomorrow. I'll email the invoice to Gus at the Christmas shop Conningworth dot com. If you could pay it immediately, that would be helpful.'

Sutton was aiming to feel normal... Helpful? Not so much.

'Goodbye.' Instead of ringing off, the woman inhaled sharply. 'I must say, I was expecting a bit more of a professional attitude from the staff of what I've been told is one of the best Christmas shops in the country.'

Sutton considered telling her she had the wrong number but before she could, she heard the click of the call being disconnected. Turning back to her task of pulling on her boots, she bent down, feeling dizzy and exceptionally nauseous. She couldn't throw up. Doing so would be the Christmas star on what had already been a pretty crappy morning. She glanced at the old-fashioned grandfather clock opposite her. Man, it wasn't even nine yet.

Sutton wasn't even surprised when she heard a sharp, hard knock on the front door. At this point, aliens could land, and she'd just shrug her shoulders. To be fair, she had a lot going on.

Knock, knock, thump.

Jeez, this house was busier than Kings Cross Station! All she wanted to do was pull on her shoes, grab her coat, and her backpack and go. But the simple task was taking much longer than anticipated. She needed coffee. It was hard to adult without coffee. It was doubly hard to adult without coffee when you had a brain-splitting hangover.

Sutton hobbled to the door, her foot in one unlaced boot. Holding her other boot in her hand, she pulled the door open and saw two men on the doorstep, one a gorgeous blue-eyed blond, the other of Caribbean African descent. The blond held two brightly wrapped presents, his long nose buried in what she was sure was a cashmere scarf. He wore sharply pressed jeans tucked into spotlessly clean gumboots. His friend – lover? Husband? – looked casual in straight-legged track pants, trainers and a thick hoodie, under a sleeveless puffer jacket.

'Can I help you?'

Cute and Cuter exchanged a long, who-is-she look. 'Hello. Is Gus in?'

Sutton hopped from one foot to the other as cold air swirled around her. 'Sorry, no.'

The blond wrinkled his nose. 'Oh, damn, have they left already? We wanted to say hi to Gus, Felix and Rosie before they went off to school.'

'Eli, I told you we were too late. And his Land Rover is gone.'

Eli, the blond, pouted. 'I was hoping you were wrong.' He pointed to his chest, then placed his hand on his partner's shoulder. 'I'm Eli, this gorgeous creature is Will. We're Gus's neighbours.'

Eli pushed past her and stepped into the hall. Will rolled his eyes and followed his partner inside and Sutton shut the door behind them. She rocked on her feet. Um…what was the protocol for letting strangers into a strange man's house? What if they ripped him off and Gus pointed the finger at her? She couldn't take the chance so she yanked open the door. 'Maybe you should go. I'll tell Gus you stopped by.'

Eli sent her a reassuring smile before nodding to a framed corkboard behind her. Sutton slowly turned and in amongst the twins' art, a voucher for a bookstore and a list of numbers was a photograph. In it, each of the men held a twin, while Gus stood behind the foursome. Both twins had their arms wrapped around Eli and Will's necks. Once she saw the photograph, Sutton's panic receded.

'You can start breathing again,' Eli said. 'We really are good friends and neighbours.' He gave her a bright smile and Sutton squinted at his whiter-than-white teeth. 'So, I'll make coffee while you tell us who you are and where Gus found you. Are you a one-night stand or will you be back?'

Sutton blinked at his departing back and turned to look at his partner. 'Help,' she whispered. She wanted coffee but she didn't think she could cope with being interrogated.

Will smiled and patted her arm. 'Eli is spectacularly nosy but if you tell him to mind his own business, he will. Maybe.'

Sutton had her doubts. But on hearing the sounds of fresh coffee beans grinding, she hurried to the kitchen. She'd slam down a quick espresso, maybe two, and then she'd split.

Eli gestured her to the window seat. Sutton did as she was asked and pulled on her boot. She eyed the coffee machine, hoping Eli would get on with the crucially important task.

'I noticed the Santa inflatable is looking very sad and deflated,' Will said, leaning his shoulder into the wall next to her. 'And half of Gus's decorations are flattened. What happened?'

Me. Tequila led me into temptation.

Sutton followed Will's gaze and twisted to look behind her. The smirky Santa lay across the lawn, looking thin and grotesque. And yes, it did look like a spree killer had annihilated the snowmen. She didn't blame Gus for feeling pissed off.

'Thank goodness his house isn't in the village because it's not a great advertisement for Kate's Christmas Shop.'

Wait! What? Sutton was momentarily distracted by Eli pushing a cup of espresso into her hand. She inhaled the divine smell, *yum yum yum*, and took a brain-reviving sip. Then another. She held up her finger, silently telling the pair she'd be with them in a second. She drained the first cup and handed it back to Eli. 'More,' she muttered. 'Please.'

Eli turned back to the could-launch-rocket-ships-complicated coffee machine and Sutton looked at Will. 'Run that by me again... Does Gus own the Christmas shop? The one in the village?'

'Kate's Christmas Shop. Yes. It's open year-round,' Will replied, sounding proud.

There was so much wrong with his sentence. Like festive music in shops, Christmas shops should only be open in December. Secondly, who was Kate?

'Well, he also owns a tour and team-building company, but in December, he takes on the role of Mr Christmas,' Eli added.

So Gus was the Mr Christmas they'd gossiped about in the pub last night. The one who ran everything Christmas-related in town – the Christmas market and the tree-lighting ceremony. He was supposed to be old and a little weird, not young(ish) and sexy. What was this crazy world she'd tumbled into?

'Gus is Mr Christmas?' she repeated. Maybe if she said

the words a few more times, they would begin to make sense.

Eli's beaming smile was as bright as the African sun. 'He is! He's crazy about anything to do with Christmas. He concentrates on the Christmas shop in December. It was his wife's, but she died.'

His wife was dead? That was a scenario she hadn't considered. When? How?

'I'm so happy we're back for Christmas, Will. The twins are finally able to understand Christmas, and we can help make it *fantastic* for them.'

Sutton smiled at Eli's enthusiasm. Christmas had never been a big deal back home. Firstly, there was never much money for presents, and if there was, then her siblings got something and she, as the much older child, didn't. *You're a tough girl, Sutton, and you're old enough to understand, they aren't!* She was always at the bottom of her mum's list of priorities, the child who was more helper than daughter, taken for granted, a convenient outlet for her mum's frustration. There'd only been a couple of slaps, but lots of yelling and emotional...well, abuse was a strong word.

Her mum was always worse at Christmas, and Sutton now understood that the pressure of the season probably got to her. Along with Christmas presents, January was also the start of the new school year, and that meant finding money for stationary, textbooks, and new uniforms. Tensions ran high during the long summer holiday – the six weeks starting at the beginning of December – and, as she knew, it was difficult to keep three energetic boys entertained in a small flat with no money.

Was it any wonder she didn't get Christmas?

Sutton brushed away her memories and tuned into Eli telling her about Christmas in Conningworth.

'I'm so excited about the Christmas market that's happening quite soon, in two weeks. Followed by the lighting of the Christmas tree on the green. Kate's Christmas shop donated all the decorations. There'll be sledging down Conningworth Hill. There should be snow this year. Christmas carols on the green – Gus is organising it all!'

Eli ended his pronouncement with a breathy sigh, making it sound like Gus was the answer to all Conningworth's Christmas prayers and more. 'He's a total Christmasholic, insanely into the season.'

No, actually, he wasn't.

The man who kicked the crap out of Santa last night wasn't a fan. She distinctly recalled Gus saying he effing loathed Christmas, if he saw another Christmas bauble he'd effing puke, he hated effing tinsel and Christmas carols made his effing ears bleed. She'd heard all that, right? That wasn't a figment of her drunken imagination?

Was he even allowed to hate Christmas if he owned a Christmas store? Wasn't that against the laws of nature or something? She took a second espresso from Eli and wrapped her hand around the small cup. Eli's phone buzzed with an incoming message, and he looked at Will. 'I messaged Gus, but he's had to go into the tour company to do something. He said he'll bring the twins over later. Marvellous.'

Sutton caught Will's excited grin. It was obvious the two men loved the twins and they seemed very fond of Gus. Eli passed Will a cup of green tea – ugh, gross.

'So Gus likes Christmas, huh?' Should she tell them what happened last night?

'No, he loves Christmas! *Adores* it.'

'Because of his dead wife?' Sutton pressed. Sympathy for Gus rolled over her. She didn't know anything about being married, and she hadn't had many long-term relationships – or any – but she did know how it felt to lose her best friend. And hers wasn't even true loss, a dead-not-coming-back loss. Losing Layla, even the possibility of losing Layla, hurt. Burying your wife, and your life partner at a young age had to be exceedingly traumatic.

'Well, maybe it started like that,' Eli replied. 'He's not the type to wear his heart on his sleeve, but now he loves it for himself and his children.'

Wrong, so wrong. No, the Christmasholic of Conningworth loathed Christmas.

'What would you say if I said Gus doesn't like Christmas?' Sutton asked, testing the waters.

'That you are nuts,' Will cheerfully told her.

'And you being here just reinforces how much he loves this time of the year,' Eli earnestly assured her.

Her? It did? How?

'He's always been resistant to asking for help with the twins, but he knows he can't run two businesses and various events and give the kids the attention they need. He's a very hands-on dad.'

Where was Eli going with this and what did it have to do with her? Her head hurt, and she didn't have the mental energy to keep up with his rapid-fire explanation.

'I first thought you were a lover, but Gus doesn't bring lovers home. But then I remembered that Moira's been nagging Gus to get some help with looking after the kids over Christmas. It's a crazy busy time for him and he can't run two businesses, be Mr Christmas and look after the twins. We're so glad he hired you.'

Eli didn't jump to conclusions, he took flying leaps. And who was Moira?

'So glad,' Will agreed. Right, so it didn't take them long to move from her being a one-night stand, a potential lover, to her being a nanny. Her ego ran into the corner and covered its head with its arms, wholly mortified by her super-swift downgrade.

'We're happy to help him look after the twins, we always are,' Will continued. 'But we weren't sure whether our cruise would be extended or not.'

Cruise? As in ship? As in...oh God, oh God. Oh...*sod it*.

'Do you two work as onboard entertainers?' she asked, her voice croaky. Please say no. Dear God, *please*...

Will nodded. 'We live in Sunshine Cottage, two up. You go past the entrance to Conningworth Hall and we're the next house opposite. You *must* come to visit.'

She was going to kill Jason, she really was. He'd assured

her his uncle – Will, obviously – would be away until the new year!

'When did you get home?' she asked, panic lacing her words.

'Oh, we haven't even been home yet,' Eli replied. 'We landed early this morning, caught the first train to Kendal and Old Bill gave us a lift to the village. The nice thing about having a lock-up-and-go house is that there isn't any rush to get home. And we don't have to worry about animals.' He looked around, frowning. 'Talking about animals, where are Pig and Pepper?'

Not wanting to explain about the originally cream, now brown couch, Sutton ignored his question.

'Does anyone look after your house for you? Do you have any family?' Sutton croaked.

Will frowned. 'I have a nephew who I can call if there's an emergency, but he's useless. Gus keeps an eye on it for us while we're away.'

Holy shit! What if Gus had checked on the cottage and found her in their house? What if she'd bumped into them while she was looking for the key? How would she have explained what she was doing, why she was there? Close call, Sutton. Too close.

Thank God she'd avoided being busted for trespassing and squatting. But now she didn't have anywhere to sleep tonight. Bit of a problem, that.

Eli placed his hand on Will's shoulder. 'I suppose we should head out, darling.'

'We should,' Will gently agreed. 'I can't wait to see the Chaos Crew of Two later on.'

Despite her where-was-she-going-to-go panic, Sutton grinned. From the little she'd seen of them, it was a perfect name for the twins.

'We'll leave you to get settled in,' Eli suggested, following Will into the hallway. Settle in? Here? Her mind whizzed through her options. Huh. Maybe she didn't need to move on, maybe this house was where she could stay for the next three weeks.

She just had to get one so-called, very fake Christmasholic to see things her way.

Chapter Four

G us walked into the kitchen, saw her sitting in the window seat, and sighed. 'You're still here.'

Sutton gripped her coffee cup tighter and pushed the tips of her bare toes into the fabric covering the cushions on the window seat.

'Yep.'

'How's the headache?'

'Horrible,' she admitted. Her hangover was exacerbated by a stress headache, and not helped by Alex's rare can-you-help-me call. And her guilt at not being able to help her baby brother added another layer of pain. 'And I'm about to add to yours.'

He closed his eyes. 'Oh, God, what have you done now?' he asked.

'I let your dog into the house, but I didn't know he was wet, and he climbed onto the cream couch,' she told him, machine-gunning the words.

'If I had the money, I'd offer to pay the bill to have it cleaned, but I don't, not right now anyway, so you'll have to add it to what I owe you.'

'You might end up having to sell a kidney at this rate,' he replied, sounding resigned. 'And Pepper? The pig?'

The pig looked so mournful, and hard done by, Sutton figured it didn't really make a difference if he slept with his mate or not. He couldn't do any more damage to the already wrecked couch.

'I felt sorry for him, so I helped him up,' she admitted.

'I have no words.'

'Sorry, again. So, the dog is Pig, and the pig is called Pepper.'

He raised his hands. 'Don't ask me, I'm just the dad, and the guy who pays for the dog food and the vet's bills.'

Gus walked up to the coffee machine and lifted the lid to the compartment holding the beans. He cursed and opened a cupboard above his head and sighed.

'Your friends took a bag of beans before they left,' Sutton said. Eli brazenly tucked the bag under his arm before they left the kitchen, blithely informing her Gus wouldn't mind. Gus did, in fact, mind.

'I'm going to kill them,' Gus muttered. 'How hard is it to remember to order coffee?' He walked over to the stove, picked up the kettle and shook it. It was empty so he shoved the spout under the tap.

Sutton touched her wet hair. 'I took a shower,' she told him, needing to be upfront and transparent.

'I noticed.' He roughly spooned instant coffee into his

mug and leaned back against the kitchen counter, looking grumpy and delicious. God, he was just her type. Unavailable and emotionally distant and a little fucked up.

She lifted her cup. 'I made myself some coffee too.' But that was where her honesty ended. She didn't think he needed to know that she was responsible for using the last of his beans, that she was on cup number four, and she was feeling super-jittery. But that could be the combination of caffeine and crime.

'Your neighbours are lovely,' she said, swinging her legs around and dropping them to the floor. *And very chatty*. She put her coffee cup on the windowsill and gripped the edge of the long cushion with both hands.

'You still haven't explained where you were heading to last night. And don't tell me you were going up to the hall. I spoke to Moira, and she says she had no bookings last night.'

'What's the hall and who's Moira?'

'Conningworth Hall is right next door, a stately home now run as a B&B and events venue. Moira is Lady Moira Conningworth, the wife of Viscount Conningworth, who passed away twenty years ago.'

'The twins' mum, and my late wife, inherited the Barony of Conningworth after her father died. It's one of the few hereditary peerages that are passed onto the oldest child, rather than the oldest male in a family.'

Sutton blinked. Okay, so his wife had been a baroness. 'Does that make you a lord or something?'

He shook his head. 'No, thank God. But Rosie, as the

oldest, will inherit the barony one day. But that's not the point – we were talking about your movements last night.'

Right, yeah. Those.

'The only other house along this road is Sunshine Cottage.'

Sutton tried to keep her expression blank, but when his frown deepened, she knew she was in trouble. 'Were you heading for Will and Eli's place last night? Why? You don't know them.'

'How can you be so sure?' Sutton asked, lifting her chin and trying to project bravado. She had none, but she thought faking some was a good idea.

'I've known them for over ten years, and they've never mentioned you, not once. And because Eli never stops talking, I know about all their friends, their families…much more than I need to.'

Sutton winced. Damn it! There was no point in continuing with the lie, it would get her nowhere. And he could refute her claim with one quick call.

'I have a friend, well, an acquaintance, I met him in London, and he is Will's nephew. He comes up here now and again—'

'Jason? Yeah, I know him.'

Sutton lifted her shoulder. 'Jason said they would be away, that I could –' Sutton hesitated '– live there until they returned. He told me where to find the key.'

His eyes iced over. 'Squat, you mean.'

Tomato, *to-mah-to*. 'Jason, obviously, got their schedule

mixed up. I was planning on spending last night, and the next few weeks, in their house.'

Disapproval radiated from him, and Sutton felt fourteen years old, caught smoking a joint and drinking vodka and Red Bull. She met his eyes and felt the power of his gaze pinning her to her seat. Sutton swallowed. It was now or never, do or die, make or break. *Enough with the clichés, Alsop, and get on with it. Be brave.*

Sutton looked away and sucked in a deep breath. She wasn't good at this, at pushing herself into situations where she wasn't wanted; she far preferred to do her own thing and make her own way. But she was out of options.

'I need a place to stay and a way to earn some money to get me back on my feet.'

What she was about to do wasn't nice, it was a dirty play, but she'd run out of road. 'If you don't let me stay and if you don't give me a job in the run-up to Christmas—'

'You'll what?' he asked, when her words trailed off.

Oh, yeah, he was cool. She could easily imagine him on the battlefield, dressed in fatigues, eyes narrowed as he considered how to storm a fortified compound or throw himself out of a helicopter. He wasn't someone you wanted as an enemy, and she did feel like a tiny, ill-prepared nation about to wage war on a superpower.

After the boys left and before he came home, she'd concocted a plan. She'd found the video clip of him she took last night pummelling Santa and thought she'd blackmail her way into a job by threatening to tag his businesses on social media. But she couldn't do it, not even for a warm bed.

But, God, where could she go? *Do?* She'd never felt more scared or helpless in her life.

She pulled the corner of her bottom lip between her teeth. 'I was going to blackmail you into letting me stay and giving me a job.'

His eyes sharpened. 'And *how* were you going to blackmail me?'

'I have a video of you beating the crap out of Santa and shouting that you hate Christmas. I thought that Mr Christmas wouldn't want that getting out.'

'Mr Christmas would not,' he agreed, still calm.

'I'll delete the video. Sorry, it was a really *shitty* idea,' Sutton babbled, her hands over her face, her feet hitting the floor. 'You've been nothing but kind, and I'll get out of your hair.'

She'd have to call her mum and ask her for some emergency money to get back to Heathrow. She had a return air ticket and could fly back as soon as a seat became available. It would be a horrendous end to her long-planned trip, the worst. She'd planned on looking for, and securing, an OT job in the new year, but she didn't have enough money to survive until Christmas Eve. She had accommodation booked and paid for from Christmas Eve until after the new year, breakfast included. But she had nothing to live on between now and then. And crucially, nowhere to stay.

Gus's eyes met hers, and she was surprised by his lack of anger. Why wasn't he furious? Threatening to kick her out, calling the police? Yelling?

'If I offered you some money, would you take it?' he quietly asked her.

Sutton bit her lip. Despite being in a dire situation, she never, not once, thought of asking him for money. She already owed him for the broken lights and the cleaning bill for the couch. But if he gave her some cash, she could find a cheap place to stay, hole up and make some plans. But paying for accommodation was expensive, and she doubted he'd give her enough for more than a few days. Would that give her enough time to find an under-the-counter job? Probably not. A free place to stay and food would be a far better deal. But she wasn't one to look a gift horse in the mouth.

'I'd so appreciate that.' At the very least, she'd asked for enough to get her to Heathrow.

'Actually, I have a better idea,' Gus stated after a minute's silence. Air invaded her lungs again and Sutton sat up straighter. 'Eli sent me a message earlier, congratulating me on hiring a nanny for the twins for the holidays. So, what do you say?'

Was he asking her to look after his kids? *Ugh, no.* She'd borne the lion's share of taking care of her siblings, three active boys. When her half-brothers were old enough to look after themselves, she made the conscious decision to keep as far away from kids as she possibly could. She'd even chosen to specialise in working with adults who'd had a stroke, a car accident or any other significant or traumatic brain injury, thereby avoiding school-going children.

But beggars and choosers and all that.

Of course she'd look after the twins if it allowed her to stay in the country. Hell, she'd do pretty much anything to stay. The UK was where she hoped to settle, to make her home. She aimed to find a steady job and settle down because she wasn't close to her mum, and her siblings were scattered across the world – Alex studying in the US, Jamie working as a dive master in Thailand, and Brynn heading to Saudi Arabia when he finished his nursing degree. She could be anywhere, go anywhere.

She needed to live in a new place and start a new chapter. She had her Occupational Therapy degree, and she'd worked hard for it. With it, she could get a good job, support herself and live a normal life. Maybe she could get a dog or a cat and take weekend trips to places like Prague and Oslo. Companies would start interviewing in the new year and she needed to stay in the UK for as long as she could. Leaving now would be disastrous.

But while Sutton really appreciated his offer, she couldn't understand why he'd made it as she'd done nothing but cause him problems!

'Why would you want to hire someone who stumbled onto your lawn, drunk as a frog? Someone who destroyed some very expensive lights, passed out on your couch and let dirty dogs onto your furniture?'

'I'm offering you a job, Sutton, one that includes accommodation and food, and a decent daily wage,' he murmured, a small smile touching his mouth. 'Are you trying to talk me out of it?'

No, of course not. By offering her the temp job of looking after his kids he'd handed her a lifeline. She just had to look after his kids. If it meant her not having to sleep in a train station or a shelter, or finding a soup kitchen for a meal, she could do that, couldn't she? Of course, she could. She wasn't an idiot.

'I so appreciate the offer...but *why*? Why would you hire someone like me to look after your precious babies?'

His steady look didn't change. 'You should know that last night I went through your stuff,' Gus calmly informed her.

'You did *what*?'

'I had a stranger passed out on my couch, and I wanted to know who I was dealing with,' Gus explained. 'I needed to know whether you were a crazy woman or a danger to me or my kids, and if I needed to call the police to haul your drunk arse, as pretty as it is, out of my house.'

He thought she had a pretty arse. Woo hoo...*do concentrate on what was important, Sutton!*

And yes, when he put it like that, she understood why he needed to go through her stuff.

'After I dropped off the kids, I swung by my office and made some calls to South Africa, and I spoke to about half a dozen people, all of whom gave you excellent references.'

As they should, because she was smart and professional. *Normally*.

'I asked them if they'd hire you to look after their small kids, and everyone said they wouldn't hesitate.'

Why did the hint of admiration and respect in his voice make her feel ten feet tall?

'Going through my backpack is such an invasion of my privacy,' Sutton told him, for lack of anything else to say. And to stop herself from throwing her arms around him in appreciation. Or cry from relief.

'You trespassed on my lawn,' Gus countered. 'Broke my decorations, passed out on my couch—'

Okay, *okay*. She closed her eyes, utterly relieved. 'I'm so, so grateful, Gus. Thank you.'

Gus leaned his hip against the kitchen counter and folded his arms. The dog called Pig padded into the kitchen, sniffed his hand and plopped down at his feet, a canine carpet. 'Look, Sutton, I think you've found yourself in an awkward situation. But I'm curious as to how a woman with an advanced degree in occupational therapy, who has glowing letters of recommendation from previous employers, lecturers and hospital administrators, ends up penniless and homeless on the other side of the world?'

Since talking about Layla was like having open heart surgery without any pain relief, she ignored his question and the curiosity in his eyes. She shrugged, looked down at the floor and followed the line of the tile with her toe.

'I can only stay for three weeks,' she told him, changing the subject and trying to ignore her throbbing head. 'I have to be back in London the afternoon of the twenty-fourth, Christmas Eve.'

Was she a fool thinking the situation with Layla would be resolved by then? If Layla repaid her, would she still want her to join her in London over Christmas, or did her hurt and sense of betrayal run too deep for Sutton to be around her? She didn't know, but that was for later.

'That's fine,' Gus agreed. 'I'll be done with my Christmas commitments by then.

So, are you staying or going?' he asked.

'Staying.'

'Good.' Gus looked at his watch and pushed his hand through his thick hair. I have a meeting at the tour company in fifteen minutes, so I can't hang around here any longer, but we have more to discuss. Can you meet me at Langston Tours – it's right next to the Christmas shop – at eleven?'

Right now, she'd meet him on the moon if that was what he required. Sutton agreed to the time.

Gus nodded and walked out of the room. Sutton followed him into the hall and watched as he hoisted her heavy backpack over one shoulder like it was a handbag. He held her boots in his other hand. 'I'll carry these up to your room. Do you want to see where you'll be sleeping?'

Sutton took her first full breath in days, possibly weeks. She was in a warm house, she'd eat tonight, and she didn't have to worry about where she would sleep, and how to make it through another cold day.

For the next three lovely weeks, she could relax a little, sleep better, and breathe. Climbing the stairs behind Gus –

her eyes travelling down his back to his rather spectacular bum and down his long, muscular legs and up again – she felt grateful to life, and him, for giving her a reprieve.

She also felt utterly wiped out. And, dammit, weepy with relief.

Chapter Five

Sutton, glad to be out of the driving wind, pushed open the door to Langston's Adventure Company and brushed the light dusting of sleet off her hair. She'd had her beanie and gloves in the pub last night, but she'd lost them somewhere on the road later. As a result, she couldn't feel her fingers and if she smiled or frowned, her face might crack.

She was African-born and bred, and when the temperature dropped below fifteen degrees Celsius, she went into hypothermic shock. For her, the mile-long walk from Gus's cottage to the village was the equivalent of Scott's trek to the Antarctic.

Sutton stamped her feet and looked around. To the left were glass walls, and a small but attractive shop selling outdoor clothes, shoes and equipment. Huge photographs of people doing impossible things – hanging by their fingertips on a rockface, no ropes in sight, canoeing off what looked to be a too-high waterfall, standing on the top of a too-high cliff about to dive – adorned the high walls.

A fully loaded Christmas tree sat next to the receptionist's desk, behind which was another glass wall. Sutton looked into a massive warehouse that had been converted into an indoor climbing centre, with three climbing walls, each more than twenty feet high. A slim woman was halfway to the open ceiling, moving up one wall with ease. A man stood on a mat, critically watching her progress. At the other end of the hall was an unmanned coffee and juice bar. A huge screen to her right advertised the adventures Langston Tours offered.

Impressive.

Then again, Gus Langston was an impressive guy. She'd run through their conversation a dozen times more since he left her the second time, unable to believe her luck. While she unpacked her clothes, she unpacked his actions and mulled over his words. He'd been so reasonable, direct but calm. Rational, sensible and kind. So kind. Utterly, absolutely in control of himself, intrinsically self-confident. He was the mostly manly man – not only in looks – she'd encountered for a long time, possibly ever. An alpha guy, but not an alpha-asshole. Someone who didn't need validation from anyone, wholly confident in his decisions and the road he was walking.

Assured and decisive, but not pompous or pig headed. She *liked* him.

Dammit.

Lust she could ignore, desire was a biological need. But

like? Well, that was a scary and dangerous emotion. *Three weeks, Sutton. You won't do anything stupid like fall for him in three weeks, will you?* Note to self: you *can't*. You won't.

Besides, you're probs just confusing gratitude with like. He's given you a place to stay, a way to regroup, and saved you from what would've been an exceptionally miserable and stressful three weeks. You're just feeling thankful, and relieved. And yes, maybe that old biological need of looking for a protector is playing a part. Despite women's rights, it's still hard-wired into our DNA.

See, there's a logical explanation for everything. You just had to look for it.

'Can I help you?'

Sutton smiled at the young guy behind the counter and jammed her ice-block hands into the pockets of her puffer jacket. Her jacket wasn't warm enough for the Lake District in winter, but she'd have to wait to buy a new one – or a new-to-her one – when she found a charity shop and when Gus paid her. *If* he paid her.

No, he would, he'd keep his word. After being betrayed by Layla, people keeping their word, and her keeping hers, had taken on new meaning and was now of paramount importance to her. And that was why she was here at eleven o'clock, to talk about the twins and what he expected.

'Oh, I'm here to see Gus Langston.'

He nodded. His name tag said he was Anton, a trainee. 'He told me to send you up when you arrived. Can I take your coat?'

Hell no. Sutton shook her head. 'I'm good, thanks.'

'A cup of coffee then?'

Sutton's smile bloomed. 'I would kill for a coffee.'

Anton smiled, blushed and half stumbled out from behind his desk. Sweet boy, getting all flustered from a smile. Anton pointed to a door beneath the huge TV screen.

'Our offices are upstairs. Gus is at the end of the corridor. You're lucky to find him in, he's normally next door at the Christmas shop. Just go on up. I'll bring you some coffee in a minute.' He paused and shook his head. 'You really do need a better coat.'

Sutton opened the door marked 'Staff Only' and winced when a gust of cold air swirled around her legs. She looked back to see a middle-aged couple approaching the desk, immediately demanding Anton's attention. Damn, no chance of coffee now.

After climbing the stairs, Sutton walked through an open-plan office where five people sat at their desks. She kept a pleasant smile on her face. At the far end were two offices, both with their doors open. She stopped at the first one and saw a blond guy on the phone. Catching her eye, he pointed to the office next door.

Sutton took a deep breath and rapped on Gus's half-open door. She heard his deep voice telling her to come in and nudged the door open with her foot, thrusting her hands back into her coat pockets. Gus stood at his window, and she took a moment to look at him, enjoying his big, rangy body. His long-sleeved Henley was tight across the shoulders and arms and fell from his chest, covering the pockets of his jeans. Casual clothes suited his work environment, but man, she'd bet everything she had –

which wasn't very much – that he'd rock a suit. His clotheshorse body would make a brown paper bag look great.

She didn't need to be attracted to Gus Langston, she had enough problems to deal with, thanks all the same. She just needed to sleep in his bed – no, not his bed, a bed he owned! – and eat his food. She'd look after his twins as best she could. Sutton sighed, feeling like she needed to lie down at the thought.

Gus perched on the edge of the windowsill and stretched out his long legs. He looked at his watch. 'You're on time,' he stated, sounding a little surprised.

Admittedly, he'd seen her at her worst, but a drunken destroyer wasn't who she normally was. Normally, she was sensible, practical and ridiculously normal. 'I see clients in my professional life, remember? They tend to get annoyed if they are kept waiting.'

'You left South Africa four months ago, right?'

Sutton nodded. 'I travelled around Europe, then Ireland, and spent a little time in Scotland.'

'That's an expensive trip considering your weak currency.'

She was aware. It was also why she'd needed fifteen-plus years to save. She had a strict daily budget and a small amount of money set aside for emergencies. Sutton resisted the urge to check her phone to see if she'd missed any calls or messages. But she knew she hadn't. Layla was still ghosting her.

Sutton pushed away the panic. For today, for the next few weeks, she had what she most needed, a bed to sleep in, food to eat, an endless supply of coffee and an under-the-counter income.

Gus stood up and walked over to her and held out his hand. 'Let me take your coat.'

Nuh-uh. She shook her head. 'I'm fine.'

He looked down at her, his eyes raking her face. Then his gaze dropped down to focus on her hands in her pockets. 'Your lips are an interesting shade of blue and I bet your hands are too. I take it you walked here?'

She shrugged. 'No car.'

Gus raked a hand through his hair and cursed. 'I was late, frazzled and didn't think. Why didn't you call me, or call for a taxi?'

She raised her eyebrows. 'You didn't leave me any contact details and I didn't think this village was big enough for a taxi operator.'

'It isn't. Old Bill Rodgers hauls people around for a little extra money...something you wouldn't know. You should've called me.' He grimaced. 'But, yeah, no contact details. Let's sort that out right now.'

Sutton unlocked and then handed over her phone, waiting as he added his number to her contacts and added hers to his. Then Gus placed her phone on his desk and tugged her hands from her pockets. Sutton sucked in a shocked breath when her hands disappeared into his. He looked down, frowned and started rubbing her hand between his, the motion sending prickles into her fingers and up her arm.

She bit her lip but didn't jerk her hands from his as the

heat slowly returned to them. Even though they stood apart, she felt the heat rolling off him. She wanted to push her nose into his neck, have his big arms wrapped around her, his thigh between her legs.

Sutton looked away, wishing she could step into his arms. It would be lovely to feel like she could rest in someone else's strength. But that wasn't the way life worked; she knew she could only ever rely on herself.

Sutton abruptly pulled her hands from his. 'Thanks, I'm fine.'

'You need some decent cold-weather clothes,' Gus told her, stepping back.

She couldn't afford them. Ignoring his comment, Sutton looked around the room, her interest caught by a wall of photographs. She moved closer, her eyes bouncing from frame to frame. Gus was in many of the pictures, doing impossibly difficult things. In some photographs he was barely recognisable, his smile framed by a bushy beard. Miles of snow-covered mountains formed the backdrop of many photographs.

'Your operation is impressive,' Sutton said, trying to sound casual. 'How did you come to start your business?'

Gus perched on the edge of his desk. 'After I left the army, I worked part-time for an adventure company, but I also guided biologists and anthropologists on their research trips into remote, often dangerous regions. I merged the two ideas, and gradually built the business up to where it is today.'

'Do you still consult?' Sutton asked, interested. She

should be talking about his kids, and the role he wanted her to take on, and not his business and his past.

'I wish I did, it was the best part of the job,' Gus replied. 'But I can't be away from the twins, so I subcontract people to do those trips.'

Sutton instinctively understood he missed being active, missed the challenge of that aspect of the job. But he was a single dad, and she appreciated his desire to put his kids first. Raising children, and looking after them as a single parent, was hard.

And after she was done looking after Gus's twins, she'd be done. If not for ever, then for a long, long time. She was mostly happy being single, and loved not being responsible for anyone else. Kids required sacrifices. She'd forfeited her teenage years to help raise her siblings, and she'd given enough to whatever gods were in charge of child-raising.

And talking about the twins, they needed to get on with it. Sutton gestured to his visitor's chair. 'May I?'

'Please.' Gus pushed the chair out with the toe of his boot and Sutton sat down, crossing one leg over the other. She lifted her chin, and folded her arms across her chest, tucking her still cool hands under her arms. Gus noticed her gesture and frowned.

'So, let's talk about how this will work,' Sutton began.

'Sure.' Gus stood up, walked around his desk and sat in his expensive, highly ergonomic desk chair. He rested his forearms on his desk, thoughtfulness creeping into his expression. 'As I explained to you, I have a lot on my plate. In between running this place, spending most of my time in the Christmas shop next door and organising the Christmas market—'

'When is the market?' Sutton interjected.

'On Saturday the sixteenth,' he replied. 'It's a full-day affair, culminating in a tree-lighting ceremony that evening, and a dance at the village hall.'

Judging by his sour lemon face, the dance was not his idea.

'How were you going to look after them and work if I didn't come along?'

He lifted one big shoulder. 'Moira and I would make it work, somehow fit it all in. Making childcare plans, juggling the balls of pickups and playdates don't crack the list of the top twenty hardest things I've had to learn over the past three years, Sutton.'

His quiet statement hit her harder than she expected it to. She bit her bottom lip as she considered the implications of his words. He'd lost his wife in a car crash, and was left with year-old twins to raise, businesses to run and a life to lead without the woman he loved.

Judging by the frustration she witnessed last night, he knew what it meant to feel overwhelmed and resentful, hard done by and deeply, fundamentally sad. He understood how it was to hold up the sky, to be the barrier between the people he loved and complete chaos. How often did he wish he could be somewhere else? Someone else? Once a month, once a week, a couple of times a day? And, because he was a dad, he'd immediately be swamped with guilt because, apparently, parents of kids weren't allowed to be human.

Did he have a Layla? A best friend he could talk to, someone who got him on a fundamental level, someone he could be completely honest with, a person who knew where his skeletons were buried. Sutton clenched her fists, and looked down, her throat tightening. Did *she* still have Layla? And if she did, could they ever go back to what they were before? She'd left her without resources in a foreign country – could she ever forgive her? Why didn't she move heaven and earth – take out a bank loan, borrow from someone else – to repay her? She would never put Layla in an untenable position; why did Layla think it was okay to do that to her and why wouldn't she talk to her, and explain her reasoning? Maybe she had a good reason... Sutton wondered if she was clutching at straws, trying to find a way of justifying Layla's behaviour. She didn't want to lose her – she was her longest, albeit platonic, love affair.

Sutton rubbed the area above her heart and closed her eyes. Would this ever not hurt? Would the pain ever lessen? Probably, in time. Most hurts faded...

'Are you okay?' Gus asked.

She met his intelligent blue eyes and saw the questions in them, the curiosity. He opened his mouth to speak but a sharp rap on the door distracted him. He stood up and Sutton slumped in her chair, grateful for the interruption.

After talking to his employee – something about a tour group in the spring – he apologised and sat down again.

Needing to move on, she jumped in with a question about the kids' kindergarten and asked about their daily routines.

Gus handed her a printed copy of their schedule and contact numbers of all the relevant people in their lives, from their teachers to their grandmother. She read the list, and when she was done, she knew what time to drop them off at school, when to collect them, what they ate and when. She waved the piece of paper in the air. 'You've been busy this morning,' she commented.

He shook his head. 'I wish I could tell you I have it all in my head, but I don't. The only way I can keep track of everything is to make lists, lots and lots of lists.' He nodded at the paper. 'Their school term ends on the 15th, and they go back in the new year. That's when your days will get busy.'

He frowned, looking thoughtful. 'You'll be spending a lot of time with the twins, and I need a way to explain you.'

A little lost, and a lot hungover, would work. Oh, he meant how to explain her presence in his house, in his life. Easy. 'I'm the temporary nanny you hired.'

'But from where?' He shook his head. 'And having said I wouldn't hire help, I've done a U-turn, something I don't often do.'

'Aren't you allowed U-turns? People do change their minds,' she pointed out.

'I was pretty vociferous on the point. Hiring you will raise eyebrows.'

'*So?*'

'So, I live in a small village that runs on gossip. People

talk, far more than they should. Having been a constant topic of conversation too often and for too long, I prefer to avoid it if I can.'

Good-looking single dad, aristocratic wife killed in a car accident, two young children. Yep, she could see why people talked about him. Add in a new woman living with him? Okay, maybe it was better to head off the gossip before it started.

'I suppose we could tell people we connected through doing one of those DNA genealogy tests,' Sutton suggested. 'I could be a second or third cousin on your mum's side who's looking for a place to stay while she's in the country.' They said the trick about lying was sticking to the truth as much as possible.

He tipped his head to the side. 'You're pretty sharp.'

'You should see me when I'm not hungover,' Sutton replied. 'I guess my eight years at uni paid off.'

He waited for her to explain and when she didn't, he tapped his finger on his desk. 'C'mon, you can't leave me hanging. Why did it take you eight years to get your degree?'

She looked away, a familiar mixture of embarrassment and pride rolling through her. Embarrassed because she was kickstarting her career late, proud of what she'd achieved on her own. 'I put myself through uni while working two jobs. I needed to support myself, so I couldn't take the full range of modules each year.'

Sutton forced herself to meet his eyes, and saw, maybe, a hint of respect pass through all that blue. But it was gone too soon for her to be sure, and she wondered if she was simply projecting her need for affirmation onto him. She liked impressing people. She liked impressing impressive, confident, hot men even more.

But Gus wasn't someone to toy with, he was the man handing her a lifeline, hauling her out of the deep hole Layla kicked her into. She had to keep her distance and ignore the lust rolling through her. He was her boss…

'So you have a degree in occupational therapy…' He winced and looked a little rueful. 'I'm not sure what being an OT involves. You work with kids who have learning challenges, right?'

It was a common misconception. 'So, basically, we teach people how to adapt their movements to complete a task. That could be helping children with their schoolwork, helping them improve their writing or anything involving any kind of activity or task. I *can* work with children, but I prefer to work with adults who've been impacted by trauma, whether that's a stroke, a car accident or something else that's derailed their life. I help them to do as much as they can, given their injuries.'

'And you enjoy it?'

No, she loved it. It was exactly what she was meant to do. And she couldn't wait to start a new job and get back into the swing of hospital visits and appointments. She loved seeing people progress, and helping her patients reach small, and big, milestones. 'I do.'

Sutton folded the sheet of paper and leaned forward to tuck it into the back pocket of her jeans. Gus picked up a set of car keys and handed them over. 'These are the keys for a car I keep as a company vehicle. I had an intern run to Kendal to purchase another set of car seats for the twins.'

She picked up the keys and looked at the familiar logo on the keychain. 'You're assuming I drive,' she commented.

A half grin lifted the corners of his mouth. 'I went through your purse. I saw both your South African licence and an international driver's licence in there.'

'Do I have any secrets left?' Sutton asked.

'Oh, I'm sure you have plenty,' he told her, his voice deeper than before.

The air still sizzled between them, and little explosions of fireworks erupted on her skin. The room seemed to take a huge breath, the tension in the air causing the walls to shuffle inward, making the space more intimate and cosier.

Everything faded, her past and his present, her money issues and his challenge to give his twins what he thought they needed. Their eyes locked and Sutton couldn't break his stare. It was a made-for-movies moment, one that didn't need a soundtrack.

Man. Woman. Want. Need.

Then Gus leaned back, and the loaded-with-promise-and-sexual-innuendo moment vanished as his sexy mouth tipped up into a smirk. 'Your music playlists are dreadful, by the way.'

'There is nothing wrong with my choice of music!'

'Eighties teen pop – sweet enough to make the enamel drip off your teeth.'

She liked those songs, they made her feel upbeat and

happy. 'I cannot believe you went through my stuff,' she muttered.

'I cannot believe you offered to help beat up Santa, killed a couple of snowmen, passed out on my couch and considered blackmailing me,' Gus retorted.

Hot adventure guy, 1. Sutton, 0.

———————

On the second morning of her Conningworth Confusion, as she'd named this period of her life, Sutton stood at the bathroom sink, contemplating her messy hair. She'd washed it last night and it hadn't been completely dry when she went to sleep. It now looked like she'd shoved her tongue into an electrical socket.

'What are you doing?' Rosie demanded from the other side of the door. She'd found the twins at the end of her bed this morning, watching her sleep – creepy! – and while her nanny duties were only supposed to start after school, she climbed out of bed and stumbled down the stairs to use the bathroom, closely followed by the twins and Pig.

The twins groaned and Pig barked when she closed the door in their faces.

'Whatcha doing?'

'How long are you going to be?'

Sutton rolled her eyes. She'd forgotten that four-year-olds did not understand the concept of privacy. As the new girl in the house, they found her endlessly fascinating. Unfortunately, their fascination would only last until she told them to pick up their toys or when she insisted they eat their vegetables.

From the moment Gus told them she would be looking after them for the next few weeks, they peppered her with questions. *Where do you live? How tall are you? Where does the sun go when it is dark? Do you have a sister? A brother? A baby? A monkey? Do you have a baby who is a monkey? Why don't crabs have eyebrows?* The best interrogators in the world could take tips from the Langston twins.

'Sutton, I need to pee!'

Sutton yanked the door open to see Rosie sitting on the hallway carpet, having been abandoned by her brother and Pig. Sutton narrowed her eyes at her, suspecting her plea was a ploy to see what she was doing.

'Do you really need to go?' she demanded.

'No, I got bored with looking at a shut door.'

Sutton had to respect her honesty. She left the door open and turned back to the sink. Rosie sat down on the edge of the bath, her deep blue eyes staring at her in fascination as she dragged her hairbrush through her hair.

'Have you brushed your teeth, Rosie?' she asked, while pulling her hair into a ponytail and snapping a hair band into place. She was quite proud of her calm tone: she usually needed two cups of coffee and an hour of silently contemplating her navel before she felt ready for any type of conversation.

Rosie put fingers in each side of her mouth and pulled her lips apart. 'Yes! See?'

'Good job,' Sutton told her, removing her mascara from

her makeup bag. She didn't wear much makeup, but her light, thin eyelashes needed a lot of help. She brushed the mascara on, then slicked a little eyeliner into the corner of her eyes. Hey, she was living with someone – and not in the fun sense – who could feature on the cover of *Men's Health*. She preferred to look the best she could without making it look obvious that she'd tried.

'Are you looking forward to school today? Is anything fun happening?'

'We're practising for the play. I'm an angel.'

Yes, Sutton knew. She'd only been around for a short time, and they'd had at least five conversations about her costume.

'My best friend's mum is taking her to buy a Christmas tree today.'

Sutton picked up a note of despondency in Rosie's voice that she'd yet to hear from the outspoken, confident little girl. She looked in the mirror and saw Rosie's bent head and slight pout. 'Do you want to go buy a Christmas tree too?' Sutton asked her.

'No, Ben will cut one down for us, Nan has already picked it out. But Daddy needs to say yes, and he keeps saying he'll get around to it, but then he doesn't.' Rosie lifted her head, and Sutton caught the faint sheen of distress in her blue eyes. 'I don't think Daddy likes Christmas very much, Sutton. It makes him sad.'

And they said kids were blissfully unaware! Sutton took a moment, not knowing how to respond. 'What makes *you* sad, Rosie?'

Her little shoulders lifted. 'I'd like to make Christmas cookies with Daddy but he doesn't have the time. I want a Christmas tree, and go to the pantonine—'

'Pantomime.'

Rosie waved her correction away. 'I want to go shopping for presents, for Nan and Daddy and Pig and Pepper, and for my friends at school.'

'Felix?'

'No, I'm mad at him,' Rosie informed her.

Fair enough. 'Well, maybe I can help you with that,' Sutton suggested. 'We can go Christmas shopping one afternoon, and then maybe we can watch a movie too.' She'd have to find out where the nearest cinema was, but it couldn't be too far away.

Rosie beamed at her. 'Just you and me?'

Nice try, kiddo. 'I'm afraid we'll have to take your brother too.'

'Ugh.'

Sutton smiled at her disgusted face and replaced the cap on her mascara. The Langston twins were a handful – lively and energetic and smart – but they were also kids trying to navigate a world without a mum. Sutton knew that if Kate was around, she would be doing everything she could to make this first Christmas the twins would remember amazing. Apart from being crazy busy, and not having the time, Gus had his issues with Christmas. Maybe she could step into the breach...

In doing so, she could give herself the experience of a true Christmas, something she could remember for the rest of her life. The snowy, cold, hot-cider and mince pie Christmas she'd dreamed of as a kid. There wouldn't be presents under the tree for her, but that didn't matter, it was about the experience, not what you received. She could experience the season through the twins' eyes, soak in their excitement and maybe she could put her Christmas issues/ghosts to rest.

She would have to run this by Gus and see if he would fund the extra expenses involved. But she knew he would, and Sutton planned to make the next three weeks as festive as possible.

For the twins. And for her. Turning back to her morning routine, she scrabbled in her bag to find her nose spray. If she didn't take a dose every morning, her sinuses played up. She squirted a dose into each nostril, put everything back into her toiletry bag and, recalling how hard it was to clean eyeshadow, lipstick and mascara off walls, placed the bag on top of the bathroom cabinet where the twins couldn't reach it. Judging by Rosie's pout, the thought of playing with Sutton's stuff had crossed her mind.

Rosie tugged on the hem of her cream-coloured jersey. 'What did you put up your nose? And can I have some?' Rosie demanded.

God, no! 'It's medicine for adults, Rosie, you absolutely cannot have any.'

'But what is it?' Rosie demanded, hands on her hips. Sutton saw the light of battle in her eyes and knew she wouldn't stop nagging until she got an answer that satisfied her. Felix was easier to distract, and more laid back, but this child was as determined as all hell. Sutton suspected she might run the world one day.

'It's my special nose medicine,' Sutton explained. She thought about her stuffy head and how listless and low she felt when she was suffering from a sinus flareup. 'It makes me feel like I can breathe better. Being able to breathe better makes me feel more energetic.'

Rosie wrinkled her nose. 'What does energetic mean?'

Sutton ushered Rosie through the open bathroom door into the passage. 'It means you feel like you can run and climb and do anything you set your mind to.'

'I need some energetic,' she told Sutton as they walked down the hallway leading to the stairs. 'Having a boy twin is haustive.'

Haustive? Sutton frowned. She'd already ascertained Rosie had an incredible vocabulary and was exceptionally erudite. Felix was less talkative and tended to let Rosie forge ahead.

'Give me another word for haustive, Rosie,' Sutton asked.

'Tired, Sutton. He makes me tired,' she stated with all the drama of a hysterical Victorian aristocrat.

Right. Noted.

'Sutton?'

Sutton turned and looked up. Gus stood at the end of the passage, outside his bedroom. He held carrier bags with the adventure company's logo in one hand. With his two-day-old stubble and shower-damp hair, dressed in jeans and a navy crew-neck sweater, he looked scrumptious. *No lusting after your boss, Sutton!*

'Can I speak to you for a minute?' Gus asked her.

'Sure.'

'We'll see you in the kitchen in five minutes, Rosie,' Gus told his daughter.

'I wanna come too,' Rosie told him, following them up the short flight of steps to Sutton's loft bedroom. Sutton looked at Gus. This was his fight, not hers.

'I don't have the energy…' he muttered and followed Sutton and his daughter into her room. Sutton winced at her unmade bed and noticed her bright blue bra lying on the back of the chair in the corner. Luckily Rosie seemed more interested in what was in the three bags Gus dumped on the end of her bed.

Gus raised his eyes at her rumpled bedcovers and picked a pillow off the floor. Having been in the army, he probably made his bed the minute he got up, complete with hospital corners and with the linen so tight you could bounce a coin off it. She suspected Gus longed for a tidy house, and for everything to be in its place.

But, as a single dad with twins, and pets, he was fighting a losing battle. She admired his ability to pick his battles.

'Ooh, pretty,' Rosie squealed.

Sutton, standing as close to the door as she could, looked at the cherry-red jacket Rosie pulled out of the bag, her eyebrows lifting. She instantly recognised the brand; it was one of the more expensive items his shop stocked. And way beyond anything she could afford.

'Is it for me, Daddy?' Rosie demanded, laying the jacket against her cheek and batting her eyelashes. God, this kid.

'It's a bit big for you, sweetheart. No, this one is for Sutton.' Gus plucked the jacket from her hands and held it in one hand. His expression fell somewhere between confused and irritated, as if he wasn't sure why Sutton was there and what he should do with her. 'You needed a new coat, and this is a sample our supplier sent us.'

Nuh-uh. Suppliers didn't send £300 coats as samples. Sutton rocked on her heels, unsure how to react. She needed the coat, she wanted it – honestly, she couldn't think of anything she wanted more – but if she couldn't pay for it, then she couldn't accept it.

'Thanks, but I'm fine.'

'No, what you are is freezing. It's winter, and you need, at the minimum, a decent coat,' Gus said, in his commanding-officer voice. He gestured to the bag. 'There's a black one if you prefer. I had to guess your size, but I think I've got it right. I also included thick socks, a waterproof pair of boots – you'll be walking the kids and the dogs – a beanie and gloves.'

Oh, the thought of being properly warm made her weak. 'I can't—'

'You can. You will,' Gus told her, looking resolute. Sutton could easily see the squaddies in his unit quaking in their boots at the expression on his face. She was so tempted, but she was already living in his house, eating his food, and he was helping her – although he didn't know it – out of a jam. She couldn't accept his charity as well.

'I so appreciate the gesture, but I can't afford to pay you for the clothes, Gus.'

He raked his hand through his hair, obviously frustrated. 'And I don't want to see you with blue lips, Sutton.'

Rosie pulled the beanie onto her head, and it fell over her eyes. She let out a wail of distress and Gus snatched the beanie off her head. He hauled Rosie up into his arms and his little girl laid her head on his shoulder, her blue eyes watery. 'I couldn't breathe, Daddy.'

'It was on your head for two seconds, Rosie-Roo, you could breathe,' Gus told her, his hand almost spanning her small back. His eyes met Sutton's. 'She's intensely claustrophobic and hates the dark.'

Sutton didn't blame her. She did too. 'Noted.' She looked at the pile of clothes on the bed. How she longed to accept them!

Gus lifted his wrist to check the time and grimaced. 'We need to get moving, or I'll be late getting the kids to school,' he said, moving to the door, his daughter still in his arms. When he brushed past her, she inhaled the scent of shower gel and shampoo. 'Add the clothes to my IOU, Sutton.'

She tried to smile. 'I'll have to sell another kidney.' How lovely it would be not to dread going outside, to be able to walk and not feel like her fingers and toes were about to fall off. 'Thank you, I appreciate it.'

'I wish everything was as easy to sort as that,' he said, smiling. Did he look at her mouth a little too long or was she imagining that? Moving on. Sutton glanced at Rosie.

'Actually, can we have a conversation at some point about the fruit of your loins, and my facilitating certain activities that will ensure their maximum enjoyment of the season?'

He frowned at her wieldy, cumbersome sentence – she didn't want to get Rosie's hopes up – but he twigged on quickly enough. 'Are you sure you want to do that? The music might cause your brains to seep out your ears, the screams of delight will give you a headache and I might have to reinflate the man of the season so that you can punch the cra— stuffing out of him to relieve your frustration.'

She grinned at him, loving the glint of humour in his eyes. He was such a sexy man, and even hotter when he smiled. 'I'll take my chances.'

His smile was low and slow and oh-so-steady. 'Sure. I'd appreciate that.'

Yay! 'Can we start with a certain coniferous plant?'

He frowned, and a hint of distress jumped into his eyes. Did he object to a Christmas tree? Why? Then he nodded. 'Yes, I'll arrange that.'

'Can I bring your offspring down to the shop so that they can choose how they want it…embellished?'

'There are boxes of the stuff in storage. I'll haul them out.' Right, he didn't sound enthusiastic, but he wasn't saying no, either. She could work with that.

'Why are you using big people's words?' Rosie demanded.

'So that little people can't understand us,' Gus told her, heading for the door.

Sutton followed him out of her messy room, darting a look at her bra. She rolled her eyes on noticing the matching panties on the seat of the chair, the thin thong on display.

'Nice underwear,' Gus softly murmured. 'I like the colour.'

Oh, kill her now. Again, how should she respond? *Thanks? Should I model them for you? I have the same set in deep violet?* Sutton slapped the forthright and flirty imp off her right shoulder. No lusting after your boss, Sutton. Your sexy, *nice* boss.

'So, you said something about me walking the dogs?'

Judging by the amusement in his eyes, he knew she was trying to change the subject. But, thankfully, he followed her lead.

'They'll take you for a walk,' he replied as they walked down the stairs. 'At the end of the garden is a gate leading to the grounds of the Conningworth Estate. Unless you want to spend an hour drying Pig off, I suggest you keep him from swimming in the stream and duck pond.'

'And how do I do that?' Sutton asked. She stopped and stood on the third step up, and pushed her hands into the front pockets of her Levis.

'He's nutty about tennis balls. There's a bucket in the hall, take three or four, or five or six, and keep throwing them for him,' Sutton said, placing Rosie on her feet at the bottom of the stairs. Her tears forgotten, she ran into the kitchen.

Gus started to pick hats and coats off the hooks next to the front door. Shoes and boots sat on a rack next to an old brass coal bucket filled with walking sticks. His wife had put a lot of thought, and money, into decorating the house, and pre-kids it would've been quite a showpiece. But the toys and the crayon drawings, the dogs' leashes, chewed plastic bones and ratty ropes, the detritus of family life softened the sharp edges of the design. And she thought the house looked better for it.

It would look amazing with a huge Christmas tree in the space next to the steps, and the banister decorated with ivy.

Gus made a pile for Felix – hat, gloves and jacket on top of his school bag – and another for Rosie. His cell and wallet lay in another shallow Raku-fired bowl, a twin to the one in the formal lounge with its still dirty couch.

'So, my mother-in-law will collect the kids from kindergarten today. She has them every Thursday. She'll give them tea and I'll collect them when I'm done at work.'

Oh. Sutton was surprised by her surge of disappointment. She'd been strangely looking forward to spending time with the kids later, getting to know them a little better. Now her day stretched out before her, with little to do but to take the dogs for a walk.

'Um…*okay*.'

'Problem?' Gus asked, placing his hand on his hips. He'd pushed the sleeves of his jersey up his arms. His fingers were long, his hands broad, and raised veins ran along the back of his hands and up his arms. Sparks skittered up her arm. So not helpful.

'No, of course not,' she stuttered, tipping her head up to look into his eyes. He looked puzzled, so she opted to explain. 'I know I'm, supposedly, on holiday but it's been non-stop for months, trying to pack too much into too little time. In Cape Town, I was working and studying. I'm not used to having downtime, and time drags when you have nothing to do.'

'You still look tired.'

'I suppose I am,' she admitted. Would he understand if she told him she was emotionally tired? Mentally wiped? Maybe. But he'd never know how relieved she was to feel safe, to be warm, to know she had a place to stay for the next few weeks. She was also grateful for any money he'd give her for looking after the twins...she just needed to earn enough to survive until Layla repaid her. But would she? She didn't know. The thought of losing all the money she'd saved terrified her.

Gus dropped his hand. 'I still, occasionally, see fear in your eyes,' he said, keeping his voice low. 'You're safe here, Sutton, I promise. I'm not going to change my mind and kick you out. You can relax.'

Maybe she could. Just a little.

'After you take the dogs for a walk, can you walk up the road and pop in at the Sunshine Cottage? Will borrowed a charger cable from me and I need it back. And they owe me a bag of coffee.' Gus seemed to have an innate understanding of when to back off and she sent him a grateful smile, happy he'd changed the subject.

Sutton nodded. If Will and Eli invited her in for coffee, she could kill an hour, maybe two.

'In between your Christmas adventures with my kids – I

think you're mad, but I would be stupid to say no to your offer – if you need to fill some hours while the kids are at school and if you want to earn some extra money, I could use some help,' Gus stated, looking thoughtful.

She owed him so Sutton didn't have to think twice. 'Sure. When and what do you want me to do?'

'We have a coachload of tourists coming in to visit the Christmas shop tomorrow, so it will be a crazy morning. I also need to make a lot of calls chasing up loose ends – lighting suppliers, vendors, permits – for the Christmas market. You can do one or the other.'

She wouldn't mind doing both. 'I can help out with both.'

He leaned back, his head against the wall. 'I don't know how I managed to get myself roped into this,' he told her, sounding exhausted.

'How did you?'

Gus took his time replying. 'About ten months after Kate's funeral, I joined Moira, my mother-in-law, for dinner at the hall. She invited a few family friends. I was furious – if I'd known she'd invited other people, I would've stayed at home. Anyway, during the meal, the Christmas market came up, and it was on hold. It was Kate's baby, she was organising it and nobody wanted to take it on. Someone, either my mother-in-law or someone else, said it would be wonderful if the market went ahead, to honour Kate. Everyone looked at me, and I felt under fire.'

He was so capable and confident, and she found it hard to imagine him being less than together. But grief, and pain, had a way of ripping a person apart. She'd seen it when her dad and stepdad left, and had a taste of it from Layla recently. 'So you agreed to organise it?'

He pulled a face. 'Agreed is the wrong word. They assumed I would do it and the next day Moira handed me a file with Kate's notes. Kate kept files on everything, the kids, the Christmas shop, the events at the hall, everything. I'm surprised I never found a file on me, detailing my likes, dislikes, how to handle me, my favourite sexual position – *shit*.' He looked aghast. His cheeks turned ruddy and Sutton, taking pity on him and a little charmed by his embarrassment, moved their conversation along.

'So you took over the Christmas market,' she prompted.

He sucked in a deep breath and managed a quick smile. 'Yeah, I figured the more I had to do, the less I'd think, the better I'd be.'

He rubbed the back of his neck as waves of tension rolled off him. He was floundering, and Sutton sympathised. She hated talking about her past and she suspected he did too.

'I'm happy to help you however I can, Gus,' she told him, keeping it simple. Helping him would make her day go faster, always a good thing. She was in a strange village, she knew no one, and she knew that if she was alone for too long, she'd start brooding about her best friend and her betrayal.

How could they have gone so off track? Had everything they shared been a lie?

'And there's some money within the budget to pay for casual labour so I could swing some money for you.'

She wanted to wave his words away, but she was too broke to be generous. 'Thanks. I appreciate your offer.' The extra cash would be extremely helpful. 'I'm pretty broke.'

'I figured. The lone fiver in your wallet and the bank machine slip showing a balance of thirty-something quid were big clues.'

Sutton threw her hands in the air. 'How many times did you go through my backpack?' she asked, pretending to be peeved. She understood why he did it and she didn't mind, she had nothing to hide.

'Only once.' He lifted his eyebrows. His eyes settled on her face and he looked puzzled, and she knew he was still wondering why she was broke and homeless.

Sutton rubbed her throat and stared at a spot past Gus's right shoulder. Strangely, she found herself wanting to explain, maybe he could make sense of the madness. But the words stuck in her throat, and she shook her head.

Gus lifted his hand and his warm fingers curled around the back of her neck. Sutton, desperate to lean into him, closed her eyes, wishing she could rest in his arms, suck up his strength. He'd have an unsentimental, thoughtful view of what happened, an unemotional take on what was one of the defining situations of her life.

Her eyes landed on his mouth, wishing he'd kiss her. How would he taste? Would his lips skim across her mouth, would she feel it in her toes? Her ovaries perked up, interested.

He'll do, they insisted. He'll do nicely. He'd be an excellent distraction and a couple of hours spent in the company of a sexy man would make her feel a lot better. And quickly. He could be a temporary salvation, a way for her to step outside of herself and her memories.

Except…*no.* She stepped back, and he dropped his hand. He was the owner of the roof over her head, the provider of early morning liquid motivation, also known as coffee and her source of badly needed cash. Yes, he made her feel squirrelly and swirly, but sleeping with him, even kissing him, was stupid. In capitals and italics. She was not a stupid girl.

Tequila aside, she tried not to be.

They had to operate on a level, sensible, practical playing field. They each had their roles to play: he needed help with his kids, and she needed a free place to live until she got a job, made a plan or, if miracles did happen, Layla did the right thing and repaid her what she was owed.

Kissing, touching, *sex*, wasn't on the table. But, she couldn't help wishing it was. It had been so long, and Gus was the perfect candidate to break her dry streak.

It was time to focus on something other than how he'd feel under her hands – amazingly wonderful, masculine, superfine – and how much she wanted him under her, over him, her body squashed between his and the nearest wall.

Sheez. Sutton turned her head to check the paint on the wall hadn't started blistering.

Get it together, Sutton. 'So, I'll walk down to Eli and Will's at about eleven. That'll give me time to walk, and dry, the animals. And do some laundry.'

'Sounds good,' he nodded. 'But feel free to use the car.'

'I will, but I like to walk when I can. I don't run –' or exercise, but he didn't need to know that '– so walking is how I burn calories.'

The distinctive sound of a phone hitting the floor made their heads spin.

'Dad!' Felix yelled from the kitchen. 'I put your phone on airplane mode, but it doesn't fly!'

Gus groaned. 'On days like these, I understand, on a visceral level, why some animals eat their young.'

Chapter Six

I n Will and Eli's small and very warm hallway, Sutton
shrugged out of her new jacket – and shoved the black
gloves and the beanie into the inside pocket and zipped it
up so she didn't lose them too.

Sutton looked around, her eyebrows lifting at the small,
cluttered space. She was glad she'd dropped the animals off
at Gus's cottage before coming here. She could easily
imagine Pig's tail whistling across a table and sending
figurines and glass sculptures crashing to the wooden floor.
Unlike Pig, she didn't have a wildly uncontrollable tail, but
she still kept her elbows tucked in.

Will ushered her into their old-fashioned kitchen where
Eli stood by the stove, a leather apron over his sweater and
jeans. The smell of lemon and chicken stock wafted over to
where she stood, and her stomach reacted with a loud
grumble. She was beyond starving.

'Darling!' Eli cried, sending her a lovely, I'm-so-happy-to-see-you smile. 'Wine? Coffee?'

Will pulled out a chair from under the battered wooden table and Sutton sat down, smiling her thanks. 'Coffee, please.' She rubbed her hands together. 'It's bitter out there.'

'Give me another day and I'll start bitching about how sick I am of the cold.' Eli stirred the contents of his saucepan. Was he making risotto? She loved risotto and hoped he'd offer her lunch.

'So how's nannying going, Sutton?' Will asked, turning to the important task of making her coffee.

'I think Rosie might be the end of me. She's frighteningly bright.'

'Her mum was like that,' Eli told her. Turning off the gas, he joined her at the table while Will opened a packet of biscuits.

'Did you know her?' Sutton asked, curious, helping herself to a biscuit and wishing it was a hunk of the newly baked bread sitting on the counter.

'Mmm. Kate was the girl next door, and I was the gay next door.' He looked up and smiled at Will, who carried her cup of coffee to the table. 'I met Will just a few weeks before she died, and I was a mess. He got me through that awful time.'

The love between them was tangible, a living, breathing thing and it wrapped around Sutton, warming her up from the inside out. Sutton sipped her coffee, her eyes widening when she realised Will had dumped whiskey in it.

'I'm working, Will!'

He winked at her. 'I won't tell Gus if you don't.'

'Actually, I'm not looking after the kids until much later this afternoon,' Sutton explained. She'd never mix alcohol with child minding, so she'd be okay. 'They will be with Molly...Moira?'

'Moira.' Eli placed his hand on his chest. 'The delightful Lady M.'

Sutton looked at Will, not sure if he was being sarcastic or not. 'He worships the ground she walks on,' Will explained.

'Moira was the first adult I told I was gay. When my parents threatened to disown me, she went and spoke to them, and we found a way forward,' Eli explained. 'She's the reason I managed to have a relationship with them. Moira's, basically, my second mum. And God, she adores her grandkids.'

Sutton gestured to the kitchen. 'Was this your parents' house?' With its old Aga and low ceilings, it had a fairy tale feel, an old-fashioned air.

'Mm. I inherited it when my mum died about fifteen years ago.'

Sutton murmured a low 'I'm sorry'. She asked Will where he was from, but Eli waved her question away and answered for him. 'London, dead normal, very liberal, very accepting parents. So endlessly undramatic.'

Will rolled his eyes at his partner's comment. Sutton wanted to know more about Kate and wondered how she could broach this. Truthfully, she wanted to know more about Gus, but Kate was a big – probably the biggest – part of his story.

And she doubted Gus, being the strong and silent type, would tell her anything. He was the most interesting and compelling man she'd ever met. Good looking, sure, but his self-assurance was even more attractive than his blue eyes and rugged face. He was a man, mature and confident, sure of himself and his place in the world. Sutton hadn't come across many men like him in her life: her father took off when she was young, she had no idea where he was, and her stepdad did the same when life demanded more from him than he was prepared to give. From the little she knew of him, Gus looked life in the eye and accepted its challenges and responsibilities.

And him being a *man* was something she found shockingly attractive. 'Tell me more about Conningworth, Lady Moira and the family,' Sutton asked, wrapping her hands around her cup. 'What was Kate like?'

Eli placed his chin in the palm of his hand, his blue eyes thoughtful. 'Kate took the responsibilities of the barony she inherited very, very seriously. She believed, rightly or wrongly, it was the family's job, as Conningworths, to look after the village. When she returned from uni, she flung herself into village affairs, determined to make this part of the district as much a tourist attraction as Windermere and Kendal. She opened the hall to tours, persuaded Moira to convert it into a B&B and started hosting weddings and teambuilding events. That's how she met Gus – he organised an orienteering weekend for her.'

Sutton wrinkled her nose. 'Is orienteering where you have to race and navigate?' She couldn't think of anything she'd less like to do.

'Sounds awful, doesn't it?' Eli grimaced. 'Anyway, they got together, and the village adopted Gus, and tourists started trickling in. Kate began organising events – she set up a weekly run/walk through the estate, the weekly farmers' market and various speciality markets throughout the year, culminating in the Christmas market. More tourists came and she decided it was time to open the shop she'd always wanted—'

'Kate's Christmas Shop.'

They nodded, looking sober. 'A week before the grand opening, she was killed in a car crash somewhere outside Manchester.'

The back of Sutton's throat burned. 'That's awful.' Poor, poor Gus. And it is so sad those gorgeous children would grow up without their mum.

'It was a tough, tough time,' Eli agreed. 'It was the village's turn to look after the family, and we set up babysitting and food rosters, organised to have their house cleaned, to do the laundry. Gus bounced back – no, that's the wrong word—' Eli flapped his hands in the air, grimacing.

'Gus had two babies and businesses to look after, and he had to pull it together,' Will calmly explained.

Eli bit down hard on his lower lip, his eyes bright with unshed tears. Sutton wanted to squeeze his hand, but because she wasn't good at spontaneous gestures of affection, she kept her hands wrapped around her cup. She envied Eli, he was so open, so unafraid to show his feelings or to put himself out there. She didn't know how to be like that with anyone but Layla.

She was her person, the yin to her yang. Layla was an only child, but Sutton juggled her schoolwork and her younger siblings. Unlike other kids her age, she had to walk her siblings home, supervise their homework, make them supper, and get them bathed and ready for bed. Her mum would make it home for dinner most nights, but the bulk of household and child-minding chores landed on her too-young shoulders. After dinner, she hit the books, sometimes studying into the early hours to get all her work done. She now understood she was chronically sleep-deprived as a teenager. But when you didn't know better, and simply had to carry on, you did.

Later, when the boys were old enough to, mostly, look after themselves she split her time between studying for her degree and finding a way to pay for it. She hadn't had time to make friends. Occasionally she partied, and had the odd one-night stand, but she never allowed people to get to know her. Or her them. Time was a precious, precious commodity and she guarded it fiercely.

Besides, she'd had Layla, always there, and she'd never needed anyone else.

Eli tapped Sutton on the hand, and she was relieved to see his tears were gone and curiosity had strolled back in. 'Now we—'

'You,' Will interjected.

'—*we* need to know why you destroyed Gus's decorations and passed out on his lawn?' Eli asked. 'We nagged him for an explanation, and he told us.'

'You nagged him, and he told *you*, Eli.'

'I thought Gus could keep that a secret,' Sutton protested. Gus folded like a pack of cards!

'Don't worry, your secret is safe with us,' Will replied, narrowing his eyes at Eli. 'The love of my life is Conningworth's biggest gossip, on sea and land, but he won't say a word if you ask him not to. And Gus has asked him not to, so he won't.'

Eli placed his hand on his heart. 'I adore Gus.'

'Partly because he's a genuinely good guy, and partly because, in summer, Gus runs shirtless,' Will told her, a smile on his face.

Sutton was rather jealous Eli had seen his bare chest and she had to use her imagination. She sighed and then realised two pairs of curious eyes hadn't left her face. 'Well, spill the tea, girlfriend!' Eli demanded.

And Sutton, who never talked about anything serious to anyone but Layla, did. She did, however, leave out her plan to squat in their house.

Conningworth Hall was, as Gus told her as he drove his SUV through the ornate iron gates and onto a Pemberley-like road bisecting a thick wood, a classical Grade II listed house, owned by his wife's family for nearly four hundred years.

'The family had some dodgy moments hanging onto the place in the fifties, but Kate's grandfather made some money importing and exporting wine and managed to find the funds to repair the roof and treat the dry rot,' Gus explained. 'You'll get your first glimpse of the house around this next bend.'

Sutton watched and waited, and there it was, an enormous house built of warm honey-coloured stone. Sutton, because she wasn't a romantic, decided she was glad it wasn't her job to clean the many, many windows. It was impressive, lovely and a bit overwhelming. Owning a house was a daunting idea; owning a house this big was something that would keep her awake at night.

Earlier in the day, she'd walked in the opposite direction, away from the house, towards the stream, and explored the fields and woods of the estate. The gardens were winter-denuded, but she could easily imagine how stunning they'd look in spring and summer, bursting with buds and wildflowers. What looked to be a massive rose garden ran the length of one side of the house, and she noticed benches under large trees.

They drove past the imposing and recessed front door and skirted the side of the house. More windows. 'Will and Eli told me visitors can tour the house,' Sutton said, half turning to face Gus.

'In spring and summer, and it's surprisingly popular. The family managed to hang onto most of their art and furniture collection. There's a Reynolds and a William Nicolson and an exceptionally fine collection of Chinese jade and Sèvres china.'

Being the custodian of so much history could be both a challenge and a burden and Sutton hoped Rosie wouldn't resent inheriting the barony one day. And that Felix would understand why it wasn't his. It was a situation rife with complications, and Sutton didn't envy Gus having to guide his kids through those tumultuous waters. Sometimes being poor, and having nothing to inherit, was easier.

Gus steered the car around to the back of the house and into a massive courtyard. Bright blue pots next to a series of red doors suggested the stables had been converted into self-catering accommodation at some point. Gus parked in front of another bright red door, this one leading into the big house, and told her they were heading into the private family entrance.

'Moira has a self-contained apartment down here,' Gus explained. 'She keeps the rest of the house shut up during winter, unless there's a function or if there are guests.'

Sutton tipped her head back to look up. And up. 'It must be a bitch to heat.'

'It really is, and damned expensive,' Gus agreed. He opened his door and Sutton winced when sharp blades of icy air hit her lungs. Man, she needed to toughen up.

'Do you get along with your mother-in-law?' Sutton asked after he opened her door and waited for her to climb out. She didn't want to. It was nice and toasty in the car and she could meet Lady Moira another time, couldn't she?

'Stop being a wuss,' Gus told her. 'It's not *that* cold.'

She'd seen the temperature on his car's dashboard earlier, four degrees Centigrade. Below twenty it was chilly, below ten was stupidly cold. And the wind blowing down from the fells cut through her and made it feel like minus four.

'It is *that* cold and you didn't answer my question,' Sutton told him, pulling her beanie over her head.

Gus placed his hand on her back to guide her to the red door. 'I do. She welcomed me into her home and her life,' he said as they stepped into a mudroom filled with coats, dogs' beds and bowls and a huge washer and dryer.

'Aren't mothers-in-law supposed to be grim?' she asked as he shed his coat and flung it over the washing machine.

'Mine isn't.'

Okay, then. Good for him. An old sheepdog looked at them from a plump dog bed in the corner of the mudroom, and Gus dropped to his haunches to scratch black and white ears. 'This is Candy,' he told her. 'She was Kate's dog.'

He rubbed his hand over her head and down her neck. 'How are you doing, old girl? Staying inside where it's warm, huh?'

Clever dog.

After another minute stroking Candy, Gus stood and steered Sutton into a surprisingly modern kitchen. She took in the industrial oven, the sleek marble counter, and sighed at the massive Aga on the far side of the wall. 'Does the Aga work?'

'Yeah, it heats Moira's private quarters,' Gus replied.

'But the house relies on an oil boiler for heat. Costs an effing fortune.'

Sutton heard the flying feet of the twins, and they barrelled around the corner and headed straight for her. Felix reached her first and skidded to a stop. 'Sutton, Rosie says you come from Africa and it takes six days to get there.'

'Just half a day on a plane, guys,' Sutton told him, placing her hand on his head. Rosie was two steps behind her twin.

'How do the planes stay up in the air that long?' Rosie demanded, looking puzzled. 'Why don't they fall out of the sky?'

She looked at Gus, who raised his hands. 'Pass,' he said. Damn, he was quick.

Sutton was saved from explaining the intricacies of modern flight by the gentle tip tap of heels coming down the hallway. Kate's mum looked just like the lady of the manor should, dammit, cool, calm and oh-so classy. She wore wide-legged trousers the colour of brushed steel, a black cashmere jersey and a gold belt that spanned her still-trim waist. Her silver bob was perfectly curled, and her make-up pitch-perfect. One look at her and Sutton felt she needed a tip-to-toe makeover.

'Moira, this is Sutton. Sutton, Lady Moira Conningworth,' Gus introduced her, before bending down to drop a kiss on both the kids' heads. Sutton smiled at Lady Conningworth and was astounded by the hostility in her green eyes. Eeek! Sutton darted a look over her shoulder, mentally judging how long it would take her to scuttle out of her perfect house.

What did Gus tell Moira about her? How did he explain her? Taking a deep breath, Sutton pulled a smile onto her face, stepped forward and held out her hand. 'It's lovely to meet you,' she said, not knowing what she preferred to be called. Moira? Lady Moira? Your Majesty, With-A-Stick-Shoved-Up-Your-Arse?

Gus's haughty mother-in-law ignored her hand and narrowed her eyes. Wow. Okay, then. This was awkward.

Gus frowned and Sutton tucked her hands into the back pockets of her skinny jeans. 'I told you about Sutton, Moira.'

'The one who passed out from too much tequila?' Moira's accent wasn't cut glass, it was laser sharp.

Great! She made it sound like Gus caught her having an orgy on his lawn. Look, it wasn't her finest moment, but she only killed a couple of neon snowmen, she didn't harm anyone but herself. And her sore cheek, still bruised, was punishment enough.

'Sutton temporarily needed a place to stay, and I need help with the twins, as you've been telling me for months now,' Gus stated, sounding cross and confused.

Moira folded her skinny arms across her chest and didn't take her eyes off Sutton. 'You said you got references,' she asked Gus.

'I told you I did. I would never allow anyone to look after my kids if I didn't feel completely comfortable with them. Sutton is who she says she is.'

'I think you missed something, Angus,' Moira stated, in

her hoity-toity accent. She lifted her hand to her hair and Sutton noticed a tremor. Okay, she was properly upset. But what could she have done to distress her? All she'd done today was walk the dogs and visit Eli and Will.

'I simply cannot forget she was –' Moira looked at the kids, who were smart enough to sense the concern in her voice. Their eyes bounced from Sutton to their grandmother, and back again '– *foxed* when you first met her.'

'Moira—'

Sutton was a big girl and didn't need Gus defending her. 'In my defence, overindulging is not something I do often, Lady Conningworth,' she stated. 'I'm not proud of my behaviour but I won't flog myself for it either.'

Gus raised one eyebrow and sent a '*not helping*' glare her way.

'Did you have a fox, Sutton?' Rosie asked. 'Was it hurt? Did you find it?'

Rosie's questions reminded the adults there were little ears in the room. Gus was the first to react. 'I think we have our wires crossed, Moira. Let's you and I talk this through, in private, while Sutton takes the twins to the car.'

Sutton planted her feet and shook her head. If she was the subject of conversation, she'd prefer to stay. Gus's eyes met hers and she caught the tiny shake of his head, his silent request to let him handle this situation. She pursed her lips. She fought her own battles, and she didn't like someone else climbing into the boxing ring for her.

'Twins, say goodbye to Nan,' Gus said, his eyes not

leaving hers. Felix and Rosie immediately ran over to their grandmother and flung themselves at her. Moira bent down and hugged them both, her eyes closing as her lips kissed their heads in turn. It was obvious she adored them, and they turned her world. Moira was super-protective of them, and Sutton had done something to raise her mama-bear instincts.

But what? Well, what except for passing out from being drunk? She'd never met the woman and she'd only been living with the Langston family for thirty-six hours. She hadn't had time to do anything else wrong!

'Sutton?' Sutton took her eyes off the kids to look at Gus. 'Take them to the car and let me handle this, okay?'

Sutton felt two little hands slide into hers and she looked down to see a twin on either side of her. She looked at Gus again and nodded. He'd get to the bottom of this, whatever this was…

This wasn't a battle she needed to fight. She had someone to do it for her. And the idea terrified her. She never allowed anyone to sort out her mess. In fairness, there never had been anyone to fight for her. Her dad and stepdad were long gone, her mum was too busy and she looked after her siblings, not the other way around. And Layla? Well, she tended to make sure Layla was okay, not the other way around.

Damn you, Layla. If it wasn't for you then I wouldn't be in this situation! I could be exploring Bath, or Oxford, staying in cute B&Bs and eating in pubs. Maybe even seeing a show or going clubbing. Ok, maybe not clubbing, but…

Sending Gus another uncertain look, Sutton allowed the kids to lead her out of the kitchen and into the mudroom. She helped them into their coats and pulled hers on before stepping outside. It was fully dark outside, and Sutton got the kids into their car seats and made sure they were buckled in tight.

Felix looked at her, his blue eyes reflecting his concern. 'Why is Nan mad at you, Sutton?'

Sutton managed to smile at him. 'I don't know, Felix. If I knew, I'd say I was sorry.'

'Did you forget to wash your hands after you had a pee?' Felix asked her, looking horrified. 'She doesn't like that!'

'I'm not sure why she's upset, sweetie,' Sutton told him, shutting his door. She walked around to where Rosie sat and belted her into her car seat, biting her lip.

Gus wouldn't let Moira talk him out of letting her stay, would she? Two days ago, she desperately needed to stay, now she wanted to hang around. This was where she wanted to be, where she could catch her breath, and let down her guard.

Just a little. And just for a little while.

———

Gus loved his mother-in-law but thought she should stop watching reality shows and documentaries.

'Sutton is *not* a drug addict, Moira.'

Moira twisted her hands together. 'But how do you

know?' she demanded, her eyes bright with fear. 'Rosie said she put something up her nose this morning! That she saw her!'

Gus didn't think it was fair to convict Sutton on such flimsy evidence. 'Rosie is four, Moira,' he stated, struggling to hold on to his patience.

'She's a very observant and bright four!' Moira shot back. Moira thought the twins walked on water and that they could do no wrong. Gus gripped the bridge of his nose, pushing away his irritation. Yes, he understood how protective Moira was over his children, but nobody was more so than him. Did she really think he'd put his precious children in the care of a drug addict? *Seriously?*

Sure, hiring Sutton the way he did was unconventional, but something in her called to him. She was tough, but vulnerable, trying her best to make the best of a bad situation. She was broke, homeless and in a tight spot, and if he could help her, he would.

'Look, I admit she didn't give me the best first impression,' Gus explained, 'but I understand more about her situation than you do.'

She'd drunkenly told him about her tough childhood – he'd had one too, so he could empathise – and he understood how her friend's betrayal rocked her. It was tough to discover the one person you thought had your back, didn't. Sutton hadn't mentioned her past again, and he understood. It was too personal and too hurtful to be shared with someone who was barely more than a stranger, and her boss. Tequila loosened her tongue, and she'd be mortified if she knew he knew. Sutton didn't like to be perceived as weak, or in need of sympathy.

He got it. He didn't like feeling that way either.

'Moi, I went through her backpack. I did not find anything that pointed to her being a drug user. She's clear-eyed, and clean.'

Besides, and he wouldn't tell Moira this, she didn't have money to spend on drugs. He gritted his teeth at the thought of her having less than fifty pounds to her name. It made him feel sick, and very pissed off. Girls, and women of all ages, had found themselves in worse situations with more money.

Gus rubbed his jaw. 'I called six people in South Africa, and they all gave me good references,' Gus told Moira, wanting to get back to Sutton and the kids. 'I promise you, she's *fine.*'

'Okay. I trust your judgement." Moira cocked her head and her green eyes, Kate's eyes, turned speculative. 'You like her,' she stated.

Oh, *fuck*. Not this now. For the last six months, Moria'd been pushing him to date more, to think about what the rest of his life would look like. He couldn't deal with another when-are-you-going-to-start-dating-again conversation.

'Moira,' he pleaded.

'You need a long-term, stable partner, someone who will help you raise the twins.'

He looked around, wondering how much it would hurt to throw himself out of the nearest window. 'I have you to help me raise the twins,' he spluttered.

'What if I find a lovely lover and I relocate to Cyprus with him?' Moira demanded.

Wait! *What?* 'Is that a possibility?'

'It might be,' Moira crisply replied. 'The point is, you need something more than casual sex, Gus.'

He did? Uh...not in this lifetime. And what did she know about his sex life? 'I'm not an idiot, Gus, I know you see a woman in Kendal for no-strings sex.'

And there went the power to his brain. He wasn't a prude, but he wasn't comfortable talking about this with the woman who'd birthed his wife. 'You need happy sex, loving sex, wild sex—'

La la la la la.

The image of Sutton, dressed only in the blue bra and matching, skimpy panties, flashed across his mind. Her skin looked soft and creamy, and he wanted to know how it felt to have her legs locked around his hips. But she was his nanny, she was in a vulnerable position, and he would *not* take advantage of her.

He didn't want a relationship and having one, having *anything*, with Sutton was impossible. He lifted his hand, needing to move this conversation along. Or to blow it to smithereens with some C-4. 'Right, I'm done discussing this.'

Moira ignored him. 'And, now that I know she isn't a druggie, I think Sutton looks like a nice girl.'

Christ on a bike! 'She's my *nanny*, Moira. End of.'

'You're a young, good-looking guy and you need to move on.' An arrow hit his chest, its point as sharp as it was three years ago. How could he explain to her, explain to anyone, that he felt guilty for *not* feeling guilty about having sex, and one-night stands? He should, but he didn't. Not after what— *aarrgh!*

'Just don't close yourself up to the possibilities…'

'Bye, Moira.' Gus turned his back to her and walked away. She couldn't keep talking to fresh air. Then again, this was Moira, and anything was possible.

'Tell Sutton I'm sorry, and that I'll swing by to apologise! Maybe she can come to tea.'

He lifted a hand in acknowledgement and strode into the kitchen, then the mudroom, grabbed his coat and hurried out the back door. Then the humour of the situation hit him, and he started to laugh. Only Moira could get it so wrong. Sutton met him by the bonnet of the car, looking adorably confused and very worried. 'What's her problem?' she crisply demanded, and he heard the fear in her voice.

Gus gripped the bonnet of the car, and leaned forward, his laughter louder than before. Sutton gripped the lapel of his coat and shook it. 'What happened inside? Why did she treat me like I was something disgusting she found on her shoe?'

She shivered and Gus noticed the blue tinge to her lips. It was time to get her out of the cold. He took her hand, tugged her around the car and opened her door for her. After Sutton climbed inside, he jogged around the car, slid behind the wheel and started the engine. Sutton immediately put her hands over the vents, waiting for the blast of hot air.

'The esteemed Lady M thinks you are snorting coke,' he explained.

She stared at him, shocked. '*What* did you say?'

'Moira, Lady Conningworth, thought you took a hit this morning.'

She waved his words away. 'I heard you... But *why* would she think that?'

Gus tugged his seatbelt over his chest. 'You can thank my blabby-mouth daughter for giving her the wrong impression.'

'I don't understand any of this,' she told him, utterly confused.

'Sometime today, I presume this morning, Rosie saw you put something up your nose...'

'Rosie was in the bathroom with me when I used my allergy spray.'

There you go.

He smiled. 'Rosie informed Moira, in delicious detail, that you have special medicine for your nose. Apparently, it gives you energy and makes you feel good.'

Sutton covered her face with her hands. 'I didn't think she was old enough to explain my allergies.'

'With Rosie, it's always better to explain,' Gus cheerfully told her as he put his car in gear. 'She repeats everything, word for word. I told Moira how you came into our lives. I explained you've been travelling and how you ended up on my lawn, but maybe I was in a rush and didn't give her enough information. After hearing you liked to shove stuff up your nose, she added two and two and came up with twenty-three. She thought I was harbouring an international drug mule.'

Sutton groaned again. 'Holy Mary Mother of God!' she muttered, closing her eyes.

'It's all sorted, Sutton,' he told her, needing to reassure her.

'I was hammered when I met you, and your mother-in-law, classy to the tips of her toes, thinks I'm an addict. Wow. I'm two for two.'

'My friend, Angela, is going to be Mary in our Christmas play,' Felix stated from the back seat. 'I'm a donkey.'

'And I'll be an angel,' Rosie added.

'Thoroughly miscast,' Gus murmured. He looked at her red, mortified face. 'Look, I reassured Moira you are not working for Escobar, and she's mortified at her mistake. She'll apologise. Expect a call, or possibly even a handwritten note.'

Sutton nodded and stared straight ahead, still embarrassed. 'The truth is that if I didn't drink so much, if I wasn't a backpacker, then she wouldn't have thought I was a cokehead.' Sutton tried to smile. 'It's okay, Gus, I can appreciate her being protective of the twins. They're her grandkids, and in her place, I would have questions about a misfit traveller moving into your house too.'

She was sensible and generous. He appreciated both qualities.

'Are you okay?' he quietly asked.

She bit the inside of her cheek. 'I didn't mean to cause any trouble for you,' she stated. 'I know you are fond of

Moira, and she adores the kids. I'm so embarrassed she knows what I did, how we met.'

He started the car and briefly squeezed her knee. 'It's fine, Sutton. She's fine. It was a misunderstanding, that's all.'

'She'll invite you for tea,' Gus added, quickly reversing so they could drive out of the courtyard. 'I'd take her up on it. Moira makes a mean chocolate cake.'

They passed Sunshine Cottage, Christmas lights blazing. 'Thanks for defending me,' she said. 'But how could you be so sure that I didn't indulge?'

He tapped his finger against the steering wheel, flicking her a glance. 'You keep forgetting I searched your backpack while you were passed out on my couch, Sutton,' he informed her, keeping his voice low-pitched and steady. 'If I'd found anything, I would've kicked you out on your pretty arse. And called the police.'

Fair enough. 'You did miss my blue bra.'

He darted a look at her. Was she teasing him? Flirting? Heat, and a hit of adrenalin, coursed through him. He shouldn't respond, he should be sensible and play it cool.

But, just for one minute, he wanted to be a man, and not a widower, and not a single dad. He wanted to be a guy sitting next to a girl, someone who could still flirt. It had been so long.

'I absolutely did not,' he assured her, keeping his voice low. 'Of the three matching sets, the red one is my favourite colour.'

'Raspberry,' Sutton said, her voice huskier than it was

before. Was her throat also tight-with-lust? 'Raspberry, blueberry and blackberry.'

'Blue, purple and red,' he said, sending her a hot look. 'I couldn't give a shit about their fancy names. What colour are you wearing now?'

'Daddy said a bad word!' Rosie crowed from the back seat, her little feet hitting the back of his chair. He swallowed his groan. 'Daddy, say sorry.'

Gus swung the car into his driveway and mouthed a 'fuck' at Sutton. 'Sorry, guys.' He parked, switched the engine off and looked at Sutton. The temperature in the car shot up and all the moisture in his mouth evaporated. She looked like a woman who wanted him. Naked, and panting his name.

He'd shut this down in a second, when they left the car, the flirting would stop. It would have to. But he could have a few more seconds of feeling…well, normal.

'Red, blue or purple, Sutt?' he demanded, his voice carrying heat and lust and so much want.

Sutton's words came out breathy and a little growly. 'Red, Gus.'

Damn, her smile was one he wanted to feel on his skin. He wanted to stroke his fingertips down her spine, across the delicious curve of her butt. He craved the taste of her mouth and needed her nipple against the roof of his mouth.

She wanted him. He wanted her.

And Felix, as he loudly informed them, wanted to poop.

Chapter Seven

Sutton's first item on the Christmas agenda was to get a Christmas tree up and the Saturday after she arrived in Conningworth, she took delivery of an eight-foot-high tree from a taciturn man named Ben who was, according to Rosie, Nan's *right-hand man*.

And, Felix added, her left too.

Ben ignored the dancing, excitable twins and helped place the enormous, kickass tree on a stand. After silently downing a cup of strong, bark-coloured tea, he stepped over the many boxes on the hall floor (Gus had them pulled out of storage and delivered) and melted away.

With the scent of the freshly cut tree wafting through the hall, Sutton stood back to admire it, loving its fat, dark green branches. It was the perfect tree and totally different from the anaemic, thin and utterly fake trees everyone used back home.

Pig and Pepper wandered in from the kitchen and nosed

the boxes, and Pig gave Felix a full-face lick, something the little boy didn't even notice, as he was trying to separate a ball of tinsel into its different strands. Most of the boxes were taped shut and Sutton looked at the feminine writing on the sides, *'Baubles'*, *'Fragile'*, *'Handblown'*. Kate had lovely handwriting, and Sutton imagined her wrapping up her decorations, and carefully labelling the boxes, never imagining she wouldn't see another Christmas again.

She swallowed the lump in her throat, and put her hand on Rosie's head, hoping that Kate, wherever she was, knew her kids were happy and healthy. And that Gus was doing an amazing job raising them.

Rosie tugged on her thigh-length jersey. 'Sutton, I need the knife-thingy.'

Words to freeze the blood. Sutton slapped her hand against her back pocket, relieved to find the sheathed box cutter still nestled in her pocket. Four-year-olds and knives would result in blood and a trip to A&E.

'You're not allowed to open the boxes, Rosie,' she reminded the little girl. 'I'll open them, remember?'

And she'd removed anything breakable before the twins could get their hands on them. Gus wasn't against having a Christmas tree but he wasn't enthusiastic about it either – why on earth not? – and she didn't need any snarky comments about breakages from him. Not that he would, of the two of them, she was the one who tended to run her mouth.

'Then what can I do?' Rosie demanded, pushing out her lower lip.

'Help your brother with the tinsel,' she suggested. Her suggestion didn't go down well, and Rosie glared at her. The little girl opened her mouth to object, but the doorbell chimed, and one big head (Pig) and three small heads (the twins and Pepper) shot up. Sutton threaded her way through the boxes to the front door and yanked it open.

Gus's mother-in-law, Conningworth's first citizen, stood on the porch, her green eyes, silver-blonde hair and white coat bright, a perfect contrast to the dreary, wet day. Sutton pushed back her shoulders. She wasn't twelve and, crucially, she was innocent of all charges.

'Good afternoon,' she said, aiming for polite.

Lady Conningworth pulled her hand out from behind her back and thrust a mug at her. Sutton frowned and took the mug. What was happening here? Was mug giving some strange English way to apologise?

'Damn, it's the wrong way round.' Lady Moira yanked the cup from her grasp, and handed it back to her, the writing on the mug now facing Sutton.

'Nan!' Rosie shouted, springing up and pushing past Sutton to fling her arms around the older lady's knees. 'We're putting up a tree. Come see!'

Pig barked, and Felix lifted a ball of tinsel that looked more tangled than it had before. Sutton looked down at the mug in her hand. The red circle had a line through it and the words *Just Say No* were emblazoned across the circle. So, Gus's mother-in-law had a sense of humour. Good to know.

Their eyes met across Rosie's head. 'I am sorry,' she said,

looking rueful. 'I shouldn't have taken my granddaughter's word as gospel.'

Rosie looked up at her. 'What's gospel, Nan?'

Moira dropped a kiss on her head. 'It means you need to go to Sunday School more often.' She straightened and met Sutton's eyes. 'Am I forgiven?'

Sutton placed the cup against her breastbone. Yes, of course she was. 'Absolutely. Come in, but be careful, there are boxes everywhere.' Sutton pulled the door open, and Moira looked past her and clapped her hands, delighted. 'Yay, a tree! I love putting up the tree.'

Sutton knew the process would go a lot quicker with some adult help. 'Then come in and give us a hand.'

'No Gus?' Moira quietly asked, wrapping her arms around Rosie's small shoulders.

Sutton shook her head, watching Moira's face. She thought she mouthed an obscenity. No, she was imagining things, there was no way the esteemed Lady M would drop an F-bomb. 'Gus is working at the shop today,' she told Moira. 'He told us to get on with it.'

Moira clapped her hands, covered in gorgeous, soft leather gloves, together. 'Then that's what we shall do. But we need chocolate cake. And champagne.'

She'd indulge in the first and not the second. Moira peeked into the hall and nodded her approval. 'What an excellent tree! It's huge and we're going to need some help. Do you mind if we ask Will and Eli to join us?'

Sutton quickly nodded. Four adults to help wrangle two overly excited children. She'd be a fool to say no.

'I'll scoot back to the hall and grab the chocolate cake I made and a couple of bottles,' Moira told Sutton. 'I'll pick up the boys on the way back.'

'They might have other plans,' Sutton suggested.

Moira smiled at her. 'Trust me, they'll jump at the chance to decorate the tree, boss you about, eat my cake and drink my champagne.'

Alrighty, then. Rosie looked up at her grandmother. 'Can I come with you, Nan?'

Moira looked at Sutton. 'Can she? I have car seats in my car, and I haven't had anything stronger than tea to drink today.'

Sutton appreciated her asking for permission. And since she knew Moira often collected the kids from school and took them out and about, she couldn't see why not. She snagged Rosie's coat and helped the little girl into it and rammed a beanie on her head. Pig pushed his nose into Rosie's neck, and she wrapped her arm around the big dog's neck. 'Can Pig come too, Nan?' Rosie asked.

Moira grinned at Sutton. 'Why not?'

She pressed her car fob and the back door of her Range Rover opened automatically. Pig belted off and leapt into the back of the vehicle, his tongue lolling. Pig wore a collar of red, white and gold tinsel around his thick neck.

Moira smiled and took Rosie's hand. 'We'll be back in fifteen minutes, tops. Do you want to put on some milk for hot chocolate? I have some baby marshmallows at home. Do you want hot chocolate, Fee?'

Felix nodded enthusiastically. 'I love your hot chocolate, Nan! It's *yum*.'

'Of course it is,' Moira smugly replied. 'Because why?'

Rosie looked at her brother and sighed. 'It's your turn, Felix.'

Felix took a deep breath. 'Because *M* is for marvellous, *O* for outstanding, *I* is for incredible…Nan, do I have to?' he whined.

Moira rolled her finger and Felix released a huge sigh.

'*R* is for ravishing, and *A* is for amazing,' Rosie jumped in, impatient to get going. 'Nan, let's *go*!'

Sutton laughed. 'How long did it take you to teach them that?' she asked, shivering in her jersey and jeans.

'Not as long as you would think,' Moira gaily replied, placing her hand on Rosie's head and smiling at Felix. 'Good little minions, you earned your hot chocolate.'

Sugary hot chocolate meant they'd soon be bouncing off the walls. 'Do you think sugar is a good idea?' Sutton asked, doubtful.

Moira waved her concerns away. 'If they get too much, we'll just send them home with the boys. The other day they told me they are thinking of changing careers, staying home more and maybe having a baby via surrogacy. It's never too early to start practising.'

Sutton grinned. 'I like the way you think,' she said.

Moira tipped her head and sent Sutton a low, slow smile. 'And I like you. You and I, Sutton, we're going to be great friends.'

As Rosie and Moira walked to the car, with Moira

belting out a rap version of *All I Want for Christmas Is You*, Sutton knew she had absolutely no choice in the matter. And she was, strangely, very okay with that.

———

The tree in Gus's hallway wasn't just a tree; it was a full-blown explosion of Christmas…well, deliciousness. It was the Ronaldinho, or maybe the Elton John, of Christmas trees, and more than a foot taller than him. Its branches, pointing in every direction, screamed 'Look at me, I'm fabulous!', and dipped under the weight of the ornaments.

Gus quietly shut the front door and tipped his head back to look at the angel at the top of the tree. It was Kate's angel, the one her dad gave her when she was eight, one of his wife's most treasured possessions. Someone had taken the time to weave twinkling fairy lights between the branches, giving off a warm, cosy glow in the dark hallway.

He walked up to the tree and touched a glass bauble with the tip of his finger, causing it to sway. He'd been with Kate when she bought this set from a glassmaker in Venice. There were many he didn't recognise and wondered if every ornament Kate owned – and she'd owned a lot – was on the tree. It looked like it. Then again, it was a big tree.

Gus placed his phone and wallet in the bowl on the hall table, cocking his head at the yelling coming from the conservatory. Years of experience told him it was a yell of excitement, so he sat down on the chair in the hall and unlaced his boots. Kicking them off, he rested the back of his head against the wall behind him and closed his eyes. It had been a long, long day at the shop, with loads of visitors all day. He'd smiled and smiled and offered shortbread and put through credit card payments. He'd been so busy he hadn't even had time to go into the storeroom and bang his head against the wall in frustration, something he'd done more than once before.

The melody of 'Hark the Herald Angels' drifted over to him and he heard Eli's distinctive tenor. All he wanted was to come home to a quiet house, a stiff whiskey and a long bath. But he mostly craved a quiet house free of anything Christmassy. Unfortunately, there was a sodding big Christmas tree in his hallway.

'Joyful all ye nations rise, join the triumph of the skies—'

Was that Moira's soprano? And yeah, she sounded a little...buzzed? Champagne soaked? Brilliant. And where was his bloody nanny?

Gus walked into the dark kitchen and stood in the shadows, looking into the brightly lit conservatory. The furniture had been pushed back against the walls and the huge carpet cleared of toys. His mother-in-law, a glass of champagne in her hand, was curled up in the corner of the couch, her eyes on the hotly contested game happening on the carpet in front of her.

Everyone, Moira included, wore a brightly coloured elf hat and Gus immediately noticed Rosie's kept falling into her eyes. His eyes drifted over the carpet. Someone, Sutton, probably, had cut out the faces of snowmen and glued them to paper cups and bowls, which were lined up in a zig-zag pattern.

A pile of rolled-up socks, his socks, sat on the carpet and his son picked up a sock ball and narrowed his eyes. He rolled it, missing three 'pins' and hitting one. He spun around, delighted at his accomplishment.

Eli high-fived him. 'Ten points for Felix,' Moira grandly declared.

'It's my turn,' Rosie announced. She pushed back her elf hat, and tossed his socks, green this time, from hand to hand. She dropped to one knee and sent the sock ball rolling. It bounced off the back wall and knocked down two pins on the way back. She howled with laughter and Pig stood up and bolted across the room and grabbed the sock ball, shaking it furiously.

Eli and Will implored him to drop it, Felix and Rosie laughed harder, and Moira awarded Pig twenty points.

When last did he see his kids looking so happy, his mother-in-law so relaxed? He couldn't remember. Behind them, rain hit the windows but here, inside his house, his kids were laughing and the people he cared for most were having a good time. Rosie picked up her cup and took a deep sip, and Felix said something to her, causing chocolate milk to erupt from her nose. Will offered her his t-shirt to wipe the chocolate off her face before taking his turn to roll his grubby ball of white socks.

They were having pure, uncomplicated fun. And it wouldn't have happened if Sutton hadn't asked whether they could put up a tree. His kids, the people he lived for, and would die for, were happy, and tears burned Gus's eyes. He was grateful they were having such a good time, but also embarrassed that he'd chosen work over this, and that he hadn't provided the source of their joy.

'They're playing Snowman Slam.'

Gus turned and saw Sutton standing in the doorway to the kitchen, strands of her hair falling out of her loose ponytail. She wore skinny jeans and a cream-coloured jersey with a dark stain – chocolate? – on her right breast. In the shadows, his eyes rammed into hers. 'What are the rules?' he softly asked.

'It depends on who you ask,' Sutton replied. 'It changes as it goes along.'

'Was it your idea?' he asked.

Sutton lifted one shoulder which was as good as a 'yes'. 'Moira's a little...toasty,' she quietly told him, laughter in her voice.

'Did she apologize to you?' Gus asked.

'She did, in the most delightful way possible,' Sutton told him, still speaking softly. She glanced over to Moira, who was arguing with Eli about an off-side rule. 'I really like her, Gus.'

He did too. He'd lucked out with his mum-in-law. The music changed to a hard beat, and Will spun Rosie around in a twirl. Eli pulled Moira out of her seat while Felix bopped around, his arms flailing. That kid had no rhythm. Like, *zero*.

Gus felt Sutton's eyes on his face and turned back to look at her. 'Do you want to dance, Gus?'

He shook his head. He had something else on his mind. Something he needed to do, right now.

Sutton watched as Gus padded over to her and gripped her wrist, gently tugging her into the hall. She looked up and Gus noticed his eyes were a lot darker than before, a blue-black she'd never seen before. He half smiled and quietly led her up the stairs. Sutton didn't pull her hand out of his, nor did she protest.

Gus pulled her into his bedroom at the end of the hall and kicked the door closed with his foot. The door clicked shut, and a moment later his hands were on her thin jersey, pulling it up and over her head. He looked down at her red lingerie and sighed, resting his forehead against hers.

'So damn beautiful, Sutt,' he muttered, his voice deeper and raspier than she'd ever heard it.

'I swear to God, Gus, if you don't kiss me…'

She was beyond being coy, she wanted this man more than she'd ever wanted anyone before. It was a need that welled up from deep in her soul, pulsed in her womb and heated the moisture between her legs. She'd experienced sexual attraction before but nothing like this.

'Is this wrong, Sutton?' he said, his big hands gripping her hips, his thumbs drawing patterns on the bare skin above them.

'If it is, I don't care,' Sutton assured him. 'I just want you to kiss me, preferably sometime within the next millisecond.'

'I'd hate for you to have to wait that long.' Gus lowered his head, and his mouth, his clever, sexy mouth, covered hers. Sutton felt her knees wobble just a little and was glad when his arm slid around her back, and he yanked her close and anchored her to him. Her almost bare chest pushed into his. She wanted to be skin-on-skin with him, but more than that, she wanted him to kiss her properly, with heat and intent and desperate want.

Sutton clasped the back of his head and opened her mouth, her tongue tracing the seam of his lips. He hesitated, as if knowing they wouldn't be able to return if they went back there, and she had a moment's doubt. What if he shut this down, what if he put some distance between... But then his mouth opened, his tongue found hers and he took control of their kiss, ratcheting up the heat. He manoeuvred her so her back rested against the bedroom door, and he pushed his thigh between her legs, high enough to create pressure on her mound. She moaned into his mouth. His hand stroked the sides of her chest and then covered her breast, his thumb skating across her already hard nipple. This man didn't say much, wasn't the world's best communicator, but God, the way he touched her! That brief, thrilling swipe was Homer's *Odyssey*, *War and Peace*, *Romeo and Juliet*, all the best words from the best authors.

Gus pulled his mouth off hers and ducked his head, taking her nipple into his mouth, fabric and all. His tongue lathed her, causing the lace to stick to her. The added friction sent waves of lust rolling through her. She'd never felt anything like this before, had never been lost to desire, caught up in the moment.

Sutton turned her head and caught her reflection in the free-standing mirror across the room. The woman she saw, sexy and half-dressed, didn't look like her. Her face glowed with need, her hair hung wild on her shoulders and her eyes glittered in the muted light of the bedroom. She looked like a seductress, a temptress, nothing like the stressed, short-of-cash, half-broken woman she'd been these past few months.

'Sutt, God, you are so fucking hot,' Gus muttered, his lips burning a trail of fire up her chest. He grazed her collarbone with his teeth, and Sutton raked his jersey and shirt up his back, desperate to lay her hands on his hot male skin. It had been so long since she'd been with a guy, for ever since she'd experienced this heady rush of need and want and heat.

Gus kissed her again, his lips demanding more than before. She was happy to give him everything, maybe more. Maybe everything. The thought settled, burned and Sutton jerked away from him, shocked. What was she thinking? This was a kiss, a quick fumble, a biological need, there was no room for emotion here, for thoughts of…*more*.

Gus lifted his hand and cupped her face. 'Everything okay?' he asked, his thumb brushing her lower lip. He stared at her, his gaze focused and intense. 'You know this has nothing to do with how you got here and you being my nanny, right?'

She never, not for a second, thought it did but she appreciated him saying so. 'If I thought you were that kind of guy, I would be out of here so fast your head would spin.'

Gus curled his hand around the back of her neck and Sutton rested her forehead on his chest. She couldn't look at him; she needed a moment to get her thoughts in order before she faced those sharp blue eyes again. He had a way of looking at her and her words floated to the surface.

She didn't like feeling this much, and wasn't used to such an intense connection. She understood the mechanics of sex, and thought it was a rather pleasant activity when done right, but she'd never found herself lost in a man's touch, craving his mouth, the pleasure he could give her. Wanting the words, and the connection. It scared her, and knowing she could be scared, scared her more.

She needed to put this, them, into perspective, and to see this for what it was...a guy and girl who sparked off each other.

There was nothing here but animal attraction, a sexual current sweeping them out to sea. The emotions pushing their way to the surface – the feeling of her heart wanting to burst wide open, her soul skipping, her breath hitching, all as terrifying as they were sexy – had to be ignored. What was the point of letting emotion into the party? Those bastards always complicated a straightforward situation.

She couldn't afford to feel anything for Gus. He was her temporary boss, the man who'd taken her in and given her a place to stay until she got her shit sorted...

She was independent, she reminded herself, Brave. Self-sufficient…well, currently that was in doubt, but normally. She was single and she had her freedom. No money, but it was coming.

She didn't need hot kisses, strong arms to hold her, a quirky smile and sharp, dark blue eyes locked with hers.

Gus, reading her mind, lifted his hands off her and stepped back. 'Too much, too soon?' he quietly asked.

'Too much everything,' she admitted. 'It's been…*intense*.'

'I get that.'

Sutton realised her bra strap was halfway down her arm. Before she could pull it up, Gus hooked his finger under the strap and pulled it back into place. He picked up her jersey and handed it to her, and she pulled it over her head and shoved her arms into the sleeves. Dressed, she felt calmer, a little more controlled.

Gus placed a hand on the wall behind her head and leaned in, his expression unreadable. Sutton put her hands behind her back, palms against the wall. She waited for him to speak, knowing she couldn't rush him. Gus wasn't a guy who could be pushed where he didn't want to go.

'I want you,' he baldly stated. 'I've wanted you since you stumbled onto my lawn, fists up and wanting to punch Santa.'

'You beat me to it, Mr Christmas.'

He winced at his nickname before his expression turned serious again.

'I haven't been a monk since Katie died, there have been a few women, but – Jesus.' He raked his hands through his hair. 'This…you…'

He raised his hands and mimicked an explosion. Sutton thought it was a perfect explanation.

'But…'

She knew what he was going to say, she could see it in his eyes. She didn't need him to explain. 'But there can't be anything between us but great sex?'

'Yeah…*that*. I'm a single dad with two small kids, I run two businesses, and I have so much on my plate. Even if I wanted a relationship, it's impossible. Not happening.'

She wasn't an idiot, she knew a relationship was out of the question.

She had a job to find, and a career to establish. She wanted to be in London and wasn't interested in living in a small, admittedly pretty village at the arse end of the world. She'd helped raise her siblings, but she wasn't ready to take on someone else's kids, as cute as the twins were. 'Relax. If I did decide to sleep with you, Langston, it would only be for your body.'

He frowned, disconcerted. 'Sorry?'

She waved at his bed, which was, she noticed, very neatly made, with an aqua bedspread tucked in with hospital corners. His room was functional, minimalistic, and as neat as a pin. Sutton fought the urge to roll around his bed, tugging the bedclothes and tossing his pillows to the floor.

'I'm just looking for a place to regroup, the chance of earning a little money, a way to get back on my feet. I'm not ready for a serious relationship, either.'

God, between raising her siblings, working and

studying, she owed herself the time and space to live life unencumbered, responsible only for herself. She deserved some time to be selfish, to enjoy life on her terms with no reference to anyone but herself. Becoming emotionally attached to Mr Christmas and his four-year-old elves would be a ridiculously stupid move.

She looked at Gus and placed a hand on his chest. 'I like sex, it's a fun thing to do. And sex with you would be fun. But I'm scared of adding a layer of complication to what is already a complex situation.'

'You took the words out of my mouth,' he said. He leaned his shoulder into the wall and folded his big arms, his expression contemplative. Right, so they were on the same page, reading from the same book. Excellent.

'So how long do you think we can hold out?' he asked. 'I'm betting a week before we crack.'

Aw, shit. He wasn't wrong. 'Four days, if you keep looking at me like that.'

But if they didn't get out of this room, she gave them twenty seconds.

She forced herself to step back, to smile. 'So...do you want to play Snowman Slam?'

He rubbed his hands over his face. When he dropped them, she noticed his rueful expression. 'Sure,' he said. 'But only if I can use a red pair of socks.'

'I think I can make that happen,' she told him. Gus reached behind her to open the door and his hand brushed her hip. *Ignore! Ignore!* She forced her attention onto what was happening downstairs and heard the distinctive tune of 'Pink Shoelaces'.

Oh, man, not again! Eli and Will taught her and Moira the TikTok dance craze earlier and Rosie was now obsessed with learning the routine too. She heard Felix groan, and grinned as she walked down the stairs.

'*Daddy!*'

Sutton saw Rosie standing at the bottom of the steps, her elf hat over one eye and one ear. Thank God it was Rosie and not one of the adults who saw them walking down the staircase together or they'd immediately suss what they'd been up to. 'Daddy! Come and do the Pink Shoelaces dance with me!' Rosie demanded, running up the stairs to grab Gus by the hand.

He threw Sutton an anxious look. 'The *what*?'

She laughed. 'Don't stress, Eli will show you the moves.'

'Moves? What moves? I don't have moves!' Gus complained as Rosie led him into the kitchen, Sutton laughing as she followed.

Chapter Eight

'I still don't know where we are going or what we are doing.'

Gus reversed down the driveway, smiling at the whine in Sutton's voice. They'd eaten, and instead of sending the kids up for a bath, he'd taken them into the hall and started dressing them in their cold-weather clothes. He told Sutton to do the same, but she'd baulked, saying it was too cold, why leave the warm house, was he mad?

Eventually, she pulled on another jersey, and her boots, and pushed her arms through her new coat. As he did for the kids, he wrapped a scarf around her neck and jammed a beanie on her bright head.

Tonight was Conningworth's, or Will and Eli's, version of mumming and, for the first time in ten years, he looked forward to walking through the streets, watching friends entertain the village. There wouldn't be any battles between

St George and the Dragon, no skits, no Turkish Knight or Clever Legs...

Actually, what Will and Eli did had nothing in common with mumming apart from it being a way to entertain the village at Christmas time. Entertainment was, after all, what they did best.

But there would be a begging bowl and lots and lots of laughter. This was the first time in years that he felt any sort of excitement to join in what had become a unique tradition in Conningworth, one entirely dependent on when Will and Eli were home. Sometimes it took place at the beginning of December, sometimes in January, but it was always regarded as a Christmas tradition. A weird one, but still a tradition.

Gus parked, cut the engine, and as he undid his seatbelt, Sutton's phone flashed with an incoming video call. Her face lit up from the inside out, and Gus felt a smack of jealously for any man who could make her smile that way. He looked down. The face on the screen of her phone was young, mixed race and, from the little he could see, damn good-looking.

'Jamie! Is everything okay? What's happened?' Sutton demanded.

'Hey, can't I just call my big sister out of the blue?'

Big sister?

'You can, but you *don't*. You never call me! For all I know you could be married with nine children,' Sutton whipped back, her smile now as bright as the sun.

Gus felt his jealously die down and he started whistling

as he left the car to help the twins out of the car, unwilling to acknowledge his relief. When had he last been jealous? Ten, fifteen years ago?

When he opened the back door, both his kids were leaning forward, their eyes on Sutton's screen. Within ten seconds, they were having a conversation with Sutton's brother. Gus shook his head, his kids, well, mostly Rosie, were not shy about stepping forward.

'And that's Gus,' Sutton explained, angling her phone so that her brother could see him. 'I'm helping him with his twins for the next couple of weeks.'

'I thought you said you'd rather walk on hot coals than look after ankle biters, Sutt.'

Sutton groaned. 'Jeez, Jamie! When are you going to develop a filter?' She threw him an apologetic look and he lifted his eyebrows, silently telling her he'd need an explanation later.

'And anyone would be gun shy after looking after you three,' Sutton told her brother.

'I was *perfect*,' Jamie protested.

'Perfectly revolting,' Sutton shot back.

Gus had both the kids on the pavement, and he shut the back doors. He opened Sutton's door. 'It's too cold to stand around, so I'm going to start walking,' he murmured. 'Catch up with us. And enjoy your chat.'

Sutton mouthed a '*sorry*' and Gus smiled, closing her car door. Taking the twins' hands, he walked away from her, hoping she wouldn't be too long. He looked down the street, the starting point of tonight's entertainment and saw Will, Eli, and Moira, standing in a huddle and stamping their feet. Next to Eli was a cooler box on wheels, and Gus wondered what liquid beverage would be on offer tonight. Last year it had been rum, the year before schnapps.

Gus felt his phone vibrate in his back pocket and didn't bother to haul it out, knowing it was a message to everyone on the village WhatsApp group, stating that the show was about to begin. Only a precious few people, the boys, Moira, and he knew the date of the boys' annual concert. If it could be called that. A village knee's up? A neighbourhood party?

'Silent Night, Holy night...'

Gus shivered as Will's deep voice broke the silence of the cold night, and Gus watched as front doors opened down the street, his friends and neighbours hastily pulling on coats as they hurried to hear Will sing. Gus always forgot how good he was, and even the kids stopped in their tracks, their little mouths falling open as Will's voice danced on the cold air.

He looked around to see where Sutton was, and his heart settled as he saw her hurrying down the road to join them, her face alight with excitement. In her bright red coat, red and white scarf, and green beanie, she looked like a Christmas elf, and utterly gorgeous.

What did her brother mean by his offhand comment about not ever wanting to look after kids again? Was that a temporary or a forever thing? And why was he worried about it? He wasn't thinking about her in a long-term way, was he? Because that would be...

Well, not *bad*. A little strange? But, crucially, he didn't feel the urge to run down the street naked at the thought.

Sutton reached them. 'Oh, are we carolling? Awesome!'

'They'll start with a few carols, but it won't end there,' Gus told her.

'Daddy, there's Nan and she has the begging bowl!' Rosie tugged on his jacket. 'Can we go to her?'

Gus let them run off and looked down at Sutton, who arched her eyebrows. 'Are things that bad at the Hall that Moira has to beg from her neighbours?' she teased.

He ran his thumb over her cheekbone, and wished he could kiss her cold lips. He smiled at the laughter in her eyes and realised that this was, so far, the best Christmas he could remember in years. And that was because Sutton was here, making the situation lighter and brighter, pushing his dark memories away. He wouldn't say he was starting to love the season, but maybe he wasn't hating it as much as he usually did.

Will and Eli launched into 'Deck The Halls' and Gus noticed Moira pouring a shot of whiskey into the glass her neighbour held out. Right, money had to be hitting the bowl. You didn't get alcohol without making a financial contribution.

He placed his hand on Sutton's back and steered her to the group on the pavement. 'So, how do I explain this? I guess it's a combination of wassailing, mumming and Will and Eli being Will and Eli.'

'I have no idea what wassailing and mumming are,' Sutton admitted.

'Mumming goes back over a thousand years and is best described as early pantomime. Wassailing is a Twelfth Night tradition, with pagan roots.' He smiled at her. 'What the boys do has no reference to either.'

Sutton's eyes flashed with interest and excitement. 'C'mon, explain.'

'Yes, your highness,' he murmured, smiling. 'The boys start on this street, with Christmas carols, and Moira holds the begging bowl, looking for donations to whatever cause the village has voted on.' He saw the question on her lips. 'There's a box in the pub, and the villagers drop in suggestions about how the money raised from tonight should be used. It might be a family in need, a new bench for the park, whatever or whoever gets the most votes.'

'With you so far,' Sutton said, jamming her hands into the pockets of her coat.

'After the boys have belted out a couple of carols, moving down the street and onto the next, the villagers can choose between them dancing, them reciting a limerick, bawdy or otherwise, quoting Shakespeare, a song... whatever is required, the boys have to do it. Donations are made and whiskey gets dispensed.' Gus narrowed his eyes, hoping the whiskey wasn't from the stash in the Conningworth cellar. That was the good stuff, collected by Kate's dad over decades.

'You guys are so weird,' Sutton said, grinning. 'But so much fun. This is the best Christmas I've ever had, Gus.'

He rubbed her back with his big hand, smiling as he watched Felix and Rosie run ahead to the next house to ring the doorbell. They couldn't reach it, so Eli lifted each of them, and they took turns ringing the bell. The Caskills were ready for them, already dressed in their coats and hats, and they joined the procession ambling down the street. By the end of the two-hour stint, at least a hundred residents would be following the boys around town.

'I'm glad you're enjoying it,' he told her. 'So, that was your brother, huh?'

'Jamie. Technically, he's my youngest half-brother. Hell on wheels, and is currently in Thailand, working as a dive master. If I have any grey in my hair, it's from him.'

Gus heard clapping from the crowd and the shouts for Eli to do a limerick. The crowd was demanding the hard stuff early tonight, and he shouted a reminder for Eli to keep it clean. Later on, when everyone was hazy with whisky, after the younger kids were scooped up and taken into someone's home to watch a movie, the limericks, jokes and speeches would become a lot more vulgar. Funny, but vulgar.

'Captain, Mr Christmas, sir,' Eli called back, saluting smartly.

The smart-arse. Like he wasn't the guy who entertained the crowd last year with a limerick about a squirrel named Cyril who was virile.

Eli belted out the first line to 'Little Drummer Boy' and the crowd joined in. Gus looked at Sutton, still entranced by the spectacle. 'So, you don't want kids, huh? Is that something that's cast in stone?'

Because, if she didn't, *ever*, then maybe he should slam

the door shut on his suddenly wayward and uncontrollable thoughts. He wasn't thinking about proposing to her, God, they hadn't even slept together yet, but he knew the spark between them could grow into a flame, then a wildfire. He needed to know whether he should douse it now.

Sutton bit her lip. 'I'm in my only-looking-out-for-myself phase of my life, Gus. So looking after kids, mine or someone else's, isn't something I want to do now, or anytime soon. I'm not even sure if I want kids of my own.'

Oh, she did. He'd seen how she was with Rosie and Felix, kind and patient and funny. She enjoyed kids, and she'd want her own eventually. 'But I do like your kids, Gus.'

'I like them too,' he told her. 'I think I'll keep them.'

She smiled at his quip and buried her nose in her scarf. 'If I donate five pounds to the cause, can I get a shot of Moira's whiskey?'

He shook his head. 'Sorry, no. You and I are on duty tonight. We'll be driving the pissed entertainment crew home later.'

'Damn.' She pulled a face, but Gus knew she wasn't complaining. Sutton rarely drank and when she did, she limited herself to a glass of wine.

'Dance! Dance! Dance!' Someone shouted from the crowd and Gus watched his little girl jump up and down with excitement. She tugged on Will's hand and his friend bent down to listen to her. Will held up his hand for silence and the crowd, about forty people now, quietened down.

'Rosie wants "Pink Shoelaces".'

Gus rolled his eyes. Of course she did. She'd been singing and playing nothing else since the night they decorated the Christmas tree at home and Gus could recite the words in his sleep. 'But Eli and I are going to need some help to do this properly,' Will told the crowd. 'E, can you find the music?'

Eli waved his phone back and forth. 'Already loaded up and ready to go.'

Will plucked the whiskey bottle from Moira's hand and handed it to old Mr Grafham, who promptly dumped a healthy measure into his glass, and showed Moira where to stand. 'Sutton? Where's Sutton?' Will shouted.

Sutton laughed and threw up her hands. 'Will, no! C'mon.'

'We can't do it without you, girlfriend!'

Gus pushed her forward. 'Your audience awaits, Sutt.'

She rolled her eyes, pushed through the crowd and took her place between Moira and Roise, with the boys just behind her.

Felix ran over to him, and he swung his son into his arms. The catchy tune started and Eli, Will and Sutton hit the beat spot on, Moira was a fraction behind, and Rosie was trying to keep up. A couple of the teenagers joined the group and gave it their all, much to Will and Eli's delight. By the time the song finished, at least ten people were dancing, and someone demanded an encore.

Gus watched, his heart full as they danced on the pavement, his best friends and his mother-in-law, Sutton and his daughter. Sutton's beanie fell off her head and her blonde hair flicked around her face, her smile wide and her eyes bright. Her cheeks turned red from the combination of the cold and the exercise, and he thought he'd never seen anyone quite so lovely. She took his breath away.

This was shaping up to be a better-than-normal Christmas. At this rate, he definitely wouldn't need to punch another inflatable Santa.

One of Sutton's best childhood memories was making biscuits with her mother and brother. She couldn't quite remember how it came to be that her mum spent the afternoon in the kitchen with them, but she remembered it being a bright, happy, fun day. Layla was there too, and the six of them mixed ingredients, made neon-coloured icing sugar and danced around the kitchen.

There had been a lot of laughter, singing along to the radio, and it was one of the few days she felt like a kid, and not her mum's deputy. She'd been free of responsibility, and she'd loved every minute in that tiny kitchen on a rainy Cape day in winter. But her freedom only lasted until later that night when Jaimie threw up all over his bed from eating too much sugar. He'd called out to her, not their mum, and Sutton cleaned him up and changed his linen.

Still, it was a good memory and one she wanted to recreate this Christmas with the twins. Rosie and Felix were initially enthusiastic, but their attention span only lasted until the decoration stage of the first batch out. They each covered a star and a Christmas tree with too-thick icing before declaring themselves bored. They started flicking icing at each other and feeding great big blobs to Pig. Sutton decided life was safer with them out of the kitchen and sent them off to watch TV. Yeah, yeah, say what you will but the big screen was an excellent way to keep them occupied.

Sutton picked up a cookie and bit into it. If she ignored the taste of baking soda, they weren't too bad. And the too-sweet, melt-enamel-off-teeth icing sugar should cover the taste of bicarb.

Sutton sighed and looked at the clock. Gus was due home sometime soon and his too regimented soul would not appreciate the mess. She could see his eyes narrowing in distaste, the tension in his shoulders, the way he'd close his eyes in frustration. He'd be even less impressed to hear Rosie's hair needed washing because it was streaked with icing, and, despite washing his face and hands twice, Felix was still sticky.

A good nanny – she was *not!* She'd dumped the twins in front of the TV and she'd ignored Pig licking the icing and cookie crumbs off their clothes. They needed a bath, but she also needed to ice about a thousand biscuits – unfortunately, she'd made enough mixture to supply three small countries and several army bases – and clean up the bomb site.

Instead of getting stuck in – the dishes wouldn't wash themselves – Sutton sat on a bar stool at the island in the centre of the kitchen and pulled her phone towards her. She knew she shouldn't, she was already feeling overwhelmed and annoyed, but she couldn't help going to Layla's Insta page. She hadn't updated it in a while but today there were a bunch of new posts...

Before she could take in the photos, a brisk rap on the kitchen door had her snapping up her head. If Will and Eli were on the other side of the door, she'd nag them into helping her clean. Or Eli could make her a cup of coffee while she stacked the dishwasher and wiped down the counters.

Sutton yanked open the door, a wide smile on her face for her new friends. She'd miss them when she left. '*Hey, bitches...*'

Oh, shit. Sutton slapped her hand across her eyes, a fierce blush instantly heating her face. 'Oh, *hell*, I'm sorry. And I'm sorry for swearing. I didn't mean to call you a bitch. I thought you were Eli and Will.'

'That's Chief Bitch to you, missy,' Moira grinned and held out her fist to be bumped. Sutton rolled her eyes, tapped her fist against Moira's and stepped back to let her in. Sutton inhaled her perfume, something deliciously lovely and stunningly expensive, and closed the kitchen door. Moira looked fantastic in black jeans tucked into low-heeled, knee-high leather boots and a scarlet thigh-length coat. A voluminous black and white scarf was tied in one of those fancy knots.

It's going to be a frosty night,' Moira told her, unwrapping her scarf and dumping it on the table by the back door.

Sutton looked down at her icing- and biscuit-dough-streaked shirt and sighed. *Fabulous.*

Sutton picked it up and hung it on the hook next to the kitchen door. Moira reached into her coat and pulled out a bunch of twigs with long, slender and deep green leaves.

'Ta-da!' Moira cried, grinning and thrusting the foliage at her.

Sutton looked at the unusual bouquet and raised her eyebrows. 'Uh...thanks?'

'I found some out on my walk earlier and got Ben to cut down buckets full of the stuff. He also cut some holly, and lots of ivy if you want some,' Moira stated. 'I'm hosting a cocktail party in the Green room, and I'm just going to use natural foliage as Christmas decorations.'

Sutton walked back into the kitchen. 'That sounds nice,' she said. She lifted the twigs. 'Why am I holding a bunch of twigs, Moira?'

'It's *mistletoe*, Sutt.'

Sutton flicked a leaf with her finger. 'This is what everyone makes a big deal about kissing under? I'm disappointed.'

'Have you never seen mistletoe before?' Moira demanded, shocked.

'I live in a hot country at the other end of the world, Moi, so no, mistletoe isn't something we're big on.'

'So you've never been kissed under it?'

'Again, no.' Sutton grinned. 'We Africans don't need to find excuses to kiss, we just do it.'

'Ha ha.' Moira undid the buttons on her coat as she took in the messy kitchen.

'I was making Christmas cookies with the twins.' The

explanation was unnecessary since the island was littered with baked, unbaked and iced biscuits.

'You've made quite a few,' Moira murmured.

And wasn't that the understatement of the year? 'I know,' she admitted, scowling at the leftover dough she'd yet to roll. 'I also miscalculated the twins' interest and their attention span.' Sutton waved the mistletoe. 'What should I do with these?

Moira pretended to think. 'Well, you could put a sprig above every doorway in the house...' she suggested.

Oh, she'd seen the nudge, nudge wink, wink glances she, Eli and Will exchanged and chose to ignore them. Firstly, because she and Gus agreed nothing could happen between them, and secondly because nothing had happened since the night they'd decorated the tree. She'd caught a couple of his hot looks, he probably caught a few of hers, but they'd kept their hands to themselves.

'I can see that you and Gus have some chemistry,' Moira quietly stated.

Ah, *jeez*. She sometimes forgot that Moira was Kate's mother, and that she had to want to curse God or fate because her daughter should be standing in this kitchen, making a mess of baking Christmas cookies. Though, from what she knew of Kate, she'd probably make the exact right amount, no mess and she'd be able to keep the kids engaged in the process.

'I don't want him to be alone forever, Sutton. Kate is gone, but he's here. He's a good guy and he deserves some happiness.' Moira picked up a biscuit and nibbled the end.

She looked at the biscuit, disgust flittering across her face. 'That's quite an interesting flavour.'

'Too much bicarb,' Sutton admitted. She nodded to the iced biscuits. 'Try one with icing.'

'Not much better,' Moira told her.

Damn. 'Anyway, I'm not staying in Conningworth, Moira, I can't. I want to work in London, with people who've had traumatic brain injuries, mostly adults.'

'London is only a few hours from here,' Moira observed.

Oh, man, this was going from bad to terrible. 'Moira, I'm only the twins' nanny, and I'm not interested in a serious relationship.'

Moira waved her protestation away. 'Whatevs.' Whatevs? Where had she learnt that? Next, she'd be using words like *boujee* and *shook*.

She placed her forearms on the island and pushed Sutton's phone across the granite. It lit up and Moira looked down. 'Ooh, who's in Mauritius? I love Mauritius!'

Mauritius? Nobody she knew of. Sutton leaned across the biscuits to scoop up her phone and stared down at her screen, unable to believe what she was seeing. Layla lay by rolling waves on a beach, wearing a designer swimming costume, so small it barely mattered. She held an expensive multi-coloured cocktail. The bright blue water and white beaches suggested she was in the tropics.

Sutton forced the words out. 'That's Layla...a friend.' *My* best *friend*. 'It's not Mauritius, she's on Clifton Beach.'

'No, that's Grand Baie Beach,' Moira insisted. 'My husband and I went to Mauritius the year before he died.'

Wanting to prove her wrong, Sutton read Layla's captions... *Mauritius vibes!* #*cocktails* #*sunandsea* #*partypartyparty*

She swiped down, and saw another photo of her on a yacht, in another bikini, posing à la *Titanic* at the end of the yacht. *Holiday vibes. So needed this ten-day break.*

Layla was in Mauritius? On holiday? She was somewhere lovely, and warm, while she was stuck in freezing England, living in someone's house to pull together enough money to get back on her feet. What the fuck? What the actual, actual fucking fuck?

Sutton resisted the urge to throw her phone against the wall, before remembering she couldn't afford to replace it. Furious, she pulled up the comment section of Layla's post and banged out her reply. *Enjoying yourself on my money?* Then she realised Layla had disabled the comments on her post. Of course she had. Why would she want someone calling her out for spending money that wasn't hers?

'Sutton? Is everything all right?'

No, Moira, it sure as hell isn't.

Sutton pushed away a bag filled with nuclear-yellow icing and gripped the edges of the island, staring at her trainers and trying not to cry. They'd been friends all their lives, they knew the good the bad and the ugly parts of their personalities and their lives. Layla was the keeper of her secrets, and she always felt confident her name was safe in Layla's mouth. Her name might be, but her money sure as hell wasn't.

Sutton didn't recognise the woman in the pictures

online, the selfish, careless *thief*. Needing an explanation, or to vent, she placed a call to Layla's phone, but, as she expected, it went straight to voicemail. 'You can't pay me back, but you can take a holiday? You can party on a yacht and boast about it? Who the hell are *you*?'

'Sutton? Honey?'

'I need to be alone, *Moira*. Please.'

Sutton switched to Instagram and sent Layla a direct message.

I just want you to know you have broken my heart. I never thought, never imagined, you could do this to me.

The icon changed and Sutton knew her message was being read. She waited but Layla didn't reply.

What had gone wrong? How could they have gone from being each other's confidants, their safe harbours, to this? She'd left Cape Town thinking nothing would come between them. They'd be each other's bridesmaids. They'd raise their kids together and be godmothers to each other's kids. Their husbands would play golf together. They'd meet for coffee and lunch, for girl days at the spa, bitch about their boyfriends, husbands and kids. Sutton believed they'd end up in a care home together, causing mayhem.

How could she have got their friendship so wrong? Or what had she done to make Layla treat her this way? If she knew, she could sort it out and try to make amends. When she'd sent Layla the money, she'd believed their bond was as tight as before, and Layla would pay her back in a week, maybe two. Months later, she was broke, living in a stranger's house, and Layla was living it up.

In *Mauritius*.

She'd trusted Layla and it was a trust built up over a lifetime, blocks of love and time and faith built into what she thought was an impenetrable wall. No outside forces, she believed, could destroy them. She hadn't expected the danger to be on the inside.

Furious, Sutton swiped the bag of sugar and the icing bag off the counter and they both exploded, sending a cloud of sugar into the air and splattering yellow blobs of sticky icing over the floor and up the cupboard doors.

Shit. Fuck. Damn.

So Sutton did the only thing she could. She burst into tears.

'Fuck me,' Gus said from the doorway.

Well, she wanted to, but not right now, thanks.

Chapter Nine

S utton looked up from her position on the floor and watched Gus drop to his haunches, resting his forearm on his thigh. He smelled of fresh air and snow, of coffee and Christmas. She wanted nothing more than to curl up into his arms, just like Felix did when he was trying to con her into making pancakes the other day. She wanted to rest in the arms of someone stronger than her, who had, she assumed, his shit together. A more adultier adult than her.

This…this eruption had been building up for weeks now, months. She'd been tamping down her emotion, trying to be logical and reasonable, trying to keep her shit together. She'd needed to, because she needed to be sharp, sensible, *together*. She instinctively knew she had to keep her emotions locked in so she didn't sink into despair, and to keep herself from making stupid decisions because she was broke, tired and overwhelmed. But the combination of feeling completely safe for the first time in many weeks, being happy and seeing those photos was the emotional equivalent of flipping open her pressure relief valve and allowing all the steam to escape.

She looked around and didn't see Moira. Gus picked a strand of hair off her sticky cheek and hooked it behind her ear while she dragged her sleeve across her snotty nose and grimaced. She was sticky *and* snotty. Marvellous.

'Good God, Alsop, what the hell did you do to my kitchen?' Gus asked, but his voice was super-gentle, the audio equivalent of a warm flannel.

She sniffed and rubbed her wet eyes with the back of her hands. 'The cookie monster came in and puked everywhere.'

'I can tell,' he replied, a small smile on his face. 'Was it his idea to make enough biscuits to feed the county?'

Yeah, she'd thought she'd tripled the ingredients but maybe she'd nine-d it. Nine-d it? Was that even maths?

Gus pulled her to her feet and reached for a roll of kitchen towel. He tore off a couple of sheets and handed them to her and she wiped her eyes. She grimaced at the streaks of mascara on the paper.

'Where are my kids? Are they in a sugar coma somewhere?' Gus asked, picking up the crumpled bag of yellow icing from the floor. He held it by the edge and dumped it straight in the bin.

She had to think for a minute. They were in the TV room, watching the pig program with a dog and a pig. 'The cookie monster ate them,' she quipped, feeling embarrassed at him finding her in an emotional mess and trying to cover it with humour. She caught the concern in his eyes, sighed and told him they were watching TV. She glanced at the clock on the wall, happy to see her emotional meltdown had been only ten minutes long. It felt like hours.

'Let me go check on them and I'll be back,' he told her, taking huge steps to avoid tracking sugar and yellow bobs of icing out of the kitchen. Sutton looked around at the devastation and sucked in a sob. There were baking bowls and cookie trays piled up in the sink, bowls of icing on the island, all the wooden spoons she could find, and flour and sugar coated every surface with a fine layer of white. Tiny handprints and fingerprints, in pink, blue, red, green and purple icing were everywhere.

Every. Where.

Holy shit. The kitchen would take hours to clean up.

And Gus hated this type of mess. He liked things to be neat, tidy and clean, but how could anyone bake and ice biscuits with four-year-old twins without making a mess? Well, making a smaller batch of biscuits and maybe sticking to just a couple of colours of icing might've been a sensible option.

Sutton placed the icing bags in a row, picked up a snowman biscuit and bit off its head. Damn, even with icing it still tasted like bicarbonate of soda. They were, to put it mildly, vile.

She heard the sound of big footsteps behind her and turned to face Gus, who stood in the doorway to the kitchen, his eyebrows arched. He looked, she admitted, a little shell-shocked.

'Are the kids okay?'

'Sticky and messy but fine,' he replied. 'You didn't tell me Moira was here.'

Sutton wrinkled her nose. Right, she'd bought mistletoe. She recalled Moira trying to comfort her, asking her how she could help. Sutton responded by pushing her arm off her shoulders and telling her to leave her alone. Great, now it was her turn to say sorry for being an idiot.

'She must think I'm a madwoman,' she muttered. 'I'll go in and apologise.'

'She's on her way out, and she's taking the twins with her for an impromptu sleepover,' Gus explained. 'She said you need a hot bath and an enormous glass of wine, and I am to make sure you get both.'

Wine and a bath sounded like heaven. But first, she had to deal with the mess she'd created. Gus, reading her mind, looked around and frowned. 'Were you crying because my kitchen will take hours to clean, or because of something else?'

He was giving her an out, a reason not to explain, and she was tempted to take it. But she felt like she needed to talk to someone. If she didn't, she might blow. Well, blow again. She felt the pressure in her chest and knew she needed an outsider's opinion on the mess that was her life. Gus was cool-headed and unemotional and, God, she needed both those traits right now.

She needed someone to talk her down from the ledge. 'I'm considering flying to Mauritius to murder my best friend,' she told him, surprised at the conversational tone of her voice.

Her statement wasn't enough to make Gus react. 'You can't,' he informed her. 'A), you only have enough money to take a trip to the village.'

Yeah, there was that.

'And B), you're not going anywhere until you clean up my kitchen.'

Fair enough.

'I'll order a pizza from the pub, and then open a bottle of wine,' he told her. He gestured to the kitchen. 'Can you make a start here?'

She nodded. While she worked, she wondered if she had the right to burden Gus with her problems. He had enough on his plate with running two businesses, the twins and trying to keep it all together. Acting like he loved Christmas – why did he do that? – also had to take a toll. He didn't need her dumping on him, and what could he do about her situation anyway? She'd lost a few thousand pounds, it was just money. She hadn't, like him, lost his life partner, and been left to raise twins on her own. What right did she have to moan about her life when life had slapped him with so much more?

No, she'd loaned Layla the money, she'd take it on the chin. Her choice, her consequence.

But damn, if she couldn't trust Layla to keep her word, who could she trust?

After a mammoth cleaning session and eating pub pizza – not too bad, all things considered – Gus handed her a glass of red wine and sat down next to her on the long couch on the opposite side of the now spotlessly clean kitchen. Pig's heavy head rested on her foot, and she'd lost feeling in her toes ten minutes ago. The actual pig was curled up in his little basket, snoring away.

Sutton wished she was asleep. She was beyond tired. But she still had to shower and wash her hair. Like Rosie, she had strands of sticky hair and she did not want to transfer sugar to her pillow.

She yawned and balanced her glass of wine on her knee. 'I cannot believe it took us over an hour to sort out the kitchen,' she muttered, resting her head on the back of the couch. Gus placed his socked feet on the arm of the chair sitting at a right angle to him, his big hand curled around a glass of whisky.

'I couldn't believe anyone could make that much mess,' he told her.

She stuck out her tongue at him. 'So, how was your day?' she asked, hoping to distract him. She'd seen the assessing looks he'd sent her as they ate pizza, and knew he was trying to work out whether she might dissolve again.

She wasn't ready to talk about Layla yet. She didn't want to explain how hurt she was, how idiotic she felt. She just wanted to drink her wine, listen to the wind in the trees outside – it was howling again, and more snow was expected – and hear Gus tell her about his day.

'We had an American customer who all but bought out the shop,' Gus replied.

'I presume you're talking about Kate's Christmas Shop?'

'Mmm. I had to place another big, urgent order with the supplier today.'

She sat up and pulled her dead foot from under Pig's snout. His chin hit the floor with a thump but he didn't stir. He wasn't the brightest hound in the pack. She wiggled her foot to get blood back into her toes before tucking her feet under her bottom and resting her arm on the back of the couch. 'That's good, isn't it?'

He pulled a face. 'I guess. I keep hoping to have a crappy season, so I have a reason to close the damn place down,' he told her, his hand tightening on his glass.

'It seems to be a great little business.' She'd worked there and she'd been run off her feet.

He lifted one big shoulder and sighed. 'I'm not its biggest fan.'

'Yet every December you throw yourself into it. If you don't like it, why don't you sell it? Or hand it over to someone to manage?'

He huffed, then shrugged. 'It was Kate's. It's a link to Kate, and Christmas is a link to her. This is the season when the community remembers her best, it's *her* time of the year.'

Wow. She could understand why December would be a difficult month for Gus and Moira, but to have the whole town invested? Wasn't that...how could she put it...a bit OTT? 'Why do the villagers associate Christmas with Kate?'

Gus shuffled down his seat and rested his head on the back of the couch. 'Kate was, to an extent, the daughter of the village. Kate's father, Derek, and Moira were always involved in every aspect of village life – over-involved, I would say. Because Kate was their only child, she tagged along to every meeting, every discussion and every function. She became, I suppose, the town mascot. Everyone knew her, everyone has a story about her. She was the modern-day version of the daughter of the manor, keeping the peasants happy.'

She pushed a finger into his hard bicep. 'Snob.'

He turned to look at her and shook his head. 'Not at all, I was the lowliest peasant of them all. Raised in London, a product of foster homes, and I was nowhere near good enough for Lady Kate Conningworth.'

She wanted to tell him she thought he was amazingly wonderful, but the words stuck in her throat.

'I'm still surprised she chose me when she could've married someone a lot richer, someone from the polo, piles and posh set.'

'How did you meet?'

He swirled his whisky in his glass, a faraway look on his face. 'I came to the area shortly after I left the army, not sure what to do or where to go. I picked up a job at a small adventure company, and they had an enquiry from Conningworth Hall, asking whether they had any ideas for a team-building exercise. I made some suggestions, Kate liked those suggestions and within six months we were living together. She encouraged me to open my own outdoor adventure company.'

She thought of his swish offices, website and indoor training setup. He ran a tight ship, and it was a successful enterprise. Frankly, with his work ethic, she couldn't imagine Gus being anything but successful. Surprised to hear him talking about his wife, she pushed to know more. 'I heard Kate was on the verge of opening the shop when she passed away. Is that right?'

He nodded and rested his forearm against his eyes. 'She died on the Tuesday, it was due to open on the Saturday. It opened, a few weeks before Christmas, the following Saturday, with the help of various people from the community.'

'Kate was crazy detail-oriented, and she had lists for everything,' Gus said, seeing her scepticism. 'All they had to do was tick off the bullet points.'

She stared at his stubbled jaw, her eyes tracing the muscles in his arm, the thickness of his shoulder. 'You told me you make lists, too. Is that something you learned from her?'

He dropped his arm and tapped his fingers against his thigh. 'Before we met, I relied on my memory to keep things on track. In the weeks and months after she...*after*... I followed her lists, they were an absolute lifesaver. I didn't have to think, I just did whatever was next on the list.'

"Lists help me keep my life organised." He sipped and placed the glass on his knee. 'And I still use lists for the shop, mostly because I'm not interested in it enough to do my own thing—'

OK, but why? What was it about Christmas and the shop he hated? Kate died mid-November, close enough to the festive season for it to sting, but…

But it wasn't like she died on Christmas Eve or Christmas Day. She didn't understand why he hated Christmas. Sutton hauled in a deep breath and released it slowly. How could she judge? She didn't know anything about death – abandonment, sure, but not the finality of death. Her Layla drama couldn't compete or compare.

She tapped her finger against her wine glass. 'Why don't you sell the Christmas shop and let someone else organise the Christmas-related events?'

'I do it in memory of Kate, and for my kids,' he told her, with a small shrug. 'If she was here, she would be in the thick of things, trying to make Christmas special for everyone. I can't do as much as she would have done, but I can do *some* of it.

'When the twins are old enough to understand, I'll explain she started the Christmas market and everything else, and I just kept it going for her, and them.' He swirled his whisky around in his glass. 'I'm their hero right now because I put lights on the house, but later she'll be their hero.'

Oh, Gus vastly underestimated the impact he had on people. She liked that about him. Honestly, she liked him a little too much. In good, bad and sexy ways.

'You do know this house can be seen from space, right?'

Sutton pointed out, trying to push away the lump in her throat with a dose of humour. 'When all the lights are on, it's so bright in my bedroom I can read a book.'

'If you are four, you can't have too many lights,' Gus reminded her. Actually, she was getting used to the lights, most of them anyway.

'I noticed Santa hasn't reclaimed his spot.'

His smile was slow and sexy. 'I didn't want to tempt either of us to use him as a punching bag again.'

Sutton curled into the corner and yawned, trying to find the energy to haul herself upstairs and into the shower. She pulled a strand of hair in front of her face and grimaced. It was as hard as a porcupine's quill. She needed to wash it but, unfortunately, it was thick and took ages to dry. Going to bed with damp hair was marginally better than the alternative of sleeping with sticky hair.

'So, cookie making…'

She looked at Gus, who was staring at his feet, a smile on his lips. 'Not my finest hour,' she admitted. 'Do you have a hairdryer I can borrow?'

He nodded. 'Sure. I'll give it to you when we go up.'

Their eyes connected and, by the heat in his, Sutton knew he was thinking about their first-and-only kiss, how his hands streaked over her body, painting fire on her skin. She wanted him, he wanted her…

Neither of them wanted to acknowledge the raging attraction between them, neither needed the complication.

'Do you want to tell me why you were crying?' he asked. He sounded almost offhand, like he didn't care, but she'd learned to read him better. He gripped his glass with tight fingers and his mask-like face told her he cared more than he wanted to. The more uninterested and remote Gus looked, the harder he was trying to distance himself from emotion.

But he'd asked and she didn't know whether to go there or not. Oh, she wanted to, but it wasn't smart. She was madly attracted to the man and she'd spent many hours imagining him naked. Making love – no, *sex* would be fabulous and fun, and would remind her what it felt like to be desired. He'd blow away some cobwebs. A shag would do her the world of good.

Look at you, trying to convince yourself he's just a guy you want to screw, a quick smash. He's not, and you know it.

The words 'making' and 'love' kept popping into her head. Problematic. Sutton couldn't handle any version of the L-word rocking up to the party. She was too messed up, was moving on, had no intention of sticking around, and couldn't allow herself to develop any he's-the-one feelings for him.

Telling him about Layla would deepen their friendship, and everybody knew friendship was the gateway to love. Explaining how Layla scoured her heart meant cracking open that door and flirting with the possibility of becoming emotionally closer to him. It also meant sharing too much of herself. She didn't want to get attached. She needed to leave without allowing her heart to take any part in these proceedings.

But, dammit, she also desperately needed someone to

talk to. For weeks, she'd kept this to herself, and nobody knew Layla was pulling her through barbed wire and across a field of broken glass. Everyone back home thought Layla was being her usual successful self, and nothing was wrong between them. That Sutton was fine, and Layla was enjoying her best life.

Nobody suspected she was broke, living off Gus's kindness – oh, he said he needed a nanny, but he'd been prepared to do without one! – and that Layla used her money to fund a holiday.

She opened her mouth to explain but changed her mind at the last second. 'Today Rosie told me I was a moron. When I told her she hurt my feelings, she asked me what a moron was.'

He smiled as she expected him to, but his eyes didn't leave hers. 'You do that,' he murmured. 'You change the subject or make a joke when you feel uncomfortable. Why do you feel uncomfortable telling me why you had a meltdown in my kitchen?'

So they were doing this. Damn.

Sutton picked up a cushion, held it against her stomach and then tossed it aside. He wouldn't let this go. 'Do you believe only lovers can break hearts?' she asked Gus, avoiding his perceptive gaze.

His eyes narrowed as he contemplated her question. He rolled his finger, silently asking for more.

'They say only lovers can break hearts, but I know that's not true. When any type of love is involved, platonic love, sisterly love, friendship love, the heart is always vulnerable.'

Gus took his time to respond. 'Maybe it's *more* vulnerable because, with lovers, the possibility of being disappointed is a known, widely accepted, risk. There isn't as much risk in a platonic relationship…So, who broke your heart, Sutt?'

Sutton bent her legs and wrapped her arms around her knees. She rested her chin on her knee and pulled a face. 'I'm broke.'

'I know,' Gus replied, his tone dry. 'Thirty pounds and a fiver broke.'

Sutton grimaced. But he wasn't wrong.

'I'm trying to understand how you managed to travel without money,' Gus said. She knew it was his way of easing her into deeper waters gently.

'I had money,' Sutton told him. 'I saved enough to allow me to pay for accommodation, food, transport and fun until the end of January.' Gus didn't say anything, happy to wait for an explanation. 'My best friend Layla and I always planned to travel together, but when it came time to buy the tickets and nail down our itinerary, she got cold feet. Fair enough, I couldn't force her to go with me, so I decided to travel on my own. She stayed in Cape Town and I went to Italy, Spain, Greece and to the Beerfest in Munich.'

More silence.

'I was in Berlin at the airport, I was heading for Amsterdam and about to board, when Layla called me. Did I tell you we've been friends since we were five years old?'

Sutton explained, and she heard her voice hitching with emotion. She would not cry, not again. She blinked back her tears and dug her chin into her knee, the slight pain-pressure keeping her tears at bay.

'Get it out, Sutton. You'll feel better when you do.'

She stared at the painting behind him, the colours a blur. 'She was in a jam, her company – she owns a nail bar franchise – had a cash-flow crunch, and she asked if she could borrow two thousand pounds. She said she'd pay me back in a week, it was super-temporary, and I wouldn't even notice the missing money,' Sutton added. 'In the line, waiting to board, and not thinking twice, I transferred the money via my banking app. Layla asked for help and I gave it to her.'

'And she hasn't repaid you,' Gus said, frowning. 'Asking you when you were about to board, and didn't have time to discuss the loan, was excellent timing on her part.'

Sutton cocked her head. She'd never thought about the timing.

'For the first few weeks, I let it go, I had some money. But then I started to get concerned. I needed the money when I got back to England from Europe. I started sending her daily messages, and she promised to pay me, then got upset with me because I lacked trust, and I was a bad friend for questioning her word. That went on for about two weeks.'

'Classic gaslighting,' Gus murmured.

'When I told her I was running out of money, she started

ghosting me. I'd leave her messages and she'd send me WhatsApp messages, supposedly showing me she'd tried to call me. I sent her direct messages on social media, which she read but never responded to.'

'Ouch.'

Indeed.

'I was out of options and then Jason, a friend of a friend, suggested I come here for a few weeks. At least I'd have a roof over my head. You know the rest.'

'It doesn't explain me finding you on the floor earlier.'

Sutton picked up her wine glass and took a large sip. 'I was trying to find the energy to tackle the kitchen and I thought I'd take a break and check her social media accounts. I pulled up her Insta account but Moira arrived. She's trying to set us up, by the way.'

Gus's half-smile heated the special spot between her legs. 'I know.'

'I let Moira in, we chatted and she accidentally nudged the phone with her hand and it lit up with Layla's beach pictures. I had a meltdown because I realised the bitch is on a beach in Grand Baie.'

'Pretty impressive alliteration.'

She thought so.

'Sucks.'

Oh, hail the master of understatement! Gus half turned to face her, hitching his leg up onto the cushion. 'What have you done to try and get your money back?'

'Begged, threatened, demanded, but nothing has worked,' she told him. 'I messaged her, saying she didn't have to handle things this way, that we could work this out if she talked to me.'

'But it's not really about the money, is it? Or not all about the money. It's about the betrayal, the disappointment and the utter disrespect she's shown you and your friendship.'

In just a few sentences he had nailed the essence of her feelings. He *got* it. And for the first time in months, Sutton felt like she'd been seen and heard. 'So my anger is justified?' She just needed to make sure.

Annoyance flickered across his face. 'How can you even doubt that? Of course you have a right to be angry. She made a promise and didn't keep it. And now she's ducking and diving.' He placed his hand on her knee and squeezed. 'If anything, I think you are trying to find an excuse for her, to minimise what she's done.'

She considered his words and knew he was right. 'She's been my friend for most of my life, Gus. I want her to be better than this.'

Something flickered in his eyes, an emotion she couldn't identify. 'Wishing something is different doesn't make it so, Sutt. People are who they are. You can't mould them into being someone you want them to be because it makes you feel better.'

Sutton dropped her knees and sat cross-legged on the couch. 'I feel like such an idiot because this woman is the keeper of my secrets, she knows the most intimate things about me. She's the only person who knows where and how I lost my virginity—'

'Is there more than one way of losing your virginity?' Gus asked, popping his tongue in his cheek.

She blushed and waved his words away. 'You know what I mean! My point is, she's been a witness to my life. We spent a night in jail together because we got stroppy with a misogynistic policeman, went on a southern African road trip, snuck into clubs when we were underage. We figured out how to navigate our periods together, birth control, boys, how to be reasonable people with only one parent.'

His attention sharpened. 'Did you lose a parent?'

'Sort of. My dad took off when I was small and then my stepdad left my mum with four kids under ten to raise. I did my fair share of potty training and bedside stories when I was younger.' She cocked her head. 'Do you know your parents? Do you have any contact with them?'

He shrugged. 'Mum died, Dad is an alcoholic. I'm not sure where he is at the moment. He pops up every few years and lets me know he's alive. As I said, I grew up in the system, foster and group homes.'

She knew those could be tough and she winced. 'Was that...horrible?'

'Wasn't fun,' he conceded. 'It made me grow up fast. As soon as I could, I left. I had two choices, crime or the military. I chose to join up. Regular meals, clothing, less chance of getting knifed or beaten. Or dead.'

Sutton couldn't take her eyes off him, she could listen to him all night. 'Did you go anywhere dangerous?' she asked.

He nodded. 'Sudan, and I did a stint in Afghanistan. It

seems like a lifetime ago. I've been in business as long as I was in the army.'

She thought about the quiet village, its pretty cottages and clean streets, the daily wish-wash of village life. 'Wasn't Conningworth boring after the army, after doing what you did?'

'It's stable, Sutton. And I like stable,' Gus told her. He nodded to her half-full glass of wine and told her to hand it over. She did and Gus sipped, before handing it back to her. 'So, what's the plan for after you leave here?'

Slam! The door to his personal life was closed, and locked. His question was also a subtle reminder she was leaving, and she could never be a part of his life. Of course she couldn't – a life spent in a village in the Lake District, being a stepmum and partner, wasn't what she wanted. Or not yet, at any rate. She needed to establish her career, to use her degree, to make a difference. To live a little. Or a lot.

She told him about the Fort Johns Hospital and how she was hoping to interview for a position with them. 'Working with stroke patients, people who've undergone life-changing injuries, is my dream job. They will be opening the interview process in the first week of the new year, and I want to be in London so I can do face-to-face interviews. I think they are better than video calls.'

'Will you be allowed to work here?'

She wrinkled her nose. 'It's a specialised position, but I have some experience and I trained for this. If Fort Johns Hospital tells your government they need my skill set, I'll get a work permit. But I have to get the job first.'

'Maybe if you get it, I could bring the twins up to see you one weekend, and we could take in the sights,' Gus softly suggested.

She smiled, happy to know that when she left, she would be able to keep them in her life. 'You do know London is not nearly ready for your daughter, don't you?'

He mock-shuddered. 'My daughter will either be the president of the world or the leader of a gang in the biggest prison in the UK.'

Sutton grinned. She loved how he saw his kids clearly but still loved them with every part of him, right down to those impressive big feet. She glanced at them in their black woollen socks. They said that... Oh, God, was she going to repeat the cliché, even mentally? Couldn't she be a *little* more original?

She closed her eyes and shook her head. When she opened them, she saw Gus's flirty, sexy-as-sin half-smile. 'I would give anything to know what you were thinking,' he told her, his voice deepening.

She could either lie, flirt or give it to him straight. 'I was wondering how big your dick is, considering how very big your feet are.'

He placed his arms on the back of the couch and stretched out his legs. 'Why don't you come over here and find out?'

Right, why on earth did she think she would catch him flat-footed? Gus was a grown-up, a *man*, he'd been around, and a little bit of sexual straight talk didn't frighten him. She dropped her eyes and took in his long, rangy body, loving the way his long-sleeved T-shirt hugged his chest and arms and drifted over his flat stomach. He wore khaki fatigue pants, the ones with side pockets, and his thick erection tented them. She placed her tongue on her top lip, eager to touch, to taste, to explore him.

She returned her eyes to his face and saw the challenge in his eyes, but also understanding. Sutton knew she was in the driving seat. She was living in his house and could be considered vulnerable – she had little money and nowhere to go – but making love was entirely her choice. He wouldn't pressurise her into doing anything she didn't want to. If they made love, or didn't, it wouldn't change anything outside this room.

Tomorrow morning, whether they bonked their brains out or nothing happened, she'd still have a place to stay, a job to do. Gus would not yank away her safety net.

'Sex is sex. Everything else we agreed upon has no relevance to what happens between us.'

He often read her mind…how did he do that? While she didn't need his reassurance, she did appreciate his words. Man, she adored straight-talking people, she always knew where she stood with them. And after Layla's lies and deceit, Gus's honesty was a breath of fresh air.

'Thank you for saying that,' she told him.

He held her eyes for the longest time before he lifted his chin in a 'come here' gesture. 'Now why don't you come over here so I can kiss your sexy mouth?'

Chapter Ten

Sutton didn't hesitate; she simply scooted across the sofa and slung her knee over his thigh, settling her core on his hard erection, and lowered her mouth to his. She wanted this, wanted the connection, for him to touch her and make her feel like a woman. It had been so long since she'd had sex. And while holiday sex had been an option, she hadn't met anyone on her travels she wanted enough, or liked enough. And because she'd been so busy in the months leading up to her trip, dating was at the end of her long list of priorities.

'It's been a while,' she told Gus, worried her rusty skills might disappoint him.

He gripped the back of her neck and looked into her eyes, amusement and ruefulness turning the navy to cobalt. 'It's pretty simple, Sutt. We kiss, then we touch, and at any point you want to stop, you tell me, and I stop. Even if I'm balls deep inside you. You say the word and I'll pull it back.'

She couldn't imagine that happening, but she appreciated him saying so. Needing to feel his mouth under hers, she placed hers on his and explored his surprisingly soft lips, enjoying the occasional tickle from his stubble. She traced the seam of his mouth with her tongue and when he opened for her, slipped inside. Her fingernails dug into his muscled shoulders, and she spread her knees, trying to get closer. She loved his mouth, tasting whisky and hot man, sin and sex, control and chaos.

Sutton pushed her fingers into the hair at the back of his head to keep his head in place, enjoying her foray into his mouth. His hands landed on her hips, he squeezed her and then, in a split second, she lost control of their kiss. He took over, his tongue sliding over hers in a deep kiss, frying her synapses and heating her skin.

She pulled her mouth off his, her breath coming in soft pants. 'More,' she told him, her voice raw with need.

He watched her for just a few seconds, and then moved, banding his arms around her waist and lifting her as he rose to his feet. She thought about his core strength, and was briefly impressed, but his next kiss was a blowtorch to dry kindling, sending flames running through her system. Sutton locked her hips around his waist, wishing they were naked.

Gus carried her across the room and into the hall, his mouth fused with hers. He started climbing the stairs, and Sutton ran her hands down his broad back, over his hard ass. She lifted his shirt and pushed her hands between his belt and his bare skin, under his underpants, and groaned when her hand wouldn't go any further.

'Want you, want you,' she chanted, placing her mouth on his neck, and sucking gently on his skin. 'I can't wait to get naked.'

'Shhh,' he warned her. 'We do not want the twins to wake up.'

She giggled. 'They're with Moira, remember?'

Shock skittered over his face. 'Shit, they are.' He grinned at her. 'Then let's make some noise, baby.'

Sutton smiled against his mouth. This was their time, adult time, sex time. Gus and Sutton time.

Gus carried her down the long hallway and kicked open his door. He lowered her to the bed, and stepped back, toeing off his trainers. And when he pulled his T-shirt up and over his head, Sutton leaned back on her elbows and looked at him, taking in his V of chest chair, his flat nipples, the scar on his collarbone.

His low-riding trousers showed off his washboard stomach and the hint of sexy hip muscles made her mouth water. Needing more, she reached for the buckle on his belt, but his hand around her wrist, gentle but strong, stopped her progress.

'Fair's fair,' Gus told her, reaching for the hem of her shirt. He pulled it up and stood back to look at her violet-coloured bra, and sighed, appreciation in his eyes. 'So sexy,' he murmured, his finger tracing the swell of her breast. Her nipples were on fire and they needed attention. Her whole body did.

She was a hot ball of need and want, and when their eyes collided, she swallowed. She was okay with wanting this man, sex was a biological need. But she wasn't comfortable with knowing he got her; he seemed to be able to easily tell what she was thinking, how she was feeling. What she needed in bed and out of it.

Oh, shit, why was she having these random, this-might-be-more-than-sex thoughts?

She was leaving in a few weeks, this wasn't real life…

But God, the way he made her feel was real enough, amazing and sexy and hot.

Gus flicked open the clasp of her bra, pulled it down her arms and bent his head to tease her nipple with his lips. She arched her spine, her arms coming up to lock his head in place. He created a highway of supercharged heat from her breast to her womb, to the space between her legs. She wanted him, now, immediately…

She might even come if he kept rolling her nipple between his teeth…

Gus groaned, pulled back and attacked his remaining clothes. His trousers and underwear went flying and he pushed off his socks with impatient fingers. Sutton leaned back on her elbows and took him in, six feet plus of raw male energy. Tonight, he was all hers…

Gus bent down and placed his mouth on her stomach, his hand expertly undoing the buttons of her jeans. He pushed his nose into the V of her panties, and pushed the denim down her hips.

'You smell like sugar and flour,' he murmured, his deep voice rolling over her skin.

Judging by the way he dropped open mouth kisses on her stomach, and nibbled her hip bone, he rather liked her eau-du-baking scent.

He lifted her onto the bed, widened her legs and dragged his finger over the wet patch on her panties. 'So hot,' he murmured. 'Love that I can make you so wet so quickly.'

He had no idea. He just had to look at her a certain way and she started to gush. No man had ever affected her like this before. Sutton ran her hand over his shoulder, down his chest, before reaching down to hold him in her fist. He was so big and at her touch he pulsed, then hardened.

Gus placed his hand on top of hers, and helped her fist him before he closed his eyes and pulled her hand away. 'If you carry on doing that, this will be over before we even start.'

She pouted, tried to reach for him again, but he batted her away. Then he diverted her attention by sliding his finger under the seam of her panties and dragging his finger through her landing strip, quickly finding, without a problem, her clit, and the pulse of her passion. He stroked her and she lifted her hips off the bed, panting softly.

He kissed her, then pulled back to smile at her. 'Like that, do you?'

She looked for his mouth, found it and slid her tongue

inside. It was a *'hell, yes'* kiss, a silent *'take me now'*. Without breaking their kiss, Gus pushed her panties down her hips and when they were out of the way, pushed her legs open to give him complete access. His clever fingers stroked her, rolled her, and when he slipped two fingers inside her, she felt the first of what she knew would be many orgasms. His thumb buzzed over her clit as his fingers tapped her inner channel, causing a dizzying, straight-up sensation she'd only ever felt before on a high ride at the fair. Normally it took her longer than this, a lot longer, but she was close to coming, about to gush over his hands.

She ripped her mouth out from under his and shook her head, her hair flying. 'I'm close, come inside me, now.'

Gus pressed down on her clit and smiled. 'Do you really want me to?'

She shook her head. 'I want to come, I need to…but you…I want you inside me.'

He used his free hand to stroke a strand of hair out of her eye, a gesture as sweet as his between-her-legs action was hot. 'Oh, I'll be inside you, Sutton, don't doubt that. You'll come on my cock, and later with my mouth on you, but right now I want you to come on my fingers.'

Because he sounded so sure, so officer-commanding, it was her pleasure – her complete, mind-dissolving, body-heating, breath-stealing pleasure – to do as he said.

They both had a sex hangover the next morning and Sutton, after a shower that did nothing to shock her out of her sex-drunk state, stumbled down the stairs, in desperate need of coffee.

Walking into the kitchen, she saw the twins sitting at the table, looking bright-eyed. Gus leaned against the counter, navy stripes under his hooded eyes. He'd showered, but looked, as she did, shattered.

He handed her a cup of coffee. 'How are you feeling?' he asked, his voice rough. She shivered, recalling the way his lips moved against her bare skin, how he kissed her between her legs, how she returned the favour.

They'd dozed for about an hour and they were now paying the price. 'I need something more than coffee but less than crack,' she informed him, wrapping her hands around the huge mug and sipping. Needing to get off her feet, she sat next to Rosie at the table and valiantly resisted the urge to lay her head on the table and drift off.

'What's crack?' Rosie asked.

'A fun time had by Irish people,' Sutton quickly replied. She didn't need Rosie passing on to Moira, or anyone else, any more drug-related comments.

Rosie looked like she had a follow-up question but thankfully Felix stole one of her bread soldiers and an argument ensued. Sutton hoped no blood would be spilt; she didn't have the energy to do anything more than breathe.

Felix, in a magnanimous but highly suspicious manoeuvre, handed Rosie her bread soldier but Sutton didn't question his actions. She was in a *'let sleeping dogs and arguing children lie'* state of mind. She glanced at Gus, who was scrolling through his phone. He frowned, then lifted the phone to his ear, his scowl deepening. He winced, closed his eyes and she saw his mouth move in a series of silent f-bombs.

Mr Christmas wasn't happy. He should be, she'd blown his mind, and other parts, last night. And yes, she was blowing her own trumpet, but someone had to.

'Problem?' she asked, not sure she wanted to know. She had the mental energy to, maybe, make herself another cup of coffee and nothing more. She was wiped. What had happened to the Sutton who could party until the wee hours of the morning, have a shower and then sit through her classes? She missed her and wanted her back.

'Dad, do bugs die when you fart?' Felix asked.

Jesus, what a question for eight on a frosty morning. Sutton met Gus's eyes and ignored the plea for help in his eyes. She shook her head. His kids, he was in charge in the mornings, so he had to answer the hard questions.

'I have no damn idea, Felix,' he muttered. Both kids immediately picked up on the curse and Gus promised to toss some money in the swear jar. She'd checked, there wasn't more than five pounds in the tin can and she suspected he'd wildly short-changed the process over the years.

'I just asked a question!' Felix retorted, annoyed at Gus's sharp answer.

Sutton took pity on Gus and laid her hand on Felix's

arm. Noticing the twins were done eating, she told them to go brush their teeth. When she heard their footsteps on the stairs, arguing about whose turn it was to use the toothpaste first – dear God! – she leaned back in her chair.

'I know you're tired, but what's upset you?' she asked.

Gus raked his hand through his hair and then rubbed his jaw. He hadn't shaved this morning and Sutton didn't blame him; she didn't trust herself around sharp instruments either. 'I just received a voice message from the MD of the biggest supplier to Kate's Christmas Shop. I've been invited to a black-tie Christmas function Thursday night.'

'Judging by your sour lemon face, I take it you don't want to go?'

'I'd rather shove a red-hot poker up my arse,' he informed her.

Alrighty then.

'The supplier sponsors the independent retail association's annual award ceremony and Kate's Christmas Shop has been nominated as one of the best themed shops in the UK. I *should* go.'

'Being Mr Christmas, you should,' Sutton agreed, yawning. 'You can wear a Christmas jersey and an elf hat…'

'Will you stop taking the piss?' he growled. 'I can act like I love Christmas around here, and I do it because people expect me to. But I don't need to travel to bloody Manchester to do it!'

Sutton shrugged. 'So don't.'

He rubbed his hands over his face. 'Being nominated is a

big deal. It's a prestigious award and there will be press coverage. Snubbing the awards would not go down well.'

It looked like he was going off to Manchester to a Christmas party. Man, she would love to see Mr Christmas in a nice suit and showing his rather fine arse off. 'Do you want me to look after the twins?'

He stared at her, and she saw the indecision on his face. He swallowed, rubbed his jaw and took a sip of his coffee. Sutton knew he was looking for the right words to say no. 'I'll ask Moira if they can have a sleepover.'

He wasn't comfortable leaving the twins with a woman he'd only known for a little over two weeks, and Sutton didn't blame him. He was a good father, and super-protective over the twins. But it still stung. Okay, she was stranded in another country with no money, but she was, in real life, reliable and responsible.

'They've had sleepovers with Moira before,' Gus said. Right, he was trying to let her down gently. She heard the silent subtext: *I might've slept with you but I don't know you, not really. Not nearly enough to leave my children with you.*

Sure. Made sense. She understood...intellectually. Emotionally, it was a knife through her heart. She would never do anything to hurt the twins, she'd be super-vigilant and neurotically attentive. But why should he believe that? She was the woman who rocked up on his doorstep in a snowstorm, drunk, broke and bolshy. She wouldn't trust her Tamagotchi to someone with that track record.

Gus rubbed the back of his neck. '*Fuck.* The last thing I

feel like doing is socialising with strangers, especially since the Christmas market is on Saturday. I have so much to do.'

Yeah, it would be a pain in the balls. For him. But her silver lining would be having the house to herself for the night. She could stretch out on the couch, eat pizza in her yoga pants, drink red wine, scoff a bar of chocolate and binge-watch *Love Island*. Heaven.

'One of the best things about twentieth-century life is the ability to be constantly connected. You can work on the train, make calls and send emails,' Sutton said, trying to sound encouraging. After months of living in dorm rooms in youth hostels, she was *quite* keen to be on her own.

'If I go, I'll drive.'

Whatevs. She could order anchovies and pineapple as toppings for her pizza, and no one would give her grief. Bliss. She could sleep in the next morning and wouldn't need to listen to Felix telling the world about his morning poop – why were boys so fascinated by bodily functions? – and mop up Rosie's tears because she couldn't remember her dreams.

A quiet morning in a warm house would be *amazing*…

'You should come to the Christmas party with me.'

Say what?

Sutton lifted her thousand-pound head and looked at him through half-closed eyes. Okay, she had a sex hangover and wasn't fully on fire, but did he say she should go with him to what would be a smart Christmas party?

'That would be a hard no,' she told him. She held out her coffee cup hoping for a refill and when he ignored her she pushed her way to her feet. She sent a longing look to the staircase, wishing she could go back to bed. 'And, hey, since you put me in a sex coma, the least you can do is make me another cup of coffee.'

'And, hey, since I gave you more than a few orgasms,' he shot back, 'the least you can do is come to a Christmas party with me.'

She didn't have a quick answer. Damn. So she did what any woman did when she was caught flat-footed. She pouted. Okay, it wasn't mature, but it was effective.

'I don't want to,' she whined.

'Find your big girl panties and pull them up,' Gus told her, sounding weary. 'I'm not leaving you alone here on your own.'

He didn't trust her. And he wasn't comfortable leaving her alone in his house, amongst his things – his *wife's* things. She wanted him to trust her, to like her, for him to know that while she might be in a pickle, it was just temporary, not a reflection of her life in general.

In real life, she was responsible and together, sensible. 'I'm sorry you still don't trust me,' she remarked quietly, walking over to the coffee machine and shoving her cup under the spout. She hit the machine with the back of her hand and listened to it gurgle and belch.

Gus rested his big hand on her back. He pulled her hair off her neck and dropped a feather-light kiss on her skin. So soft, yet so sexy.

'You're not with it this morning, are you?' he murmured. 'You collect my kids and look after them in the afternoons, you drive them to karate, and Rosie to ballet. You haven't lost them, hurt them or burned the house down yet.'

Point.

'I *want* you to come with me. I'd like someone to talk to, someone there to save me from looking like a sad sack of shit standing in the corner in a stupid tux.'

Aw. Her irritation evaporated and she sent him an over-the-shoulder smile. 'Sweet, but I'd bet the thirty-five quid I have left that if you went on your own, you wouldn't be lonely for long.'

He started to speak but he couldn't compete against the twins yelling as they ran down the stairs, and Pig barking in solidarity. Gus kissed her neck again and released her hair. 'I'd like to spend another night with you when I don't have one ear out for the kids, wondering if they'll wake up or bang on my door. Where I can touch you freely without running the risk of one of them seeing us and Rosie acting like a war crimes prosecutor.'

Sutton shuddered. She could imagine the questions from the super-bright four-year-old. *Why are you kissing my daddy? Why do adults kiss? Does kissing a boy feel different to kissing a girl? Are you getting married? What is sex?* The possibilities were endless.

Gus tucked his phone into the back pocket of his dark jeans. 'Yes or no?'

She wanted to say yes. She wanted to be alone with him again too, to be themselves for a night and a morning. To spend lazy morning time, to touch him freely, and to talk without little ears listening. Sutton picked up her coffee cup and looked out of the kitchen window, grimacing at the light layer of frost outside. It was another cold day and light snow was predicted for the weekend. She hoped it wouldn't impact the Christmas market. Gus had enough on his plate without having to contend with weather problems.

Now she was actively worrying about, and for, him? Crap, she had to get her thoughts under control, her feelings to stand down. She'd been living with him, innocently until last night, for two weeks...but she was starting to become emotionally invested in this little family, in him. She couldn't afford to think like that.

She needed to be able to move on in a few weeks, without any strings to be cut. Without anyone, especially herself, getting hurt. This wasn't her family, she'd just dropped into their life. She'd drop out with minimal disruption.

If Gus was just a one-night stand and if she knew she wouldn't encounter him again, she could easily move on... maybe. But she'd be spending more time with him, and with his kids, and proximity and familiarity obliterated her *'he's just a fuck buddy'* thoughts. She couldn't, she mustn't start thinking there was a possibility of something more...

She wasn't ready for serious, and she *definitely* wasn't ready to take on a man with young kids. She liked Gus before last night, and now she knew how he used his body in bed, she liked him more. Sure, he could be super-grumpy, reticent and emotionally constipated, but he was an excellent lover and an even better father. She *liked* the man, *FFS*.

Sutton knew she was wading into dangerous waters, and she needed to be super-careful. She should say no to going to Manchester with him? *No.* It wasn't a difficult word. An n, and an o. She'd used it tons of times before.

'I don't have anything to wear,' she told him. Holy hell! Seriously? 'And no, you can't buy me a dress!'

Gus folded his arms and considered her problem.

'So, Moira is…what do you call those people who are into clothes and shit?'

'Stylists? Fashion junkies? Fashionistas? *Rich*?'

Gus snapped his fingers. 'Fashionistas. Moira was a fashion editor before she married. Anyway, she collects vintage clothing, and I'm sure she could find something to fit you.'

Sutton was irritated by her surge of excitement. Okay, maybe. 'I suppose an LBJ is an LBJ, right?'

'Are you confusing little black dresses with little blow jobs?' he asked, his voice low and hot. 'Because you should know there's nothing *little* about your blow jobs.'

Sutton felt the space between her legs heat up, thinking of the way she dropped to her knees while he sat on the edge of his bed, looking up at him while she took him between her lips…

'Daddy, what's an LBJ?'

Gus groaned and Sutton laughed when she saw Rosie in the doorway to the kitchen, looking super-cute in her sunshine yellow coat and fluorescent pink feather boa. She picked up her coffee cup and hid her face behind it, trying not to smile. Gus sent her a 'please, please help me' look.

'You're on your own, dude,' she told him, laughing.

Gus put his hands on his hips and looked up at the ceiling. 'God, give me strength,' he muttered.

'That's what you said last night,' Sutton told him, enjoying herself.

Rosie stamped her foot, looking increasingly annoyed. She hated being out of the loop and sensed there was a subtext she wasn't privy to. 'Daddy, I asked—'

'I heard you, Rosie,' Gus snapped, and turned to Sutton, pointing a finger at her. 'You, enough!'

He walked Rosie into the hall, and his frustrated voice drifted back to her. 'Rosie, get your boots on and stop listening to adult conversations. Felix, put Pepper down, right now. Pig, move your lazy arse, you stupid dog. Dammit, this place is a goddamn circus. And Rosie, I swear if you mention the swear jar, I will send Santa a text message and tell him to put you on his naughty list.'

'You will not, Daddy! You will *not*!'

Sutton sipped her coffee and was enormously grateful she had six-plus hours to pull herself together before she had to deal with Rosie-in-a-strop again.

She was still congratulating herself when the little girl barrelled into the kitchen, flung her arms around Sutton's knees and squeezed. Her coffee cup rocked in her hand and the hot liquid rolled over her hand. She looked down into Rosie's wet eyes and her heart sighed. Sutton dropped to her haunches, managing not to spill any more coffee, and wrapped her free arm around Rosie's little body. The little girl pushed her face into her neck.

'Daddy's being mean to me,' Rosie said, her words interspersed with hiccups.

'Daddy's had a hard morning,' she told her, then realised how apt her words were. He'd been very hard as he slipped inside... *Will you please stop, Alsop? You are comforting this man's child, for the love of Mary, Joseph and little Jesus!* 'I'll make sure he doesn't send a text to Santa.'

Rosie pulled back, her hands still on Sutton's shoulders. She nodded solemnly. 'Will you also check he got the email we wrote, the one Daddy sent on his 'puter?'

'I will.' Wondering what Rosie asked for, she stroked her hair off her too-lovely face. 'What did you ask Santa to bring you, Rosie-Roo?'

'A mummy,' Rosie told her, sounding deathly serious. Sutton sighed. Aw, this too little girl, growing up without a mum. She needed someone to cuddle, to teach her how to plait her hair, how to deal with mean girls. She needed someone to introduce her to romcoms and musicals, to help her dress her Barbies in stylish outfits.

'I want a mummy because there are too many boys in this house, and they irritate me. Also, girls are easier to boss around than boys,' Rosie blithely informed her. 'You can be my mummy if you want. But you have to do what I say.'

Right, okay then. It would be a strong woman who took on Rosie Langston. Sutton lacked the bravery Rosie's stepmother would undoubtedly need. It was a very good thing she wasn't thinking about Gus long term...

Chapter Eleven

K ate's Christmas Shop lost out on the best-themed shop award to a newly established store in London selling jewellery from recycled materials. Sutton was disappointed for Gus, but, judging by the photographs flashing on the screen behind the presenter, the winner looked sleek, modern and very, very cool.

Wearing a dress borrowed from Moira, a dark green cocktail dress by a famous designer whose name she couldn't remember, Sutton nudged Gus's shoulder with hers. 'Sorry.'

Gus took a sip from his glass of beer, not looking remotely concerned. 'All good. I would've liked those tickets to Spain. The hotel looked amazing.'

'I can't see you taking two weeks in Spain and leaving the twins behind,' Sutton said. They stood at the back of the crowd, close to the wall and too far away from the bar. A pity, because her glass was empty. She was sure there was wine trapped in a bottle she needed to rescue.

'I would've given the tickets to Moira. She deserves a break,' Gus said, his breath on her shoulder, speaking quietly as the person on stage stuttered through their acceptance speech. 'God, this is torture. Is it nearly over?'

Sutton glanced at the program in front of her. 'Yep. We're done.'

'Thank fuck,' Gus muttered. 'After the speeches wrap up, I'll find Owen, thank him and we can go back to the hotel.'

Sutton wrinkled her nose. While she did want to spend the rest of the night making love to Gus, she'd also heard the DJ earlier and he sounded good. She wouldn't mind sticking around for a while. She loved to dance, and it had been ages.

Gus touched her nose with the tip of his long, blunt finger. 'Your nose wrinkles when you want something.'

She frowned, and her hand came up to cover her nose. 'It does?'

'Mm. So, what's up?'

She looked toward the dancefloor on the other side of the room. The DJ, wearing expensive headphones worked his desk, his body moving to a beat only he could hear. 'Do you dance?' she quietly asked Gus.

'Not if I can help it.'

Damn. She wasn't surprised. Gus was athletic and in complete control of his body, and she could easily imagine him striding over fields and up mountains, scaling rockfaces, but she couldn't see him shimmying his arse on the dancefloor. While she was very good at arse-shimmying.

Gus looked at his complicated watch with its many dials and tipped his head back to look at the ceiling. 'I suppose you want me to dance, right?'

Sutton grinned at him. 'You know what they say? That dancing is the vertical expression of the horizontal intention?'

'In other words, foreplay,' Gus said, surprising her by kissing her bare shoulder. She felt a tingle skitter through her and suddenly she was reevaluating her need to stick around. Why did she want to dance when she could get naked with Gus? She only had x amount of time with the man, and she wanted to spend it on the dancefloor. Her priorities were skewed.

Their eyes collided and heat blasted through her as Gus's hand drifted from her hip and up her ribcage, his fingers curling to slide over the side of her breast. A few inches and he could touch her nipple... She turned to look at him, her hand sliding under his jacket to glide over his hard, shapely arse. Their eyes collided and held, and Sutton heard the MC inviting the guests to grab a drink and hit the dancefloor. Music flowed over them, a sexy, salsa beat, and the DJ, from miles away, exhorted the room to sign up for karaoke.

'If you keep looking at me like that...' Gus warned her, his eyes moving from her eyes to her mouth and back again.

'If you keep touching me like that...' Sutton replied, her

voice husky with need. This wasn't her, she wasn't the type of girl who got all hot and horny from a look and a guy's hand on her ribcage. But Gus did something to her. He made her want to slap her mouth against his, to push her breasts against his chest. She wasn't someone who liked public displays of affection, and she hated horny people getting hot and heated in front of her, but she now, for the first time, understood how things could get out of hand in a public place.

But she and Gus were adults, and neither of them wanted to attract attention, so she put some daylight between them.

Sutton gestured to the now heaving dancefloor. A dark-haired woman dressed in a black leather mini skirt and a neon yellow handkerchief top shimmied and shook, attracting attention from men and women alike. It was obvious she'd had, like Layla, years of training. 'Layla and I closed down many a club when we were younger. We'd spend the whole night dancing, oblivious to anything but the music.'

Gus looked interested so she continued. 'We'd stumble out of the party or club at four or five in the morning, just as the sun was coming up. Then we'd head to an all-night canteen place we found close to campus. We'd drink coffee and energy drinks, stuff our faces with vegetarian curry and talk until it was time to go to our first lecture.'

'You miss her.'

Yeah, she missed her. Sometimes it felt like she was missing a limb or a vertebra. If things were normal between them, Layla would know about Gus, would be bossily ordering her not to fall for him, telling her she couldn't get involved with a single dad of twins. Layla would remind her she wasn't ready for kids, her own or someone else's.

Sutton saw the list of performers flash up onto the large screen on the stage. Two spotlights, one yellow, and one red, hit the stage and a ripple of excitement surged through the crowd.

'We're a minute away from our first karaoke performer, folks. Sign up now to take your turn!'

Sutton cocked her head and lifted her eyebrows and gestured to the stage. 'I will if you will,' she told Gus.

'I would rather shove hot bamboo sticks under my nails,' he growled.

'Is that a no?'

'It's a *hell* no with bells on.'

Sutton grinned and watched a young woman stumble up onto the stage, a microphone in her hand. The young woman had sat opposite them earlier, and Sutton remembered she was a buyer for one of the stores up for an award. A cacophony of wolf whistles and jeers broke out, and Sutton winced at her song choice. She'd done enough karaoke to know it was a lot harder than it looked.

'This isn't going to end well,' Gus murmured in her ear.

'I'm impressed by her ability to hold her liquor. She's had a few Long Island Iced Teas. I would've fallen after two,' Sutton replied, keeping her voice low.

'Or found a few Christmas decorations to destroy.'

Sutton pulled a face and nudged him with her shoulder. 'Haha. Will I ever live that down?'

Gus kept his eyes on the stage, but she saw his smile. 'No.'

'And I will never let you forget you kneed Santa in the nuts. I think you're heading to hell for that,' Sutton said, laughing. Then she remembered she wouldn't be around to remind him of anything; she was taking off soon. It was a horrible thought, difficult to swallow. She didn't want to move on, not yet. Maybe not at all.

Sutton pushed her fist into her sternum, terrified. Maybe she should ease up on the wine and drink a gallon of water in the hope it would make her more sensible. She wouldn't fall for Gus Langston, she refused to.

But what if she had, just a little, already?

Refusing to spoil the evening by overreacting and overthinking, she turned her attention back to the stage and winced when Long Island Iced Tea butchered a high note. She, and the audience, just had to make it through another chorus…

There, done. Thank God.

'My ears might never recover,' Gus whined.

Sutton laughed. 'Man up, dude.'

Sutton was glad to see him looking relaxed, amusement lightening his eyes. Taking her hand, he pulled her into him, slid his lips across hers and gently spun her so her back rested against his chest. She shared his beer and laughed as a couple butchered a Taylor Swift song and a floppy-haired Hugh Grant lookalike slayed Eminem's 'Lose Yourself'.

She stroked her thumb over the back of Gus's hand, flat against her stomach. He responded by pushing his half-hard cock into her lower back, a reminder of the naked fun still to come. It was subtle foreplay, a stroke, lifting her hair away from her neck and kissing the tender spot where it met her shoulder. Occasionally she'd place her hand on his thigh and squeeze, wiggle her butt just a little, to let him know she was there, anticipating the pleasure to come.

There was a lot to be said for delayed gratification.

'Ready to go?' Gus asked, his voice low in her ear. She watched another inebriated couple stumble off the stage, laughing uproariously. They'd been dreadful but didn't seem to care. But she'd seen enough of drunken people making fools of themselves, and it was time to go, time to do what they most wanted to do…

She nodded, turned to face him and looped her arm around his neck. Despite wearing heels, she wasn't tall enough to reach his mouth, so she stood on her tiptoes, her lips skating over his. His hand drifted over her hip and onto her lower back, pulling her into him, and his hard dick pushed into her stomach. She sighed as his tongue twisted around hers. She wanted him so damn much. She'd never had this instantaneous, hot, I'll-die-if-I-you-don't-take-me feeling with anyone before, not like this. It was new and petrifying.

How would she find the willpower to walk away?

The microphone screeched, and Sutton pulled away from Gus. She winced and raised a hand to her ear as the high-pitched sound bounced around her brain. She was done, she wanted to be alone with Gus. She slid her hand into his, their fingers intertwining as they pushed their way through the crowd to the exit. Sutton made a mental checklist, coats, taxi, hotel, bed...

Naked. *Nice.*

'I'm not singing, dammit!'

Sutton braked at the high-pitched, slightly drunk, tear-soaked voice, and turned to look at the stage. Gus turned as well, and Sutton took in the tiny brunette teetering on sky-high heels. She wore her hair in a blunt-cut bob and Sutton liked her scarlet shade of lipstick. The rest of her face was bone white, and she was shaking.

She winced and knew whatever was coming would electrify the room. The crowd at the front of the room tittered and Sutton stood on her toes. Frustrated, she looked up at Gus, who was tall enough to see. 'What's happening?' she demanded.

'Some guy is begging her to get off the stage...oh *shit*, it's Owen.'

She'd met Owen earlier, and he introduced them to his wife, Alice, a lovely, stylish and witty woman who thought Owen made the world spin. Sutton decided they were who she'd like to be when she hit her early sixties. Elegantly dressed, effortlessly confident, at home in their skins and with each other.

They'd explained they were about to celebrate their thirty-fifth wedding anniversary and couldn't decide where to go to celebrate. Sutton suggested Cape Town, followed by a safari, and they'd both been thrilled by her recommendations of places and things to do.

They planned to spend the next day researching, and could they phone her if they had any questions?

'Oh, *fuck*.'

Sutton heard Gus's curse and saw Owen's wife standing off to the side of the room, her hand clutching her thick gold chain. Even though the lights were turned down low Sutton caught her tight mouth and her wobbling chin.

'No, dammit, I'm sick of you promising to tell her, promising to leave and then doing nothing about it.'

'Fuck, fuck, fuck,' Gus muttered, his hand tightening around hers. Okay, this was interesting and compelling, in a car-crash kind of way, but she didn't think Gus was close enough to the couple to be so upset over their marital drama. All the colour had leached from his face and his eyes looked a little wild.

'We've been sleeping together for a year, and with me, you don't need Viagra!' Oh, ouch! And too much information! 'I'm sick of lying and I'm very sick of sharing you with her!' The brunette placed her hand on her chest and the microphone wobbled in her other hand. 'I'm sick of being your moon, Owen!'

Your moon? What was she talking about? Sutton heard the crowd's confused tittering. 'She's his sun and I'm his moon – it's a country song, you idiots!' Was it? She loved country music but didn't recall a song with a sun and moon theme. She'd have to look it up. For curiosity's sake, of course.

'I want to marry you, Owen, I want your baby! You *promised* me a baby, Owen.'

'He's had a vasectomy,' Alice shouted.

Sutton's head, along with everyone else's, swivelled towards Alice. She now stood tall and straight, her shoulders pushed back and spine straight. Man, she looked pissed. Not a little pissed but run-a-spear-through-his-heart angry. Sutton looked at Owen, his head now in his hands. This was the Christmas party version of Wimbledon, with eyes bouncing from player to player and back again.

'That's not true. He would've told me!'

Sutton grimaced at Owen's mistress's shrill screech. Right, this evening was far more entertaining than she'd thought it would be. While she felt sorry for Alice, and it was embarrassing for Owen, she didn't know them well enough not to enjoy the entertainment factor of their drama. It was like watching reality TV in HD, up close and personal.

Tears streamed down the PA's face, but she kept a tight grip on the microphone, turning away from the emcee every time he tried to grab it from her. 'And you know all those business trips he took? Well, we went to Spain, and Santorini, and we did it in *your* bed.'

An invisible hand slapped Alice and her head jerked back. She was now bone white, and Sutton suspected she was close to snapping. She grimaced. Ok, she'd seen and heard enough. She didn't want to watch this anymore, the pain on their faces was too real, too naked, too intense. The emcee led Owen's sobbing mistress off the stage and Owen stood where he was, his fingers gripping the bridge of his nose, and stared at the floor. On the surface, Alice seemed the most composed, but Sutton knew she was deeply traumatised.

Who would Owen choose to comfort, his wife or his mistress? What facet of his life was more important to him? Excitement and, possibly, great sex with a younger woman, or familiarity, comfort and years spent together? What did he value more? She, like the rest of the room, waited to see whom he'd choose.

'Fuck him, and fuck this,' Gus muttered. Sutton watched, astounded, as he left her side to push through the crowd. He stopped in front of Alice, his big body providing a screen between him and the rest of the room. Why was Gus interfering? He was just a client, not particularly friendly with Owen, and he knew no one here. Why was he stepping up to comfort a woman he'd only met a few hours earlier?

Sutton watched as Gus put his hand on Alice's arm and lowered his head to speak in her ear. Alice cocked her head, listening intently. Gus turned, caught her eye and nodded to the exit, a silent order for her to meet him there. Then he placed his hand on Alice's back and steered her through the crowd, his fierce scowl suggesting people moved the hell out of their way.

Right. *Okay then.*

It took Sutton longer to get into the lobby. Through the windows of the lobby, she watched Gus and Alice outside, his hand still on her back. He'd retrieved her coat, and

Sutton noticed Alice wobbling on her expensive heels. A taxi pulled up next to them, and Gus reached into his jacket to pull out his wallet. He opened the back door to the taxi, helped a now crying Alice inside and handed the driver some cash. After exchanging a few words with the driver, he stepped back, and the taxi pulled away.

He watched the taxi until its lights disappeared, his face etched with grief and anger. He scrubbed his face and linked his fingers behind his head, tipping his face to look up. Instinct told her to hang back, to stay where she was, feminine wisdom suggesting he needed time to get his emotions under control. Gus, as she knew, valued control and emotional distance.

Sutton made herself useful, retrieved their coats, and then sat on the backless bench in the lobby, waiting for Gus to join her. She stroked his thigh-length coat, trying to tamp down her curiosity. Why was he so affected by what happened to Alice? Had he helped her purely because he was a good guy who didn't enjoy having a ring-side seat to her humiliation? Sutton felt a stab of self-loathing, knowing she'd initially enjoyed the show a little too much. Had the revelations of Owen's infidelity triggered something within him? Should she ask about it or should she let it go?

She wanted to know, she wanted to know *him*, needing to dig under the grumpy, reticent man who pretended to love Christmas but actually hated it, who put himself out to help the community, but took himself on punishing runs – or punched an inflatable Santa – to relieve stress and steam. The man who was a brilliant father, and an excellent son-in-law, someone trying to keep his dead wife's memory alive as much as he could.

But asking questions, and getting answers, would strengthen the bond between them, and would add more strands to the rope binding them together. The stronger the rope, the harder, and more painful, it would be to break those strands when she left. It would take energy and effort to walk away, more than she wanted to expend.

She wanted to be able to kiss his cheek and wave goodbye, happy to move on. But he was making that difficult for her... Not only because he was a great lover and she wanted more of the pleasure he so effortlessly drew to the surface, but because he intrigued her. He was smart and sensitive and had the emotional depth of the Mariana Trench. There were currents and eddies and caves to his personality, and she wanted to explore them all. She wanted to dive into him...

But that meant exploring *all* of him, every facet of his life. Gus wasn't a solitary creature who lived alone. He had the twins, and they were, as they should be, his priority. Getting to know Gus and being a part of his life meant becoming a part of *their* lives, embracing his children, his friends and even his mother-in-law, as fully as she did him. He was a package deal. Sutton wasn't ready for something so deep, nor was she ready for the long-term responsibility of having the twins in her life.

As little as they were, the twins understood, as much as they were able to (and as much as they cared) that she wasn't sticking around, and she'd be leaving before

Christmas. She deliberately kept her emotional distance from them, reminding them as often as she could she was leaving and the chances of them crossing paths again weren't high. She didn't want them to feel like she'd come into their lives to stay, and then feel abandoned when she left.

They'd had enough grief in their young lives; she didn't want to add to it. Kids were smart, they understood more than adults believed they did. And they valued the truth. It was society that taught them how to lie. To themselves and each other.

She was worried about Gus and the twins, but she'd be lying if she said she wasn't trying to protect herself too. What if she stupidly fell for Gus, how could she trust him with her heart? How could she trust anybody ever again? She'd genuinely believed Layla would never let her down, would never stab her in the heart.

But her best friend, the sister of her soul, the keeper of her secrets, had lied to her and betrayed her. If she couldn't trust her, how could she trust anyone again? No, it was better to live life alone than to take a chance on loving and losing, of trusting and being disappointed.

Sutton stared down at the carpet below her borrowed-from-Moira heels. Her deal with Gus was now exponentially more complicated than she'd anticipated, but she had to keep her head. She could sleep with the guy, but she wasn't allowed to fall for him. She could look after and have fun with his kids but not become attached to them.

She could live in his home, but she couldn't call it home. She needed to think more and feel less.

She needed to be prudent and practical. Rational and reasonable.

Gus lifted his head and saw her watching him through the window, and his expression softened. Man, how was she supposed to keep her feet on the ground, when he looked at her like she was all he wanted, the only person he needed?

Chapter Twelve

Their hotel was just around the corner from the Christmas party venue, but Gus asked Sutton whether she was happy to walk for a while instead of heading straight there. She looked down at her feet – she was unused to heels – but he didn't take the hint, looking past her head.

'I need to work off some energy,' he told her, 'to suck in some fresh air.'

She thought about suggesting he work off energy by making love to her. Or she could remind him that, compared to the Lake District, Manchester air wasn't particularly fresh. But then she caught the combination of what she thought might be grief and frustration in his eyes, and she nodded. She could walk for a while longer…

She shoved her hands into the pockets of her coat, thankful it wasn't too cold tonight. The shop windows of both the high-end retailers and the small independent shops were decorated for Christmas and Sutton had to admire the owners' and designers' creativity and flair for the dramatic. There were the traditional winter wonderland scenes with cottages and Christmas trees, and abstract snowflake and Christmas tree designs in popping colours, giving just the barest nod to the season.

Felix would love the miniature train running through the three windows of the toy shop. A troop of reindeer, with a red nosed Rudolph – who looked like he had an extremely painful bout of gout – flew through the star-studded sky above the train. Rosie would get a kick out of a five-foot automated Barbie placing a bauble on a half-decorated Christmas tree.

Manchester's main streets and squares wore their best sparkling lights and most colourful decorations, illuminating the cityscape. Sutton had seen at least five towering Christmas trees, branches laden with fake snow, and shimmering ornaments and ribbons. The magnificent Manchester Town Hall sported grand wreaths and garlands, and the granddaddy of Christmas trees, adorned with thousands of twinkling lights, made tourists and locals stop and stare.

Ten days to go and the city, and the rest of the country, had caught up with Conningworth's accelerated Christmas schedule. The lights were fantastically pretty. Many buildings were illuminated with colours and patterns, and the reflections from the lights shimmered on the pavement. If she ignored her stoic date, and her aching feet, their evening stroll was magical and romantic.

But her stomach kept grumbling. It was hours since she'd scoffed the small portions of the haute cuisine meal served at the hotel. She could murder a burger or a curry…

'So, that was quite a scene back at the hotel.'

Sutton jerked at the sound of Gus's voice. He hadn't said anything for ages, and she'd left him to his thoughts. But his out-of-the-blue comment jerked her out of her fantasies of eating Nando's.

'Uh, yeah. It was…' She couldn't say entertaining because she felt sorry for all the parties involved. Alice and the mistress were both distressed, Owen too.

And while their exploits would be a funny story told over the water cooler and in whispered sniggers in the hallway, she couldn't forget that people's lives had been turned upside down and inside out tonight.

'It was a shit show.' Gus finished her sentence.

That was one way to put it. Especially for those involved. And a nasty surprise just before Christmas.

Sutton tucked her hand into the crook of Gus's elbow. 'What you did for Alice was nice. I presume you called the taxi to take her home.'

'Yeah.' She felt the tension in his arm. He was the human equivalent of a vibrating rod. 'My wife died in a car crash.'

She looked up at his stonelike profile. 'I know, Gus,' she gently replied. Where was he going with this?

'It happened just outside Manchester. We passed the site of her crash coming in.' Oh, she'd wished he'd said something. Not because she was a ghoul and wanted to see where it happened, but because driving past the place where his wife died had to be hard for him. She could've touched his knee, held his hand…

Even tough guys could use some emotional support now and then.

'She was on a buying trip, getting some last-minute things for the shop. She had a blowout, and she overcorrected. Her car flipped and hit the barrier on the motorway. She died instantly.'

Okay. This was the most he'd said about Kate, and she wondered why he was bringing up his dead wife to his short-term lover. Because that was all she was, all she *could* be…

Gus answered her unspoken question. 'She wasn't alone. Her passenger survived the crash and was taken to hospital.'

She stopped abruptly and looked up at him. 'Was she okay?'

Gus's smile held no warmth. '*He*. They'd been talking and emailing for months, having what I would call an emotional affair for months. They'd met a couple of times for coffee and a drink. He finally persuaded her into spending a few nights with him in Manchester.'

Sutton winced and squeezed his arm in sympathy. *Shit. Damn. Fuckity fuck.*

'I thought her spending so much time on the computer and her phone was normal. She needed the time to get her shop up and running. Moira and I picked up the slack with the twins, and I thought life would settle down after the shop opened. That our sex life, our *lives*, would get back to normal.'

Sutton didn't know what to say so she kept quiet. What did you say on hearing so much pain in someone's voice?

Gus kept his hands in his coat pockets, his stoic expression not changing. 'That scene tonight, earlier, brought it all back. I know what Alice is going through. I easily recall the shock and disbelief.'

There was still so much she didn't know. He might not tell her, but she wouldn't know if she didn't ask. 'Was the man badly hurt?'

'Broken thigh and pelvis.'

Sutton considered asking whether he was just a friend or a colleague, checking whether Gus got it wrong. But he'd never accuse his dead wife of being unfaithful without proof.

'How did you find out?'

'That she was shagging someone else? A policeman gave me her phone, and he told me he took a call from her B&B, asking what time they'd be returning because they needed to do some maintenance in the room. I went there to collect her bag and found his luggage too. The double bed, the torn condom wrappers in the rubbish bin, the '*I've never been fucked like you fucked me last night*' message written in lipstick on the bathroom mirror were all pretty big clues.'

Sutton grimaced, imagining him reading that soul-destroying message, and then packing up his dead, unfaithful wife's possessions. 'Did you leave his stuff there?'

He shook his head. 'I grabbed his stuff and dropped his bag off at the hospital,' he continued, rubbing the back of his neck.

Sutton winced. 'Did you confront him?'

'I was hell-bent on it. I planned on breaking his other fucking leg, and his head. But when I got there, his wife was outside his room, crying. She was so damn thankful he was alive. And she was also pregnant. Not too far along.'

'What a prince.'

'I left his stuff at the nurses' station and walked away. I decided not to tell her, and after not telling her, it was easy not to tell anyone.' He caught her surprise and lifted his shoulders in a quick, what-was-I-supposed-to-do shrug.

'What good would it do to tell Moira her dead daughter was having an affair? And if I told one person in the village, everyone would know by sunset. The villagers loved Kate, they'd known her since she was a child, and they were gutted enough by her death. My kids were tiny, but I knew somebody would tell them, at some point, that their mum died in a car accident with her lover. I don't want them finding out about that, ever. So I kept it a secret.'

Sutton bit her bottom lip. He'd told no one, and he'd carried this heavy-as-hell burden for three years? Man, that was weighty luggage to lug around. And on top of that, he had to pretend his wife was the sweet, lovely, family-orientated woman everyone believed her to be. 'Holy shit, Gus.'

'So now you know why that scene at the hotel pushed all my buttons,' he said.

And then some. She turned over the information in her head, thinking it took huge strength and a shit-ton of willpower to keep a secret that big, to pretend something you didn't feel. And why did he tell her? 'How did you deal with the grief and the betrayal?'

He stared at a point beyond her. 'Fuck, I don't know. I threw myself into work, into looking after the twins, into running the Christmas shop, taking on whatever I could so that I didn't have time to think.' In his eyes, she caught an echo of the pain he'd endured. 'But I always wondered what I did wrong. Why wasn't I, and the twins, enough? Why didn't I suspect something?'

Everything she'd asked herself about Layla. She'd lost a friend, but he'd lost his wife, the mother of their children. She couldn't compare their two situations.

Sutton rested her forehead on his bicep, wishing she could suck the pain out of his voice, the distress out of his eyes. He was always so in control, stoic and reserved, and she knew he didn't open up often. Or ever. But she didn't know how to comfort him, or what to say. Stating she was sorry his dead wife was a Class A cheater bitch might make her feel better but wouldn't help him.

'That…sucks goats' balls,' she said, wishing she could be more eloquent.

He released a small laugh. 'Yeah, it does…*did*. I'm over it now.'

Pfft! Of course he wasn't. If he was over her betrayal, he would've found another significant other or would be dating regularly, actively looking for someone. Gus, as Eli informed her, was either celibate (not, as she'd discovered) or had one-night stands when he was out of town. He was commitment-phobic and had trust issues, and how could she blame him? She wouldn't want to fall in love again if she discovered her husband was having an affair in the weeks and months before his death.

'I found that scene with Owen, Alice and his lover excruciating,' he said, steering her left. She'd been oblivious to their surroundings and had no idea where she was. She was grateful Gus was a decent navigator, or they'd be very lost by now.

'People are so complicated,' she said, burying her face in her scarf. 'What would you have done if you'd found out she was having an affair?'

'You mean if she didn't die?'

'Mm. Would you've tried to make it work, or gone to marriage counselling, or would you've divorced her?'

Gus frowned, and his eyes narrowed. 'I've asked myself that question a few times. My pride and ego want me to tell you I would've divorced her and moved on without a backward glance. But when it happens, it's not always *that* easy to do. The twins were tiny, and I wanted a family, *my* family. I wanted to be a hands-on dad. I wouldn't have been able to do that if I left. Conningworth is my home, my business is there and Moira's the mum I never had. If we divorced, the village would've sided with Kate, and I would've lost them too.' He stared off into the distance. 'And…*fuck it*…I loved her. At the time of her death, I was so damn in love with her. You can't just switch that off.'

She understood. Love didn't just die, it wasn't a black-and-white situation. If Layla came back into her life, she would try and find a way to repair their relationship because her friend was the main witness to her life, and a participant within it. So many of her memories, the good, bad and ugly, featured Layla, and she couldn't edit her out of those mental video clips and reels. She was there, just like Kate would always play a starring role in many of Gus's memories.

'I like to think I would've done whatever was best for the twins.'

She didn't need convincing. 'I have no doubt you would've done the right thing, Gus. You're a good guy, you do what's right. Hell, you even took in a drunk waif who destroyed your Christmas decorations. I haven't forgotten that you could've tossed me out, that you really didn't need me to look after the twins. You had, have, everything, including the twins, under complete control.'

He kissed her but didn't reply and Sutton knew she was right. If he hadn't wanted her in his home or his life, she wouldn't be there.

They stopped in front of a Victorian villa, cleverly converted into a boutique hotel. Sutton tipped her head back to take in its erratic roofline, with its gables, dormer windows and decorative chimneys. The steeply pitched roof sported wrought-iron cresting, which added more elegance the house didn't need. Sutton wrinkled her nose, wishing Gus had booked a room at a bog-standard hotel. She felt bad he was paying for her to stay in such a lovely hotel with its wide bed, oriel window and spectacular ensuite bathroom. It was romantic and sexy, and she felt uncomfortable with both.

This was sex. They were, at best, *friends*. She didn't need him to romance her, she was leaving soon. She thought about telling him that and knew he would either laugh or give her his '*are you high*?' look. Gus wasn't any more into romance than she was.

She followed him through the gate and walked up to the small porch supported by ornate columns. Gus pulled open the heavy black front door, a dim light illuminating the stained-glass panels, and Sutton stepped into the cosy, comfortable lobby. She returned the night manager's cheery goodnight and headed for the wide stairs leading to their second-floor bedroom.

She turned back to look at Gus and caught him ogling her legs. He was thinking about sex, and she was glad. Sex she could handle; emotions tipped her upside down and sent her spinning. 'Like what you see?' she teased.

'You know I do,' Gus said, coming up next to her. The staircase veered up and right, and when they were out of sight of the night manager's desk, he spun her around to face him. His hands yanked at the belt of her coat and he shoved it open, his hand skimming over her ribs and cupping her breasts. He thumbed her nipples, and Sutton released a low groan.

'You are so fucking hot, Sutt,' he told her. 'I've been thinking about this all evening.'

She lifted her eyebrows. 'Taking me on the stairs?' she

teased him, glad to see the passion in his eyes. They were better at light and fluffy, keeping their relationship surface.

'That too,' he told her, feeding her a hot, open-mouth kiss. Sutton wanted him to take his kiss deeper, but Gus grabbed her hand and pulled her up the stairs, digging into the inner pocket of his jacket to find the room key. She liked his haste, loved the desire on his face, in his pants, for her. Sex she understood; need and want and attraction were easy to deal with. Deeper feelings, scary feelings, made her feel unstable, dizzy and off balance.

It was better to kick them to touch. They had no place in her life.

Yet, in their room, watching him shrugging out of his coat and jacket and yanking down his tie, emotion bubbled up. Her heart wasn't listening to her brain, it wasn't on board with keeping whatever this was surface-based. She needed to ignore it – its only job should be pumping blood around her body! – and she knew she needed to be clever, sensible, strategic…

But Gus… Gus just melted all her thoughts and fears away.

Gus dropped his hand from his shirt. Leaving it half untucked, he moved to stand in front of her and lifted his hands to hold her face, his thumbs caressing her cheekbones.

'Stop thinking, Sutt,' he murmured, his voice low and rumbly. 'Tonight, it's just you and me. Let's forget about the people we loved and who let us down. We're just a man and a woman who love how we feel when we are together. Tonight, nothing else matters.'

His voice, with its deep timbre and seductive words, was impossible to resist. As she lifted her mouth to meet his, Gus's hand moved from her face to the back of her head, guiding her to the perfect angle to be deeply kissed. His tongue delved into her mouth, and she felt him tremble as his arousal pressed against her stomach. The yellow glow of an outdoor light filtered through the room, streaking shifting shadows over his skin. Gus made her feel alive and vibrant. She was a blank canvas waiting for him to paint her with pleasure.

Sutton felt the sofa against the back of her knees. The bed could wait, so she told him to sit down and with a raised eyebrow at her bossy tone, he sat down, stretching out his long, long legs.

Kneeling beside the sofa, she ran her hand across his chest, feeling the firmness beneath his shirt, tracing the outline of his arousal beneath the fabric of his trousers. Gus shuddered, his eyes glinting with desire, appreciating her touch. In their previous encounters, he had been the one in control, but this time she wanted to take charge.

She pushed her hands under Gus's shirt, peeling it up to reveal his hard, flat stomach, the light sprinkling of chest hair, his muscular arms. She helped him out of his shirt and pressed her mouth to his biceps, savouring the play of muscles beneath her lips. She inhaled his intoxicating scent – a blend of soap, cologne, masculinity and raw desire – her lady parts warm and throbbing.

Desire for him consumed her, and it was the sweetest pain.

'Come up here and kiss me,' Gus urged, his voice husky, as he pushed his fingers through her hair, toying with her curls.

'Not yet,' Sutton softly replied, placing her hand on his chest and feeling the steady rhythm of his heartbeat. So strong, so masculine. She watched, fascinated, as his nipple hardened, and she impulsively brought her mouth to it, eliciting a low groan. Emboldened, she trailed her tongue across his chest, exploring the contours of his warm skin. Now on her knees, she caressed his sides, running her knuckles lightly over his stomach before dipping her tongue into his navel.

'You're driving me crazy, Sutt.'

But it was a good kind of crazy. Sutton smiled against his skin, tracing the defined ridges of his stomach with her tongue.

'I need to touch you, babe.'

'Not done yet,' she whispered, placing her hand on his erection, gliding her fingers along his shaft, feeling the heat radiating through the fabric of his trousers. She unfastened them and slowly pulled the zip down. Gus hooked his thumbs into the waistband and lifted his hips, helping her remove both trousers and pants in one practised move. As they fell to the floor in a heap, Sutton gazed down at him, captivated by his masculine beauty. She traced her finger along the raised vein and spread the small bead of moisture from his tip around his head.

The sight of him made her soaking wet. She could straddle him and easily take him inside her, but she wanted to make this last, delay what she knew would be their mutual gratification.

Sutton pressed her lips against his shaft, inhaling his intoxicating scent. She nibbled her way up to his tip, resting it against her closed lips.

'I'm dying here, Sutton. Seriously,' Gus muttered, his hips lifting, urging her to open her mouth.

Sutton turned her head, pushing her hair behind her ear so he could see her face. Consent was important and she wanted his permission to carry on with this most intimate of acts. 'Do you want me to continue, Gus?'

'More than I want my heart to keep beating,' he replied, his voice vibrating with need.

She savoured the note of desperation in his voice, his erratic breathing filling the room. For once, the usually confident Gus was surrendering control, and Sutton loved being in charge. Powerful, alluring, feminine and undeniably sexy. In giving, she discovered heightened pleasure for herself, a level of arousal she'd never experienced before. Sutton opened her mouth, allowing him to glide onto her tongue, her lips enclosing him. Gus tensed, his grip on her hair tightening.

'That feels amazing, Sutt. Please, *please*, don't stop.'

She wanted him speechless, unable to think, so Sutton took him deeper, swirling her tongue around his tip. She teased and tormented, taking him deep before pulling back to nuzzle his long length with her lips. She heard him panting, his hips lifted and the grip on her hair tightened. Then Gus released a low curse. Using his core strength to sit up, he gently pulled her head back. 'I'm hanging on by a thread,' he told her, his eyes glinting.

'Nice to know I can drive you wild,' Sutton teased.

'Sweetheart, you just have to walk into the room, and I get hard. Then I start thinking what hard surface would work best and how quickly I can get inside you.' Gus pulled her up to stand between his bent knees, quickly removing her clothing. When she stood naked before him, he placed his forehead against her breasts, gripping her waist firmly. 'I want you so much, Sutton.'

He kissed her hipbone, and his hands cupped her breasts, his thumbs brushing over her nipples, sending waves of pleasure through her body. 'I like you in my mouth, but now I need you inside me, Gus,' she whispered.

'I need a moment,' he told her and lifted his hand to show her the inch of space between his index finger and his thumb. 'I'm so close to coming.'

She knew he valued control, but she wanted him wild, wanton, consumed by desire. Taking charge once more, she pushed him back and straddled him, taking in his surprise when she rubbed her wet core on his shaft. Currents of pleasure washed through her – warm, wet and utterly blissful – but she managed to remember their need for a condom, and slid it down his shaft. Then, not allowing Gus any time to think or react, she took him in her hand, lifted her hips and slowly sank, inch by inch, onto him.

Gus pulled her closer, pulling her into him, her breasts

squashed against his chest. His hand drifted up her back to cradle her head. She tasted need and passion in his kiss, knowing that, right now, all that mattered was how she made him feel. And for the next few hours, she'd allow herself to fall into him, to wrap herself in him, around him, through him. To allow his heart to beat for her, for her breath to sustain him.

Theirs was a profound connection, and Sutton's stomach and heart fluttered. Would she ever feel this way again?

'Sutt, you need to let go! I can't hold on any longer,' Gus growled, lifting his hips and going deeper. She couldn't take any more of him, and her eyes crossed as she chased a whirlwind of pleasure and colour flying across a starry sky. Gus slipped his hand between them, finding her clit and rolling it under his finger. She hurtled towards that vortex, faster, faster...

The bands of the tornado flew apart and she shattered with it, splintering as she experienced the most intense orgasm of her life. Gus drove into her, and despite the barrier of the condom, she felt his pumping release. She wrapped her arms around his neck, keeping her face buried against his neck, unwilling to step off this white-knuckle ride.

Gradually, she loosened her tight grip on him, her muscles relaxing as she melted against him, confident he would support her weight. She now weighed nothing – excellent – and breathing was overrated.

Gus pulled out but his hand skimmed her bottom, her hips, her back. She knew he had to get rid of the condom –

good housekeeping was important – but she didn't want to move just yet. She couldn't.

'What the hell was *that*?' he asked, kissing her shoulder.

Sutton pressed a gentle kiss on his chest before rising, her eyes fixed on his sexy mouth. He'd shaved but stubble was just appearing, and because she loved his facial hair, she rubbed her cheek against his jaw. 'If you need an explanation then we didn't do it right,' she teased him.

'Any more right and I'd be dead,' Gus told her. She felt movement and looked down, her eyebrows raising at his half-stiff cock. No *way*. And seeing him hard, for her, caused her nipple to tighten and her clit to throb.

She had genuinely believed she was done, she'd come super-hard. Her last orgasm had been so intense she couldn't handle another one so soon. Gus smiled, pushed her knees apart and slipped two fingers into her, finding her wet and oh-so-willing.

'You need to clean up, get another condom,' she murmured against his mouth. As brilliant as sex with him was, they didn't need to make an Alsop-Langston baby.

Gus curled his fingers inside her and rubbed her clit with his thumb. 'You know what's better than having an amazing orgasm?'

Up until tonight, she would've said salted-caramel ice cream, being upgraded on a long-haul flight, a tangy cider after a sea swim on a super-hot African day. 'What?' she asked, not able to think of one damn thing.

'Having another one.'

Yes, please.

Chapter Thirteen

Late on Saturday afternoon, the day of Conningworth's Christmas market, Sutton walked down the hill into the village, beanie on her head and her gloved hands jammed into the pockets of her coat. She'd been on twin duty for most of the day, which involved her following them around the market until Moira rescued her at two, taking them back to the hall, kicking and screaming, for a nap. Thankful for the break, Sutton returned to Gus's house, made herself a sandwich and watched TikTok reels for an hour, slowly making her way through two cups of coffee.

Gus had left the house very early that morning, but not before sneaking into her room and waking her up by climbing into bed, naked. To be clear, his climbing into her bed didn't wake her, but his hand between her legs did. Before she was properly awake, he'd made her come twice. She wasn't complaining.

She'd only caught glimpses of him earlier as he rushed around, organising extra power points, consulting his iPad, his calm facade never dropping. Sutton patted the small flask she'd tucked into the inside pocket of her fancy coat. As soon as she reached the green, she intended to track her lover down, pull him behind a tree or a tent and give him a belt of whisky and a quick snog. That should keep him going until he could collapse later.

Damn, it was cold. Crisp air burned her nose and throat, and the hedges and fields were peppered with patches of clumpy snow. As she reached the outskirts of the village, coming in past the open pub and the closed butcher, the scent of pine and wood smoke drifted over her. Sutton took a deep breath. It was the essence of Christmas. Despite it being colder than a polar bear's toenails, the village, nestled in the heart of the valley, the cold waters of the lake forming one border of the town and the snow-capped mountains another, was a pretty place to live.

'Jared, you tosser!'

'Wanker!'

Sutton jumped as teenagers on bikes sped past her, trading insults. She grinned, happy to know the spirit of goodwill to all men was alive and well amongst the younger population of the village. Dodging a couple pushing a pram, their baby all but buried under blankets and a snowsuit, she looked toward the green and smiled.

The afternoon was fading but twinkling lights on the charming wooden cottages cast a warm and magical glow over the busy green. A huge, unlit Christmas tree stood in the middle. A local celebrity – a jockey or a disc jock, Sutton couldn't remember which – would enjoy the honour of lighting it up later. It looked magical, picture-postcard pretty. Good job, Mr Christmas.

She walked past the stalls, stopping now and again to linger when a stall or a product caught her interest. The stalls were lavishly decorated – she'd heard there was a prize for the best-dressed one – and Sutton sighed over the handmade chocolates, the handwoven woollen scarves and the selection of cheeses on display. Thanks to Gus, she now had a little money, but she needed to save it, so she gave the stall owners, bundled up in big coats, smile after regretful smile.

Sutton looked around, inhaling the delightful aromas of freshly baked gingerbread cookies, roasted chestnuts and spiced mulled wine. A quartet of Christmas carollers drifted through the crowd, looking a little bored and quite tired. Sutton wondered whether they were on their sixth or tenth rendition of 'O Come All Ye Faithful'.

Small bonfires in steel dishes were placed round the edge of the green, and people congregated around them, coffee or mulled wine in their hands. Kids and adults alike, under the supervision of a village volunteer, roasted marshmallows over the hot coals. Sutton stumbled as a toddler careered into her knees and she put her hand on the child's head to steady herself. She looked up into the eyes of her hot dad who grinned and apologised. Hot dad was accompanied by an even hotter mum, who scooped up her kid in a practised move and balanced the pretty toddler on her hip. She sent Sutton a suspicious look and a tight smile. *Relax, lady...jeez.*

Sutton watched them walk away. The market was a place for families, and everyone but her seemed to have someone. Grannies and granddads handed out money to pre-teens, teenage couples melted into one another, and people walked hand in hand. It felt like she was the only single person in Conningworth that night.

It didn't matter that she was sleeping with Mr Christmas. No one knew they were and she would be moving on soon.

Sutton stumbled as she was rugby-tackled from behind. Just managing to remain upright, she twisted to see Felix's sturdy arms around her knees. Rosie, dressed in a pink beanie, red jacket, blue jeans and bright yellow rain boots, held Gus's hand. Her pink-with-cold face was smeared with candy floss. Great, Rosie on a sugar high was hard to handle.

Felix also had candy floss; his was blue. But the candy floss from his face was now on the thighs and knees of her jeans. Oh, well. Looking clean and presentable was overrated.

Gus lifted his head as their eyes met. He wore dark jeans, boots and an open thigh-length coat over a red jersey, and Sutton tried to make out the figures on his Christmas jersey. Were those? No, they couldn't be...

When he stopped in front of her, she pulled open the lapels of his jacket to look at his jersey again. Trying not to laugh, she patted his chest. 'Nice jersey, Gus.'

He looked down and shrugged. 'Moira brought it down this morning and insisted I wear it. It's Christmas and, according to the law of Moira, I need to look the part. She also wanted me to wear an elf hat and pointed ears. After five minutes of arguing, we settled on me wearing this jersey.'

Right. She bit her lip. Moira? The Lady M gave him that jersey? Really? It took all she had to hold back a giggle.

Gus squinted at her. 'What's wrong with it?'

Felix saved her from answering. 'Sutton! Sutton! Sutton!' He patted her thigh, each pat getting harder. So close to laughing, she was happy to move off the subject of Gus's jersey. She looked down at his son. 'Yep?'

'I saw Santa! He's over there, and I'm going to ask him for an octopus or a shark!'

Sutton blinked. 'And where will you keep an octopus or a shark, Felix?' she asked, intrigued.

'In Nan's pond! If I can't get either of those, I want a giant squid!'

Alrighty then. She looked at Gus, who rolled his eyes.

'I might also ask for an otter. And a mouse,' Felix declared.

'I think you should limit how many nature programs he gets to watch, Gus, or else you'll end up with a zoo,' Sutton suggested. She looked down at Rosie. 'And what are you going to ask Santa for, Rosie?'

'A snake to eat Felix's mouse!' she retorted, glaring at her brother. Right, they'd been fighting but Sutton knew better than to ask. She'd learned that much.

Rosie crossed her little arms and looked across the lawn to what Sutton knew to be a makeshift but quite realistic grotto. Why did people put Santa in a cave when everyone knew he lived in a perfectly nice wooden house in Lapland?

'Do you want to sit on Santa's lap?' she asked Rosie, changing the subject.

Rosie shook her head. 'I'm not allowed to sit on strange people's laps, so I think I'll stand.'

Fair enough. 'But I don't think he's the real Santa,' Rosie added, her little nose wrinkling.

Sutton and Gus exchanged a puzzled look. Before they could reply, Rosie spoke again. 'Shall we call the police and tell them so they can lock him up?'

'Santa decided he needed a break from Santaland and sorting presents, possibly from Mrs Santa too,' Sutton lied, enjoying herself, 'so he decided to visit the boys and girls of Conningworth village.'

Rosie shook her head. 'Nope.'

Sutton, out of ideas, handed the problem over to her father. 'I called his chief elf,' Gus told his daughter, using his highly effective don't-argue-with-me voice. 'He said the real Santa is coming and Chief Elves aren't allowed to lie.'

Rosie squinted at Gus, her little hands on her hips. 'Does that mean normal elves are allowed to lie?'

Sutton knew he wanted to roll his eyes and silently praised him for his patience. 'Nobody is allowed to lie, Rosie.'

Thankfully, the thorny problem of whether the Santa in the grotto was the real deal or not was put onto the back burner by Moira's arrival. Looking smart and chic in a black coat, black trousers and a bold, fuchsia-coloured scarf wrapped around her neck, she stopped and placed her hand on Gus's back. 'How are you doing, darling?' she asked.

Gus smiled at her and bent down to kiss her cheek. Their mutual affection was easy and authentic. Sutton understood why he'd never want to hurt, or lose, her by telling her about Kate's infidelity.

Moira held a steaming cup of coffee, and Sutton wondered how she'd feel if she ripped it out of her hand. Moira, being as wonderful as Gus thought she was, handed her the cup. 'It's not blow, but it is addictive.'

They'd taken to teasing each other about Moira thinking she was a drug mule, and Sutton grinned. But calling it blow? She exchanged a *WTF* look with Gus. Moira, seeing their confusion, rolled her eyes. 'You know…the big C, snow, white lady.'

Gus darted a look at the twins. 'We've got it, Moi.'

Sutton could easily imagine Moira hunched over her computer, typing the phrase 'slang words for cocaine' into her search engine and testing them out. Sutton gestured to her scarf, which looked to be cashmere. 'That's a beautiful scarf.' And since they were talking about clothes, she'd yet to thank Moira for loaning her the dress on Thursday. So she did. 'I so appreciate it.'

'Gus said you had a nice time and I'm glad.'

Sutton shifted on her heels. Moira *had* to know she and Gus were sleeping together. How did she feel about that?

After all, her daughter had been Gus's wife. Sutton forced herself to meet her eyes and in the faded blue she saw sadness, but more than a hint of practicality. Her daughter was dead, but Gus wasn't.

Felix turned his attention to Gus. 'Daddy, are you coming with us?'

Gus tapped his finger against the side of his iPad and winced. 'Sorry, mate. I have so much to do.'

Moira shook her head and pursed her lips. 'Angus, you *need* to be there with them.'

He frowned at her. 'I'm busy, *Moira*, I have a market to run! And have you seen the length of that queue?' He gestured to a long line of parents and kids.

'Sutton and I will join the queue and we will text you when we are near the front,' Moira informed him.

Gus sent her a 'help me' look but Sutton shook her head. This was between him and his mother-in-law. Besides, she agreed with Moira. At four, the wonder and magic of Christmas were starting to resonate with the twins, and Gus needed to be there to witness memories being made. And at the very least, he needed to take photos of the kids' first interaction with Santa, real or fake.

In the queue, a child sneezed, and they all winced at the volume of snot coming out of one little person. 'To stand in that queue, I'd need a stiff drink. And an antibiotic,' Gus muttered.

Moira sent him a cheerful smile. 'Good thing Sutton and I are much, much tougher than you and we'll do the bulk of the queue-standing.' She waved Gus away. 'Go now, so that you can get back.'

Moira and Sutton watched him walk away and, when he was out of earshot, Sutton turned back to Moira. 'That's a nice jersey you bought him,' she commented. Did she know what she'd bought? Sutton wasn't sure.

'Isn't it?' Moira replied so blandly that Sutton wasn't sure whether she was taking the piss or not.

'Um…uh…did you take a proper look at the jersey? Did you notice the reindeer look like they are…' Oh God, how could she put this delicately?

Moira gurgled with laughter. 'It looks like one reindeer is doing the other doggy style,' she said through her snorts. 'I couldn't resist.'

Sutton belly-laughed. 'I wonder how many people have noticed?' she asked, wiping the tears out of her eyes.

'Lots, I hope.'

'You do know he's going to kill you, right?' Sutton was unable to stop giggling.

'*Pfft!* He doesn't scare me. Our Mr Christmas is a bit too serious about his responsibilities to the town.' Moira squeezed her arm before stopping and tucking a loose strand of her hair beneath her beanie. The sweet gesture made Sutton swallow. Damn, she liked this woman.

'I don't know why you are here or how you came to be in his life, Sutton, but you're helping him to enjoy life more,' Moira said.

'Doesn't he always?' Sutton asked, choosing her words carefully.

'We both know he doesn't, Sutton. Or not as much as our resident Mr Christmas should.'

Sutton held back when the twins approached Santa sitting on his glorious throne – a throne in a grotto? – but Gus placed his hand on her back and pushed her forward so she stood in front of him and next to Moira, close enough to hear the twins as they greeted Santa. Rosie, deciding Santa wasn't an imposter or, more likely, hedging her bets, decided it was okay to sit on the arm of his chair. Felix bounced on Santa's knee and Gus thought about all the little hands and streaming noses he'd encountered that day. He hoped the dude had a decent immunity from coughs and colds.

An exhausted-looking elf, around Sutton's age, leaned against the throne, and Gus saw her swallow a yawn.

Santa released a couple of rather authentic-sounding 'hohoho's' and asked the twins their names. They were off.

'Rosie Kate Langston,' Rosie immediately responded, never shy about putting her best foot forward.

'Hello, Rosie,' Santa replied. He patted Felix's knee. 'And you are?'

Felix darted him an anxious look. Rosie was extroverted and forthright, but Felix could be shy and reserved, and Felix wasn't a fan of new situations. Gus knew he desperately wanted to run over to him but also knew he would lose face with his sister, so he sat there, looking like a petrified mouse.

'He's Felix Angus Langston,' Rosie informed him, and everyone else within a two-mile radius. Did she think Santa was deaf?

'Keep it down, Rosie,' Gus told her.

Santa looked grateful. 'Have you been a good girl, Rosie?'

Rosie considered her answer. 'Mostly,' she replied, with her normal candid honesty. 'I have good days and bad days.'

'Don't we all,' Tired Elf muttered.

'I can work with that,' Santa answered. 'And you, Felix?'

Felix slowly nodded. 'I've been good.' Yeah, sure. Earlier they'd screamed blue murder when Sutton stirred their hot chocolate anti-clockwise instead of clockwise. She'd thought they wouldn't notice. They did. *Loudly.*

'Then what can I bring you for Christmas?' Santa asked.

Rosie took a deep breath. 'Here we go,' Gus muttered in Sutton's ear.

'I would like a new art set and a yellow scrunchie for my hair, and a new doll that cries and a doll's house, and new clothes for my doll. And I would like a big chocolate and a purple bicycle and a witch's hat and a—'

'Dear God,' He whispered as Rosie recited her list of wants. 'How the hell am I supposed to remember any of that?'

'It's mostly the same as she put in her letter.' Moira patted his arm.

Gus watched Rosie and in his baby daughter's sweet face, he caught traces of the woman he'd loved, who gave him his kids, a family, this village. Rosie had Kate's mouth, her direct approach, her inability to bullshit. So what led her to lie to him, to her having an affair? For the first time, he found he could ask the question without seething. It had been such a busy year, and they'd both been juggling babies and their businesses, her more than him. Did she feel unseen? Unappreciated? Had she felt hemmed in, did she feel like her life had just stopped when the twins came along?

Did the why still matter?

Gus jammed his hands into the pockets of his jeans, his thoughts miles away. He couldn't change the past, and being angry with her, still feeling cheated was the equivalent of beating yourself after the horse bolted. It was time to stop remembering Kate for what she did in that hotel room, and remembering her, and still loving her, for being a brilliant mum, a loving daughter and the Boss Girl of the village.

As old-fashioned as it sounded, he needed to forgive her…

'—and I want a unicorn that poops rainbows,' Rosie emphatically declared.

Sutton tipped her head to look up at him. 'Fair. Because a unicorn isn't a unicorn unless it poops rainbows,' she whispered.

He snort-laughed.

'Why don't we give your brother a chance—' Santa suggested.

Nope, Rosie was on a roll, and she clapped her hands together and looked to the heavens, an angelic little girl who could feature on old-fashioned greeting cards. *Oh, Kate, look at your warrior daughter and your stunning son. We did that.* 'I want an elf.'

Santa's bewilderment increased. 'An elf? One of *my* elves?'

Rosie patted his cheek. 'Do you need a nap?'

She's all you, Katie. 'Uh…no?' Santa replied.

'Then keep up! I want an elf, a nice one, who can live in my cupboard or under my bed. He can be my friend and do what I say, all the time. And if things don't work out, I'll give him back to you next year.'

Sutton slapped her hand over her mouth, trying not to laugh. Gus put his hand over his eyes. Only Rosie could come up with something like that. *She's your daughter, Kate.*

'Noted. I'll have to think about that.'

Rose pouted. 'That's what Daddy says and then he always says no.'

Accurate. It was his go-to phrase when he needed them to shut-the-fuck-up. Thankfully, Santa turned his attention to Felix, who was still wide-eyed with stage fright. 'And what do you want for Christmas, Felix?' he asked. Santa pushed his shoulders back, obviously expecting the same barrage of demands he received from his twin.

Gus raised his eyebrows. If he asked for a shark or an octopus, as he did earlier, Santa might lose it.

Felix's eyes widened with anxiety, and Gus mentally urged him to find his words. Rosie started to speak for him, but Santa shushed her. 'I asked Felix, Rosie.'

Gus nodded his approval. He knew Rosie spoke for Felix far too often. Felix looked at him and Gus smiled. 'It's okay, Fee, you can tell him,' Gus encouraged him, jamming his hands into the front pockets of his jeans and hunching his shoulders.

Felix leaned into Santa's shoulder and placed his mouth near Santa's ear. They all strained to hear him, including Rosie, but his words were too low. When he pulled back, Santa frowned at Gus. What the hell did he do?

Santa patted Felix on the back, gave a couple of muted 'hohoho's' and told Tired Elf he was taking a break. The twins ran over to Moira, and over their heads, Gus saw Santa jerk his head.

'You're on his naughty list,' Sutton said, jabbing him in the ribs with her elbow. Excellent. What the hell did Felix say?

Gus told them he'd be back and walked away to join Santa behind the black fabric. He was back in five minutes, feeling bemused and, God, so exhausted. Gus looked down at Felix. 'What did you ask Santa for, Felix?'

'I asked him for bread, peanut butter and jam,' Felix replied, his attention caught by a clown on stilts. 'I want to try that!'

'Over my dead body! 'Moira retorted, equally puzzled. 'Why on earth did you ask Santa for food, Fee?'

Felix looked at her as if she were daft. 'Because I like

bread, peanut butter and jam,' Felix replied, bored of the topic. 'And if I have my own, then I can eat it whenever I want.'

There was no denying the logic of his statement.

Gus pulled Moira and Sutton away from the kids. Entranced by the jester on stilts, they didn't notice. 'Santa is a social worker. He says that kids in need often tell Santa they want food because they are hungry, or they need a coat or a blanket because they are cold. It's a good way to identify kids, and families, in trouble.'

'And he thought Felix might be in need?' Moira asked, looking shocked.

Gus shook his head and grinned. 'No. He just wanted to piss himself laughing for a minute. And then he wished me luck and told me I'd need it to raise Rosie.'

He ran a hand through his hair before pushing his jacket back and shoving his hands into the front pockets of his jeans. 'Like that's news!'

An older man passed them, did a double take at Gus's jersey and laughed. Gus looked down at his chest. 'And why does everybody keep looking at my jersey?' he asked, glaring at Moira. 'What's wrong with it?'

Moira patted his arm. 'Nothing, darling. It's just a picture of reindeer pulling Santa's sleigh.'

Did he hear Sutton singing the words 'and humping as they go' or was that his imagination?

Chapter Fourteen

The next morning, after a full English breakfast, cooked by Sutton and finished by Pig and Pepper, Gus suggested a walk for the twins to run off some energy. Sutton, who loved the twins but found their zero-to-hero enthusiasm exhausting, quickly agreed. Between them, they bundled the kids in jackets and boots, beanies and gloves, found Pig's balls – the throwing kind – and left the house.

Their boots made crunchy sounds on the frosty grass as they crossed the garden to the gate leading to Conningworth Hall grounds. As soon as they reached the boundary, Pig headed straight for the pond, but a whistle from Gus, and a fast yellow ball heading in the opposite direction, had him braking and galloping away.

The twins and Pepper ran behind him, and when Pepper lagged too far behind, Rosie stopped and ran back to him, urging him on. Gus pushed his hand through his hair.

'Sometimes I wonder how I'll raise a wilful, opinionated child, then I see her kindness and I think she'll be okay.'

Sutton slid her gloved hand into the back pocket of his jeans. 'Of course she will. Rosie's a boss girl, there's no doubt about it, and that's perfectly okay. The world needs more strong, kind women who take no shit.'

Gus sent her a sweet smile, one she didn't often see. Thank God, because if she did, it would make leaving him hard. Or harder. She had just a week left in Conningworth, no time at all, and her heart plummeted to her toes. Not wanting to spiral, she changed the subject. 'That's a nice sweater you're wearing today,' she told him, her tongue firmly in her cheek. The jersey under his coat was a solid black crew neck, nothing special. 'But I prefer your Christmas one. You know, the one with the picture of reindeer humping each other.'

He sent her a sour look and Sutton giggled. 'Bloody Moira!' he muttered.

'I'm sure the lady who designed it meant to depict reindeer pulling a sleigh.'

'That'll teach me to pay better attention to what I wear, and not to trust my mother-in-law. I now know who has a dirty mind in this town.' Pig dropped two balls at his feet and Gus lobbed them one after the other, double the distance she managed. Pig looked confused, sent Gus a WTH look and sat on his foot. Gus pulled a ball from his coat pocket and threw it and Pig took off.

'So who has a dirty mind, Gus? Apart from Moira, Will and Eli?'

'Pretty much everybody.'

Sutton laughed, enjoying the glint of humour in his eyes. He was strong enough to handle being teased and she liked that. 'Next time, check the design before you pull it over your head.'

'I will certainly be on the lookout for reindeer porn,' Gus told her.

Sutton's laugh carried across to the twins, who turned back to look at her. She waved at them and lifted her eyes to meet Gus's. Her breath hitched when she saw his expression: part affection, part terror, part humour. He gripped her chin with his glove-free hand and lowered his mouth to hers, and she half closed her eyes, humming with anticipation. Then her phone vibrated in her back pocket, and she groaned, frustrated. It was a stunning winter's day, she was with her favourite people, and her family only sent voice notes and text messages. And funny videos.

Layla. It could only be Layla finally, bloody *finally*, returning her calls. Sutton jerked, reached for the phone and looked at the screen. *Best Bitch* flashed across her screen in all caps. Maybe she should change that, maybe she should drop the 'best'...

'It's Layla, I've got to take this,' Sutton told Gus, who frowned. She pointed to a bench under a beech tree, her gloved fingers trying to answer the call but sliding off.

'Shit, shit...' If she missed her call, it might take another three weeks to get hold of her ex-best friend. She couldn't miss it. 'Dammit, why won't it work?'

Gus snatched the phone from her fingers, hit the green

answer button and held it up to her ear. Sutton released the air she'd been holding and closed her eyes. She opened them to mouth a thank you to Gus, but he was already walking away from her, giving her the privacy she needed. She walked over to the bench and sat, her heart thumping.

'Sutton, are you there?'

Sutton nodded, realised Layla couldn't see her, and didn't bother with a 'hello'. 'Where the hell have you been, Layla? In bloody Mauritius? And God, where the hell is the money you owe me?'

'Is that all you care about?' Layla shot back. Her voice, always shrill, was at top volume. 'Is that how you talk to me? After everything we've gone through? After everything I did for you?'

'I'm sorry, I just…' Wait! Why was she apologising? She was the one who might've landed in an untenable, could've-been-really-bad situation if Gus hadn't offered her a place to stay. 'You borrowed money from me, promising me you'd pay it back within two days. It's been months! And then you ghosted me. Then you went on holiday!'

'I paid you back this morning,' Layla told her, her tone cold. 'Your money should hit your account any moment.'

'For real?' Sutton whipped back. Before she left home, her trust was instinctual, unwavering. Now it…wasn't.

'Look, if you're going to be bitchy and snotty, I'm hanging up. You always get like this when you feel threatened, Sutton,' Layla's tone softened, and Sutton heard her long sigh. 'Why are we fighting, Sutt? Are you really that mad at me?'

Sutton started to explain she'd been a hair's breadth of being homeless, that she'd run out of options, when she heard Layla's sniffle.

'I'm so hurt by your lack of faith in me, Sutt. I know it took longer than I said it would to repay you, but I'd never let you down, Sutton. I've *never* let you down before.'

Sutton swallowed, instantly catapulted back into a maelstrom of emotion. Layla, just a year older than her, was there when Athol, her stepdad, told her he was leaving, and Layla held her while she cried. Layla helped her take care of her siblings – feeding them, bathing them, getting them dressed, while her mum sobbed in her room. Layla made her realise that if someone didn't do something, they'd run out of money and social services would rip her family apart. Layla called her mum in to help, and they got her mum out of bed and found her a job. It was Layla who got her through those dark, dark times. Without her input, so wise despite being so young, Sutton would've drowned in the hopelessness of their situation.

She owed her. She always would. Okay, she messed up repaying her, messed her around, but was it a good enough reason to sacrifice a friendship? Everyone messed up at some point.

'So where do we go from here?' Sutton asked, rubbing her fingertips over her forehead. She was grateful to have money in her bank account, of course she was, but there was still a rip in their relationship. Could it be mended?

'I need you to get over yourself by the time we meet up in London,' Layla informed her. 'Because, shit, I'll be pissed if, after flying for twelve hours, you meet me with a sulky face.'

Whoa, she wasn't the one who messed up here. 'Hold on a sec…'

'The hotel room is booked and paid for, right? And did you manage to get tickets for a show?'

Sutton, her head reeling, had to work hard to keep up. 'Two actually, *Abba Voyage* and *Book of Mormon*. I booked them before I left and I told you—'

'And you've organised the sightseeing and transport, right?'

'Again, I did that before I left Cape Town.'

Sutton wondered if Layla included the money she owed her for their London expenses when she did the bank transfer earlier. She doubted it. Damn, this wasn't how they were. She didn't react like this. But being nearly homeless, definitely broke, had made her a little bitter.

'Just checking, there's no need to be testy.' Oh, Sutton thought there was. Layla had yet to apologise. 'I have a couple of things to sort out before I leave, but I should be good,' said Layla.

Should be good? What did that mean? Sutton tasted panic at the back of her throat. 'Are you suggesting there might be a problem with meeting me in London, Layla?'

'God, Sutton, *chill*. You are always so damn over-dramatic,' Layla retorted.

Sutton stared at her feet. The ice in her veins wasn't due to the icy wind or freezing day. If Layla didn't meet her in London, if she didn't make the effort to be there after everything she'd put her through, then their relationship couldn't be salvaged.

'It's a celebration of our thirtieth birthday, Layla. We've been planning this for half our lives. Christmas and New Year in London,' she stated, proud at how calm she felt. This UK and Europe trip was her biggest dream, sometimes her *only* dream, and spending the week between Christmas and New Year with her best friend would be the culmination of a lifetime of her scrimping and saving.

'I know!' Layla howled. 'Will you stop hounding me about it?'

Sutton pulled her glove off with her teeth and gripped the bridge of her nose with her thumb and index finger. 'If you can't make it, tell me now, Layla.'

'Will you stop overreacting, for Christ's sake? You are so fucking dramatic, Sutton, so emotionally demanding. I said I'll be there, so I'll be there, okay?'

Sutton wanted to believe her, but was she being a sucker? Was she too emotional or was Layla manipulating her? It felt like she was, but Sutton couldn't be sure because she'd never been at odds with Layla before. Not to this extent, anyway. Oh, Layla could be difficult, and she was strong-willed and selfish. When she didn't get her way, she often sulked or nagged until she did.

She'd never felt this off-balance, this unsettled, and a huge part of Sutton wanted to tell her to forget their trip, to cancel their plans. And Layla's cavalier attitude to her well-being and safety made her question her love and loyalty…

'I'm so sorry, Sutton,' Layla softly stated, sounding

genuinely contrite. 'I'm feeling so sick about the position I put you in, so guilty that you went through so much stress because of me. And you know that when I feel vulnerable, or when I know I've done wrong, I lash out.'

She did. Layla hit first, and said sorry later. It was just the way she was.

'I can't wait to see you, it's been so long,' Layla continued, sounding so much like the girl she grew up with. Sutton's eyes watered. 'This place isn't the same without you and I feel like I've lost a limb. Maybe that's why I'm so grouchy. I can't wait to see you, to have you all to myself for a week! We'll have the best time, Sutt.'

Maybe.

No, of course, they would. They'd just hit a bump in the road, all they needed to do was to reset their friendship. Layla was *her* person, it would be fine. 'Shall I meet you at Heathrow?' she asked.

Layla released a low laugh. 'God, no! My flight gets in around two, I'll be with you by three, or half-three at the very latest. I'll text you when I land.'

'And when you leave,' Sutton told her. 'I know you are bad at texting and communicating, Lay, but this is important to me. When you leave and when you arrive, 'kay?'

'You're such an old nag,' Layla replied. Was she teasing her or was there a hint of steel in her tone? Or was she just being, as Layla frequently accused her, overly sensitive? 'Look, I've got to go. See you soon, sweets! Love you!'

Layla had reached her limit of phone talking and Sutton

knew there was no point in trying to keep her on the line. And maybe that was a good thing because if she didn't start to move soon, she might go into hypothermic shock.

'Love you more,' Sutton replied, but Layla had dropped the call before she completed her sentence.

Sutton slapped her phone in her hand as she walked back to Gus, still throwing balls for Pig. The twins chased each other, and Pepper shivered, looking thoroughly miserable. Sutton scooped him up and tucked him under her jacket. He buried his snout under her arm and pretended he was dead.

He was her own little hot water bottle.

'I take it that was the elusive Layla?'

Sutton avoided Gus's eyes and nodded, shifting from foot to foot. 'Yeah.' She wanted to tell Gus she'd been repaid but thought he might ask her to leave. She swallowed, her throat tightening. He didn't have to know, did he? It was just another week…

No, of course he did. She had to tell him. 'She paid me my money…' she said, biting her bottom lip.

'And?'

'And I can move out if you like. I have money to go back to London, to support myself until I have to return to Cape Town.'

He adjusted the beanie on her head, pulling it down. 'Stay until you need to go, Sutton. Spend Christmas with us if you want.'

Oh man, she'd love to. She'd love to wake up to shouted yells in the morning, childish excitement, watching the twins rip open their presents. She wanted to eat Christmas lunch with them, and doze on the sofa in the afternoon, preferably in Gus's arms, while the kids played with their new toys. Then, later that night, she wanted to work off all the extra Christmas calories rolling around in Gus's big bed.

This was all becoming too tempting, and that was why she had to leave. She needed to put a lot of distance between her and Gus, because if she stayed, if she indulged, she risked falling in love with him. Oh, maybe she was a little there already – or even a lot – but she could *still* walk away. But if she stayed past Christmas...

Having him, and the twins, in her life would complicate her plans and her career. She'd come to the UK to work in trauma therapy, to help those who experienced the worst strokes, survived almost fatal car crashes, and experienced the severest traumatic brain injuries. She could work as a bog-standard OT back in Cape Town, but she wouldn't gain the knowledge, experience or on-the-job training she would working at a hospital like Fort John's. And working at Fort John's, if she got the job, meant working in London. Even if he was wildly in love with her, Gus wouldn't give up his career for her...

Should she give hers up for him?

Oh, it was all so complicated! He owned two businesses, and was raising the twins. This was *his* village, the place he loved and was a part of. It wasn't like he had a nine-to-five job he could walk away from. No, if they wanted to be together, she would have to make the sacrifices, and Sutton wasn't ready to do that. This was *her* time, she'd worked hard for it. She deserved it. She had to look after herself and her interests, because nobody else would.

Oh, and a crucial point, Gus hadn't asked her to stay... Because, let's not forget this either, they'd only known each other for less than a month!

'*Can* you stay for Christmas?' Gus nodded towards the twins. 'They've been asking.'

She shook her head. 'I would, but I'm meeting Layla on the twenty-fourth, we're spending Christmas together in London.' Pig dropped the ball at her feet and Sutton kicked it over to Gus, who bent down to pick it up. He stood up and in one loose movement sent the ball hurtling towards the small wood in the distance. Pig, besotted, hurtled after it, ears flying. Pepper released a gentle fart.

Gus pushed his bomber jacket back to place his hands on his hips. 'You're still doing that?' he demanded, frowning.

'Yes. Why wouldn't I?'

He glared at her. 'Oh, let me think...she borrowed money from you, didn't repay it and you nearly ended up homeless! She hasn't returned any of your calls—'

'She—'

'—and until now, she hasn't emailed you or reached out on social media. She went on holiday before she paid you back!' Gus continued, relentless.

Okay, he had a point. But he didn't understand how bad Layla was at keeping in touch. She'd called, repaid her the money and apologised. It was time to move on. 'She's a terrible communicator and she knew I was mad at her, so she didn't—'

'*Bullshit*, Sutton! Stop making excuses for her. She borrowed cash from you, put you in a frankly dangerous position and now everything is forgiven because she repaid you?'

When he put it like that, doubts crept in. But she couldn't just toss her out of her life, there was too much between them. 'Gus, you don't understand. Layla has been my rock, the sister of my soul since I was a child. She's been there every step of the way. She got me through some pretty tough times, kept me laughing, kept me going.'

He scratched his forehead. 'So she was there for you in a crisis?' Pig dropped the ball at Gus's feet but Gus's full attention was on her. 'Okay, granted. She was there. So tell me, how does that give her a pass for putting you in a vulnerable position, for causing another crisis for you?'

She didn't know.

'And, while you're looking for an answer to that question, I'd be interested to hear when last she celebrated your triumphs, your happiness.'

What was he talking about? 'I don't understand,' Sutton said, confused.

'I don't have many mates, Sutt, but the ones I do have are there for the good and bad. Malcolm and Grant were there for me in basic training when I thought I'd jack it in, and they talked me out of it. They came to stay with me when I lost Kate. They also make time to come to the important events in my life, like the twins' first birthday party. Will and Eli brought over a bottle of whiskey the night I signed the lease for my premises, and we sat on the cold floor and got wasted. They toast my small victories, the twins sleeping through the night, a new client, as loudly as they do my big ones. It's not only about being there when there's a crisis, Sutton.'

Sutton rolled through her memories. Layla didn't attend her uni graduation ceremony – she had stomach flu – and she sulked the night of her twenty-first. Sutton couldn't even remember when last she told Layla about her successes with any of her patients. She'd told Gus, Moira, Eli and Will more in the few weeks she'd been in Conningworth than she'd told Layla in a decade. Gus might have a point.

But she couldn't chuck in their friendship. Not yet. Sutton stroked Pepper's back. She couldn't believe she was having such an intense conversation while holding a pot-bellied pig. 'So, here's a question for you, Gus.' He lifted his eyebrows and waited for it. 'If Kate lived, and if she came to you and said, "Hey, I'm sorry, but we've got a lot between us, we can't just chuck it in," would you give her another chance?'

He grimaced and she carried on. 'You told me it wouldn't have been an easy decision to make, and my situation is complicated too. Love, platonic, familial, sexual, it's all complicated. She's my very best, and oldest friend, Gus,' Sutton said quietly. And she'd fight for her and her friendship, as long as she could.

'Maybe. But are you hers?' he softly asked. Gus lifted his

hand and stroked his thumb across her cheekbone. 'You've got to work this out for yourself, Sutton. I hope you do.'

He lifted his finger and thumb to his mouth and released a piercing whistle. The twins looked up and he gestured for them to come back. They didn't argue, and Sutton knew they were freezing and ready to return home.

Rosie looked around for Pepper and when she realised she was under Sutton's coat, she slipped her hand inside and stroked her pig's little butt. Then she looked up at Sutton, her blue eyes serious. 'You'd make a good mum someday, Sutton. I love you a lot.'

The edges of Sutton's heart started to melt. Then she wondered where Rosie was going with this. Oh, God, she hoped she wouldn't ask her to be their mum. None of them were ready for that.

'Thanks, Rosie-Roo,' Sutton said, deliberately not looking at Gus. 'I love you too. And I hope I have a boy and girl as wonderful as you and Felix one day.'

Rosie cocked her head to the side, incredulous. 'Yeah, you wish. Can we have hot chocolate when we get back? Stirred clockwise?'

Yes, Your Majesty.

Sutton both hated and envied those people who could wrap Christmas presents with all the precision of an aircraft engineer. Her wrapping skills were more *'let's get this done'* than *'let's make it look exceptionally pretty'*.

She was only halfway through wrapping the presents she'd ordered online for the kids, and she was already bored with it. Choosing the presents was fun, paying for them better – it was so wonderful to be able to spend money without experiencing a burning hole in her stomach – but wrapping them was something she'd happily farm out. Unfortunately, none of Santa's elves were around to help her out.

Her presents, her problem.

Sitting on the floor next to the coffee table, she picked up a plastic dinosaur and flicked its tail with her thumb. How the hell was she supposed to wrap this up? Honestly, if she was President of The World she'd make one standard size for women's clothing – earning gratitude from women the world over – and she'd make it law that all presents had to come with a wrapping rating. Buyers could factor in how hard they were to wrap before making the purchase.

Sutton opened a new roll of wrapping paper and reached for the scissors. She had to get this done before Will and Eli dropped off the twins after an afternoon at the Beatrix Potter Museum. Sutton knew Will and Eli would buy them all the books and a few stuffed toys. It didn't matter that Christmas was around the corner, the boys loved the twins and thought, as their honorary uncles, they were entitled to spoil them. And they did, with gleeful abandon.

She'd miss Will and Eli's easy friendship when she left, would miss how unjudgmental they were, and their positive attitudes. The Langstons were lucky to have them in their lives. And maybe, if she was very lucky, she'd retain contact with them after she left in a few days. *Stop it, heart, you're not withering away. This is the way it has to be.*

Her phone rang with a video call and Sutton was grateful for the distraction because once she started that *'God, I don't want to leave'* spiral, it was hard to stop spinning. She picked up her phone but didn't recognise the number. She swiped the green button and looked at the two strangers on her screen. Both were men wearing sharp suits and carefully knotted ties.

'Ms Alsop?'

'Uh, yes?'

The older of the two men introduced himself as the chief recruitment officer for the Fort Johns Hospital group. Sutton gulped. 'And this is Anders Gunderson, he's the head of our occupational therapy department.'

Oh, shit! This was, essentially, a job interview. She had tape on her fingers, messy hair and her sweatshirt had a coffee stain over her right boob. *Shitdamncrap.*

The man who would be her new boss smiled into the camera. 'I'm sorry we didn't give you a warning about this call, but two of my therapists just resigned and I need new people, *fast.*'

Sutton gestured to her clothes. 'Can I take a moment to freshen up and call you back?'

He shook his head. 'I don't mind if you don't. And carry on with wrapping presents if that's what you need to do.'

Uh, no. This was one time when she shouldn't test her multi-tasking skills. Taking a deep breath, she nodded. They wanted to do this now, so they'd do it now. Frankly, she'd do pretty much anything to get this job.

For the next half-hour, Sutton answered questions, made suggestions on patient treatments and was grilled on ethics, procedure and theory. By the end of the thirty minutes, she felt like a well-used and tightly squeezed, but still damp, kitchen towel. She'd done her best, given as much as she could. She didn't think she could do any more.

Sutton watched anxiously as they made notes, both of them quiet. Then the chief recruiter looked up and gave her a small smile. The head of the department gave her a bigger one and Sutton resisted the urge to beg them to give her the job. She'd never wanted anything as much as she did this.

'Um...when do you think I might hear whether I've been successful or not?' Sutton asked, trying to sound professional.

'Right now.'

For the next five minutes, she listened, trying to take in the information, wishing she felt confident enough to ask the caller to stop so she could take notes.

'Of course, I will detail everything we discussed in an email so you can read through and digest our offer.'

Right. They were offering her a job. Her dream job. 'If you find the package acceptable, you could start work at Fort Johns Hospital in January,' Anders said.

'I'm sorry, Anders, but I'm not a UK citizen. I have to go back to South Africa and apply for a work permit from there. And you have to send the British Consulate—'

'I've got that in hand, Ms Alsop,' the head of personnel

replied. 'We're working to expedite the process. But we'd appreciate it if you could apply for a work permit as soon as possible—'

'I would go back now, but I have commitments up until the New Year. But I suppose I could cancel—' Layla would freak at their plans being changed but this was her career, her future, and she'd just have to deal.

They laughed. 'I said I was desperate but I'm not that desperate, Ms Alsop,' Anders said. 'You stick to your plans and hopefully you'll be back sometime in January.'

'Thank you so much, I'm so excited to work with you.'

She had a job! Yay.

Anders looked down at his notes. 'I'd like you in London, but I have to tell you that we have job opportunities to work in our other hospitals, we have facilities around the country—'

'But you're offering me a position at the London hospital, right?'

'Yes. But it's all in the email you'll be sent later today,' Anders replied. 'Welcome aboard. I'll see you in the new year.'

Sutton garbled her thanks, said goodbye and shot to her feet. She had her dream job…she got it! She did a little shimmy, then a boogie. Greatest day ever!

Ev-Ah!

She reached for her phone to call Layla and then hesitated, thinking about Gus's words. Would she be happy for her? Or would she make some snotty comment, something along the lines of '*it sounds too good to be true*' or '*please check your contract's small print, Sutton, before you get too excited.*' She couldn't be sure of Layla's reaction, even if she managed to get hold of her. She'd yet to answer any of the messages she'd sent since speaking to her on Sunday. Sutton wasn't sure Layla would be happy for her and she didn't want her deflating her high.

No, she'd keep this news to herself. This was *her* win, *her* achievement, *her* success. She was allowed to fully enjoy it. Even if that meant doing it by herself.

Chapter Fifteen

'I'm home!'

Sutton, still fizzing, shoved Gus's Christmas present – a lovely framed photograph of the twins she'd captured on her phone – under a couch cushion and whipped around to face the table, still covered in Christmas wrapping paper and ribbon.

Gus bent down, dropped a kiss on her upturned mouth – so normal, so lovely – and gestured to the table. 'And this?'

'I bought the kids some presents,' she told him, picking up a bottle of kids' perfume. 'On Christmas day your daughter will smell like a hothouse trollop.'

'Awesome,' he replied, walking into the kitchen. He opened the fridge, pulled out a bottle of wine and reached for two glasses. 'Shouldn't they be back from the bunny museum?'

She smiled. 'They are.' She lifted her phone and waved

it back and forth. 'Eli just sent me a voice note informing me they are watching *Shrek* and they'll give them their tea.'

Gus grimaced. '*Shrek*? Again?'

'Apparently, it's the twins' favourite movie,' Sutton said, thanking him when he handed her a glass of Chenin Blanc.

Gus snorted. 'It's *Eli's* favourite movie and he probably bribed the kids into watching it with him.'

She took a sip, and Gus sat on the couch behind her, his knee brushing her back. He leaned forward and picked up the heavy rubber dinosaur. 'Felix will love that.'

She half turned to face him and grinned. 'Actually, that's for you.'

He poked the dinosaur's face into her neck and Sutton squealed as the cold rubber hit her skin. She batted the toy away. 'How was business at the shop?'

'Good,' Gus replied, before grimacing. 'Though I did have various people pop in to see if my sweater was PG-appropriate.'

The day after the Christmas market, some wag – Sutton's money was on Eli, though he'd vociferously denied it – posted a headless polaroid photograph on the corkboard in the pub that served as one of the town's off-line noticeboards. Gus's X-rated jersey was on display and 'Mr Christmas is on the naughty list' was neatly printed on the white border. Mmm, the handwriting was a little feminine...Moira? She wouldn't put it past her either.

'Fucking Eli,' Gus muttered.

Sutton grinned. She was going to miss the little eccentricities of this village: that the villagers gently teased

Gus, that every adult was partaking in a Secret Santa £5 present swap – she'd drawn Emily, a teacher's aide at the twins' school – and that the village took Christmas so seriously. She loved how much they adored their Mr Christmas and his little family. And how protective Gus was of them and Kate's legacy. She'd miss this place, him most of all.

But she'd…God, she'd landed her dream job. She wiggled her butt on the carpet, a little like Pepper did when she was over-excited.

Gus, because he was super-perceptive, raised an eyebrow. 'What's going on, Sutt?'

Her glass wobbled and Gus plucked it out of her hand. Unable to keep the news to herself for one second more, she blurted it out. Gus, because he was Gus, and completely wonderful, immediately leapt to his feet and swept her off her feet and whirled her around. 'That's amazing, Sutt! I'm so, *so* proud of you!'

She looped her arms around his neck, locked her legs around his hips and laughed. 'I am such a freaking rock star!' she told him.

'You really are.' He kissed her nose, then her mouth, briefly taking the kiss deeper before pulling back. 'I'd love to take you to bed to help you celebrate—'

She laughed. 'Why, how *noble* of you, Mr Langston!'

He grinned. 'But there's every chance that the kids will be back soon. So, what if we get Moira, Eli and Will over, and crack open a bottle of champagne to help you celebrate?'

'You have champagne?' Sutton asked. She'd never seen any in his wine rack.

'Moira does, she lives on the stuff,' Gus assured her. And that was just another reason to like his mother-in-law. Still holding her, his arm under her butt, Gus brushed her hair off her forehead. 'What do you say?'

He was so happy for her, and proud of her. It radiated from his eyes, and his smile was so wide it made the fine lines at the corner of his eyes deepen. Gus was sincerely, authentically thrilled for her.

This was what she wanted from Layla but suspected she'd never get. Although she'd known him for less than a month, Gus was already a better friend than Layla. The thought rocked her. And made her so sad. Tears burned her eyes, and she buried her face in his neck, sighing when both his arms tightened around her.

He gently rubbed her back. 'Hey, what's this?'

She shrugged and kept her face where it was. The circles on her back continued. 'As well as excited, you must be feeling relieved and overwhelmed, babe. You've had a tough couple of months, Sutt, and you've held it all together. Your happy tears are completely understandable.'

Yeah, happy tears. She'd let him believe that; it was far easier than telling him the truth. She was more than a little in love with him and wasn't sure how she'd manage to walk away from him. She wanted to keep the twins, and him, in her life, but how could she do that when they'd be living in different places? Her in the city, him in the country and hours apart?

She might be crazy about him, and adored his kids, but she wasn't ready to bury herself in a small village, to be a stepmum. Her staying in Conningworth wasn't an option. She needed to take the Fort John position, she'd worked too hard and sacrificed too much to pivot now. She hadn't come this far to only come this far.

She loved Gus, more than she'd loved any man before, but love wasn't enough. Love didn't stop her real dad from leaving, her lovely stepdad from doing the same. Her mum loved her, but that didn't stop her from treating her as an unpaid nanny and maid. Love didn't stop Layla from letting her down.

Sutton couldn't cope with Gus disappointing her. She couldn't risk letting him fully into her heart and her life, and him stomping all over both. Wasn't leaving now, on good terms, a better option than her falling deeper and hurting more later? And it wasn't only her who had skin in the game: she had to think of how a relationship between her and Gus would impact the twins. The kids weren't that attached to her yet, thank God. And while Gus liked her, and he definitely liked sleeping with her, she didn't think he'd dropped into '*feel more for her than I should*' territory.

Honestly, being a rational, sensible and clear-thinking adult was *exhausting*.

———————————

'I think you should stay here, in Conningworth, with us,' Gus said, his words a rumble. He leaned against the doorframe of her room and folded his big arms. Sutton sent him a glance and sighed at his stormy expression. She knew he didn't want her to leave, but, even if she hadn't been meeting Layla, what was the point of staying? They were just delaying the inevitable.

Sutton rolled a T-shirt and tucked it with the others next to her jeans. Her backpack was already three-quarters full. She darted a glance at Gus's watch and saw she had an hour before her train for London left Kendal. It was a fifteen-minute ride from Conningworth to Kendal, and she still had to say goodbye to the twins.

'I promised Layla I'd meet her in London, Gus. She's flying in from Cape Town, we've booked and paid for the hotel –' and no, Layla hadn't paid her share of those costs, but she'd tackle her friend about that when she saw her '– and we have theatre tickets and plans to visit the tourist attractions.'

'Hmpf.'

Look at him, all bolshy and bold and beautifully grumpy. She wanted nothing more than to lay her head on his chest, to sink into his warmth and strength, but she knew that if she did that, she might not be able to pull herself away. 'As I told you, we've been planning this trip since we were fifteen years old, down to the last detail. We have itineraries for every day. It's been our longest dream, the best way to celebrate our thirtieth birthdays.'

His gaze sharpened. 'It's your birthday?'

'Midway through January. Layla's is in November, so we thought December was a good compromise. We'd lie awake night after night talking about London, about doing this,' she continued. She winced at her robotic tone. Where was her enthusiasm, her excitement? Was she trying to convince him or herself?

'You *can* change your mind and do something else.'

Of course she could, but not about this. She needed to reset her relationship with Layla, to see if they could find a new normal. And she needed to walk away from Gus while she could. Before she got hurt. 'After so many years of planning? I can't, Gus. You wouldn't do that either.' Sutton picked up her laptop case and shoved it down the back of her battered backpack. 'But maybe I can come and see you guys when I return to the UK.'

'For a quick shag?'

Ouch, that hurt. She looked at him, trying to keep it together. 'What we shared might've been short, but it wasn't cheap, Gus. Don't make it sound like it was.'

He winced and nodded. He rubbed his hands up and down his face and when he dropped them, she saw his contrite expression. 'Yeah, sorry.'

She also noticed he didn't comment on her visiting them in the new year. Didn't he want to see her again? Was he the *'when it's over, it's over'* type? Was this it? The end? Were they done? Should she push the point, or see how it played out? She didn't know…

'She's going to hurt you, Sutt.'

His change of subject threw her. 'Who?'

'Your friend Layla.' Gus gripped the doorframe above his head, and his sweater rose to reveal a strip of skin above the band of his cargo pants. The muscles in his arms bulged and he looked cross and competent, frustrated and as sexy as hell. Sutton lowered her eyes, reminding herself she didn't have enough time to jump him. What were they talking about? Right, Layla.

Sutton glanced at her silent phone. Layla's plane was in the air now, had been for a while, but she hadn't received a text message from Layla telling her she was excited to see her, nor had she sent her a photo from the airport. She hadn't heard a damn thing.

She didn't know if Layla had left Cape Town or not. Oh, she could check her social media pages, or reach out to their mutual friends, but she was reluctant to do that. She wanted Layla to value their friendship enough to be on that plane.

'How will she hurt me, Gus?' Please don't say it, please don't say it.

'She won't be there, Sutt.'

And there it was, her biggest fear. 'How do you know?' Sutton retorted, annoyed by his confidence. 'You don't know her!'

'I know she's let you down, and she hurt you. Why are you going back for more? People show you who they are, Sutton, and when they do, you should believe them.'

Philosophy by Gus. Great, it was all she needed. He didn't understand, and she couldn't explain, that she needed to go to London. Not only to put some emotional distance between her and Gus, but to be able to say to herself, and anyone who later asked, including Layla, that she'd kept her word, and she'd given her all. She didn't want to have any regrets, and as long as she could prove she'd shown up for their friendship, she'd be able to hold her head high.

Her actions would show the value she put on their relationship, and Layla's would do the same. If Layla was there, they could try to repair what was now a broken and unbalanced relationship. If she wasn't, well, she'd deal with that too.

'Why can't you move on from her?'

Oh, that was rich! He said it like it was so easy to do, like moving on was something she could do with the snap of her fingers, a toss of her head. 'Like you have?' she whipped back.

He slowly lowered his arms to his sides and his eyebrows formed into a deep frown. 'What? What does that mean?'

'You haven't moved on either, Gus! You own a Christmas shop and every December you throw yourself on the altar of fake worshipping it, but you hate it! You wear stupid sweaters you hate, decorate your house within an inch of its life, and take on this role of Mr Christmas while loathing every second of it!'

'You know why I'm doing it! I'm doing it for my kids, to keep the memory of their mother alive—'

'Oh, *bullshit*. Your kids will want to know what their mum's favourite colour was, whether she liked apples or oranges, and how much she loved them, not whether she owned a Christmas shop or was a pillar of the community. It's like you take her out at Christmas and dust her off.'

'You don't know what you are talking about!' Gus whisper-shouted.

'And you don't know what you're talking about when it comes to Layla!'

Her chest was heaving, so was his. *Shit!* A fight wasn't what she wanted, she didn't want to leave on a sour note, with harsh words between them. She wanted him to remember her, this crazy, time they shared, with a smile and laughter. She didn't want his last memories of her to be of them fighting. She lifted her hand. 'I don't want to argue with you, Gus. Please let's not do that.'

He placed his hands on his hips and shook his head. When he looked up at her, his eyes reflected his torment. 'I don't want you to go,' he admitted, his voice low and rough.

'I know. I don't want to go either. But I have to,' Sutton told him. 'You *know* I do. Because if I don't I will regret not going.'

'Because I'm not enough to stay for?'

Oh, how could he think that? It was the first time she'd seen him look a little lost, vulnerable, and she was in danger of him ripping through her defences. 'No, Gus, of course not. I have to leave because *I'm* not enough for *you*, or the twins. I'm not ready to be what you need.'

'And what's that?' he asked, his eyes pinning her feet to the floor.

'A partner, a stepmum, someone who is here all the time.' Sutton stuffed the rest of her clothing into her pack, no longer caring about creases; she just needed to get it done. 'I need to take this job, Gus. I need to do more, be more, and think of myself first. Can you understand that?'

Gus nodded, his hand raking through his hair. 'I wish I could say that I didn't, but I do. I'd never want Rosie to stop doing what she was passionate about because of a man, and I can't ask that of you.'

The next sentence would be harder to say, but that wasn't an excuse to leave the words unspoken. 'And there's not enough between us, not yet, for me to stay.'

His nod was confirmation that he wasn't in love with her. Would she change her mind if he was? Probably...*not*. Love wasn't enough...

'I know,' he agreed. 'Who makes life-changing decisions after just knowing someone for a month?'

Sutton blinked back tears. 'Especially when I brought mayhem into your life.'

'It would've been an exceedingly busy but quite boring time without you, Sutt.'

Gus walked over to her and folded her in his arms. 'Maybe we'll work something out, Sutt. Not today, or tomorrow, but maybe sometime in the future.'

She appreciated him saying that, but what else could they be but over? Realistically, London was only two hours away by train, but she would be working long hours initially, and doing shifts. As one of the new hires, she'd have to work over weekends, and when and if she had some days off, was it right to disrupt the Langstons' weekly routine by dropping into their lives for a brief visit here and there? Gus wouldn't be able to spend his days with her, he still had two businesses to run, and their time together would be limited. Wouldn't that frustrate her more? Would it make returning to London harder, a sticky plaster removing several layers of skin week after week after week, a wound never able to heal?

Wouldn't it be better to just call it quits, say thanks for the good times and move on? For her and for him, for the twins. She didn't know what to do, or which way to jump, and she hated it.

She felt Gus's lips in her hair and tightened her grip around him. She inhaled his scent and stood on her tiptoes to push her nose into his neck. Being held by him was heaven; she felt safe here, protected. Cherished. But safety was an illusion, being protected a myth. She had a career to establish, a friendship to sort out, and a pair of big girl panties to pull on.

Real life wasn't a fairy tale. It was gritty and hard, with less champagne and truffles and more beer and burping.

Gus pulled back and looked at his watch. He pulled a face. 'You'll miss your train if we don't get a move on,' he told her, brushing the hair off her forehead, his expression tender. 'But feel free to stumble onto my lawn, pissed or sober, any time you like, Sutt.'

He kissed her lips, before pulling back. 'By the way, I've been meaning to tell you something since we met.'

She lifted her eyebrows, internally wincing. She still couldn't remember anything after she fell, and she suspected she'd made more of an arse of herself than Gus had let on. '*What*?'

'You punch like a girl.'

She rolled her eyes and handed him her sweetest smile, appreciating his effort to lighten the atmosphere. 'Of course I hit like a girl. And you could too, but only if you hit a little harder and aimed a little straighter.'

His big laugh rolled over her. 'God, I'll fucking miss you, Sutt.' He dropped a hard but quick kiss on her lips. 'I'll see you downstairs.'

It took all the willpower she possessed, but Sutton only allowed her tears to roll when she heard his big feet clattering down the stairs. Leaving was the right thing to do, she knew it was.

Then why didn't it feel like it?

Chapter Sixteen

I n London, Sutton sat in the lobby of the hotel off Piccadilly Circus, her eyes on the door. She'd booked in four hours ago, and after dumping her rucksack on the bed closest to the door – Layla preferred the bed next to the window – she headed back to the lobby to wait. After an hour of surfing the news on the net, she asked the person at the front desk whether Layla had left a message for her. But nope.

Layla's plane had landed two hours ago, she'd checked the airline's website, and Layla should be here by now. Even if she didn't have international roaming on her phone, there were always places where she could find free Wi-Fi, and she could've sent her a WhatsApp message or email. But her phone remained stubbornly silent.

Another hour passed and Sutton watched as twilight fell over the city, and a light, cold rain darkened the pavement outside. Guests, happy and jolly guests – it was Christmas

Eve, after all – walked in and out of the lobby, occasionally sending a curious glance.

She didn't blame them; she knew what she looked like. White-as-bone face, big eyes, her lower lip wobbling as she tried not to cry. Layla was now hours late and Sutton had to accept she wasn't coming.

There would be no walking through the streets of London tonight, taking in the Christmas displays in the windows of Harrods and Selfridges, no ducking into a pub for a pint and fish and chips. They wouldn't be spending the rest of the night catching up or trying to reset their relationship. Oh, it was hard to accept, to even consider, but Layla didn't care enough to make the trip.

Or to let her know.

After everything, how could she do this to her? This was as bad as a breakup, as hurtful as having your heart broken. Sutton twisted her wrist with her other hand, mentally begging Layla to walk through the lobby door, for her to have an excuse she could believe. Hell, with *any* excuse. But no, the next woman through the door was just a normal traveller, hauling her big suitcase behind her.

Layla wasn't coming, Layla wasn't coming...

A part of Sutton still wanted to believe there was a decent reason for Layla's non-arrival. Maybe something happened back in Cape Town to prevent her from getting on the plane. Or maybe she was sick, had injured herself, or maybe someone else was sick and injured. She was lying to herself, and Sutton hated doing that. Layla wasn't here because she couldn't be arsed to be here. It was that simple…

Find your courage, pick up the phone and find out where she is, Sutton. Sutton punched in Layla's social media handle and scrolled through her posts. In a photo, posted six hours ago, Layla stood in the centre of a group of friends, all dressed in silly Christmas hats, in their favourite restaurant. *Celebrating Christmas 2023 with my besties! No place I'd rather be.*

Right. Well, *shit*. Layla's IG post was a gut punch, and fairly clear, but Sutton still needed to hear it from the horse's – or the ass's – mouth. So she dialled her number and this time, after it beeped a few times, the call rang through. And a male's voice grunting a hello crossed the miles.

Sutton was pretty sure she recognised his voice but didn't want to get into a conversation with Lyle, Layla's on-off bed buddy. 'Put Layla on.'

Lyle didn't argue, but just passed the phone on, which involved some grunting and bedclothes rustling.

'What?'

Sutton was sitting in a London hotel, but Layla was having afternoon sex. Of course, she was.

'Merry Christmas Eve, babe,' Sutton said, her words as hard as bullets.

There was a long silence on Layla's end. 'Sutton…shit, look, can I call you back?' Her laugh was as fake as the hotel's Christmas tree. 'Lyle is about to give me my Christmas present…'

Layla looked at her phone, unable to believe what she was hearing. There was chutzpah and then there was pure, undiluted bullshit. 'Are you *kidding* me? Where the *fuck* are you?'

Another silence. 'Didn't you get my email telling you I couldn't make it?'

Really? Did Layla expect her to swallow this load of crap? 'You didn't send an email, Layla.'

'I had a problem with my visa, it didn't come—'

'How stupid do you think I am, Layla? I know your visa was approved, you told me it was months ago. I paid for the hotel, and for everything else, upfront. All you had to do was get on the fucking plane. But you're not on the goddamn plane!'

'I—'

'And the reason you're not on the goddamn plane is because you didn't want to be on the goddamn plane. Because you never wanted to do this!' Sutton shouted. Several people turned to look at her and she stared them down, daring them to mess with her. Right now, she was angry enough to take on Attila and his armies, Boudica and the merry men of Marvel. And she would kick all their arses.

'Will you stop yelling?' Layla whined. 'I've got a headache and you're not helping.'

Another lie. Layla frequently used a headache as an excuse to get out of an unpleasant conversation or situation. 'Oh, sorry,' Sutton shot back. 'I thought yelling was the appropriate response to my best friend not being here.'

Sutton rubbed the back of her neck, her eyes on the tiles beneath her feet. There was a sweet wrapper under the coffee table, and every time the lobby door opened, or someone walked through the rotating door, it jumped from one place to another. That was like her and Layla; her direction was decided by the winds of Layla's temper. And it stopped, here and now.

'I don't know what I did to make you treat me like a bag of crap, Layla—'

'You left.'

Sutton blinked, not sure she'd heard her correctly. 'Sorry? What was that?'

'You left me. You went to the UK, and you went to Florence, and Barcelona and Munich.'

She did and she'd had fun but so what?

'You weren't supposed to do that.'

Sutton frowned. 'Why the hell not?'

'I didn't go.'

Sutton frowned, trying to keep up. 'I invited you to come with me. I begged you to come with me. I mean, you had the money, and you could've let your partner run the business, you told me you would do that.'

'I had too much on.'

No, she didn't. What she didn't have was control. Over her little world, and her friends. Layla liked knowing where she was, having her boxes stacked, and operating within her little fiefdom. She hadn't been sure how the rest of the world would react to her – newsflash: it didn't care! – so she'd stayed where she was.

Understanding and clarity flashed, as bright as the African sun. Layla resented her for being brave enough to go without her. She disliked Sutton for doing something without her, for flourishing and having adventures. She was supposed to stay in Layla's shadow.

Knowing Sutton would never refuse her anything, Layla used the ruse of needing a loan, and not paying her, as a way to force her to come back home. When her manipulations didn't work, Layla repaid her and then punished her by not meeting her in London. It was games and gaslighting, manipulation at its highest form.

Sutton remembered what Gus once said to her, about Layla not celebrating her victories. 'I got a hell of a job offer a few days ago,' she said, testing her. 'It's effectively my dream job.'

'It won't work out, you'll miss home too much,' Layla shot back. 'They probably do things way differently over there and you'll find yourself messing up. I give you three months.'

Wow. *Nice.*

'Wrong answer, Layla,' Sutton said, exhausted.

'Look, can I call you back later, because we're late for another function...'

No, she wouldn't allow her to duck out of this conversation. 'It's the wrong answer because you're wrong for me, Layla, you've probably been wrong for me for a long time,' Sutton said, vaguely aware of tears pouring down her face. This felt like a death, a rip in the universe, a fracture in time. But she had to step through it, go over or through it and deal with it. 'You don't need to worry about calling me back, Layla, because we're done.'

'Jesus, Sutt, can you lay off the dramatics for a moment? I'm tired—'

'We're *done*, Layla. Don't call me, don't email me, don't do anything… I wish you well but this, whatever this is between us, is over.' Sutton pushed the ball of her hand into her eyes, not wanting Layla to hear her sobbing. She needed to be cool and calm, to sound determined and collected. If she didn't, Layla wouldn't believe her and would think she was just overreacting and being over-emotional. She had to get this right the first time.

Because she only had the strength to break up with her once.

'I can't be friends with someone who's jealous of me—'

'What the hell, Sutton? I'm not jealous—'

Sutton spoke over her. 'I can't be friends with someone who needs to keep me in my place, who can't be happy for me, who put me in a situation where my safety was compromised. I'm no longer willing to be your doormat, Layla.' It was a wound being lanced, oh-so-painful but also an intense release of pressure. 'Have a good life, Layla. Don't contact me again.'

'What? Hell, are you being serious right now?' Layla screamed. Right, the message had, finally, landed. 'What the hell are you doing?'

'I'm saying goodbye to someone who is no longer good for me, saying goodbye to a friendship I treasured but which no longer serves me. I'm saying goodbye to my past,'

Sutton calmly replied. 'Merry Christmas, Layla. I did love you and I'm so grateful for the good memories.'

'Sutton, wait…you *can't*.'

'I can. And I am.'

Sutton killed the call and fought the urge to curl up into a little ball on the hotel's couch, to assume the foetal position to avoid the sharp stabs of grief, the rolling waves of nausea, the wet, hard repeated slaps of pain. She needed to get up, and go to her room. She could fall apart there. Cry and sob.

The wound went deeper than she thought, was wider and yuckier. A minute ago, she thought she'd only need a couple of plasters, now she required a trauma surgeon and a transfusion. And no, she wasn't being dramatic. She'd been strong, and done what she needed to do, but now she felt like she'd fallen in on herself. Devastated, emotionally whipped and utterly exhausted.

She had to get to her room, the sooner the better. Pushing herself to her feet, she swayed, and half bent down to grip the arm of the chair. She didn't want to be alone, didn't think she could be. Not right now. But her family was so far away, and she was the one they called, not the other way around. The one person she would've called when her world fell apart was the source of all her unhappiness.

Sinking back down to sit on the couch, she realised she would get more sympathy, and attention, from Will and Eli, from Moira. And from Gus…

Gus was who she most wanted to talk to. If she heard his rumbly voice, she'd feel steadier, more in control, able to cope. He radiated strength and capability and he'd pass some of his strength to her.

She fumbled through her contacts, looking for his number. Finding it, she rubbed her hand across her wet cheeks and dialled. She shouldn't get her hopes up; it was Christmas Eve, and he'd be busy. What was on the town's Christmas schedule tonight? There were carols by candlelight on the green, followed by hot chocolate. But it was still early, he would still be at home, trying to corral the twins. Or, more likely, at the shop, serving last-minute customers.

'Sutt? Are you okay?'

She gulped, and her throat constricted. She managed, just, to tell him no.

She heard his F-bomb. 'She didn't arrive, did she?'

She shook her head, remembered he couldn't see her and managed another no. She placed her elbow on her knee, her palm on her forehead and wished she could teleport herself back to Conningworth. But she'd walked away, so confident about Layla's arrival, unable to imagine her disappointing her again. He'd tried to warn her, but she hadn't wanted to listen.

She wiped her tears away with the heel of her hand. 'I'm sorry, I shouldn't have called you. I can't run back into your life because I ran headfirst into a brick wall.'

'Okay, I need you to listen to me,' Gus said in what she recognised as his officer-commanding voice. It wasn't any louder than normal, but she heard steel in every word. 'This is what you're going to do.'

She was a strong, independent woman but she *so* needed someone to tell her what to do. Just this once. 'I'm listening.'

'Go to the front desk and ask someone to call you a taxi. Then go up to your room and wash your face and blow your nose. In the outside pocket of your rucksack, the one with the South African flag sewn onto it, there's some cash for the taxi and there's a train ticket. The train to Kendal leaves at six o'clock from Euston station. I'll be there when it arrives.'

Oh, that's exactly what she wanted to do, Conningworth was where she needed to be. Tonight, maybe for the rest of her life. 'Gus…'

'I'll see you later, Sutt,' he gently told her. 'Don't let me down.'

Having been through something similar herself, just ten minutes ago, she had no intention of letting that happen.

Gus punched the red button on his phone and rested the screen against his forehead. The urge to find his car keys and belt to London and find Sutton was strong, and he had to take a few deep breaths before that passed. After calling Eli over to watch the twins, he yanked on his coat and slipped out the back door, needing to walk off his anger and frustration. The cold air slapped his cheeks, carrying the faint scent of damp earth and pine. The trees, bare of their vibrant foliage, stood tall and statuesque, stoically waiting for spring.

His boots hit the ground and crunched through the thin layer of powdery snow. As always, being outside, in nature, soothed him and the hot licks of his temper faded away. Gus hit a narrow path, enjoying the solitude, and trying not to think of Sutton in London, possibly in tears, pushing her way through the Christmas crowds.

He knew this would happen, knew Sutton's friend would let her down. That was why he bought a ticket and tucked it away because he knew only one person would show up.

Because that's what Sutton did, she showed up. Sure, they hadn't met under the most auspicious set of circumstances, but showing up – for her brothers, for her friends, for the people she loved – was what she did.

Unlike Kate…

No, that wasn't fair. As he decided at the market, he couldn't keep judging Kate, and everything she did and everything she was by her affair. She'd cheated on him, but being an adulterer wasn't *all* she was. She'd been, before the craziness of being a mum of twins, running everything in Conningworth, her responsibilities to the Hall, a wonderful life partner, fun and feisty and fantastic. She'd loved the twins, and still, probably, loved him. She'd stepped out of her life for a few weeks or months – he didn't know whether she would've stepped back into it, and he would never know.

The temperature suddenly dropped, and Gus lifted his collar and buried his bare hands in his coat pockets.

He reached a small clearing, and a sense of calm settled

over him. He leaned his shoulder into a thick tree trunk, enjoying the quiet.

It was time to let the anger and the resentment, the guilt at not knowing why she had an affair, go. He needed to remember her for what she was, not what she did. His wife had been wonderful, a Christmas nut, crazy about their kids and for most of their time together, crazy about him. And he still loved her, and always would. He no longer needed to keep up the facade of loving Christmas, throwing himself into the projects she loved to remind himself she was a good person who did good things.

But Kate's story was over, and he needed to write a new one. One that included him being a little more truthful, maybe more open. Being involved in so many Christmas projects kept him from being with his kids, and he needed to spend more time with them. If Sutton hadn't helped him these past few weeks, his kids would've had a fairly unimaginative Christmas. He wanted to enjoy the season with them, and not watch them enjoy it.

He also wanted to share his coming Christmas's with Sutton. While he knew he'd have his kids around for, hopefully, forever, Sutton was a different story. She was at a different stage of her life, she needed different things than what he did. And that was...

Problematic? Frustrating? Yes. Insurmountable? No.

It was what it was. He couldn't change her, he couldn't change the situation. He could either be a part of her life, on her terms, or not. If he demanded more from her than she could give, then he'd lose her.

And, shit, he'd already lost too much, sacrificed too much. He wasn't prepared to let her go without a fight.

Gus turned to retrace his steps back to his always chaotic house and the demands of his children, and his busy life. He'd do what he could to make it work. His best was all he could ever do.

———

Sutton sat on a worn window seat on the packed train, her gaze fixed on the shadows beyond the passing landscape, but lost in the past. Ignoring the man next to her who was dictating notes on a complicated deal into his phone, and the woman opposite her making rapid charcoal sketches – she would be forever immortalised as 'Woman Falling Apart On A Train' – Sutton kept her head turned away as a series of messages pinged on her phone.

I can't believe you are doing this!

Are you seriously tossing away a two-decade friendship?

Why are you hurting us like this, Sutt?

They were all from Layla, variations on the theme, ranging from desperate to devious to bitter and bolshy. She ignored them all but couldn't stop the memories from rolling over and through her. The many afternoons they spent practising their dance moves to the latest club beats, trying to look both cool and sexy. How they screamed with laughter at horror movies, the many 'I've got my period and I hate the world' or 'Come and get me, I'm drunk' texts. Layla standing back when Sutton asked the pharmacist for the morning-after pill Layla needed, and Layla feeding her ice-cream when she had her tonsils out. Holding hair back as they puked, keeping an eye on each other's drinks in clubs. The rhythmic clatter of the train's wheels was a melancholic soundtrack to the video clips playing on the big screen of her mind, and within the sound she heard the repeated chant of 'Layla is gone...Layla is gone...'

Sutton saw her wan face reflected in the window, her swollen eyes reflecting her profound confusion. How had they come to this? She rested her head against the cold glass and wrapped her arms around her chest, her head a hundred pounds heavier than it was when she made this same journey earlier. Her shoulders sagged lower, and she clenched her fists tightly, banging them softly against her thighs.

She was going back to Conningworth, in a worse state than when she'd left. And looking worse too. But this time it was by choice, it was her choice to go back to Gus, to re-enter his life, sober this time. Sutton bit her lip. She was wasting a week's accommodation in London, giving up her tickets to *Abba Voyage* and *The Book of Mormon*, wasting the London Pass. But money, usually so important to her, didn't matter.

She needed Gus. She suspected she always would.

Nobody got her like Gus, physically, mentally or emotionally. She saw him and her body said, 'Yes, please, take me to bed.' Oh, it was easy to objectify him. He was a good-looking guy and she had, she presumed, a healthy sex drive, but her feelings for Gus went deeper than that. He walked into the room and her restless soul nodded, able to relax knowing he was near. Wherever he was, was where she wanted to be...

But, because this was real life and not a romantic comedy, it wasn't as simple as that. Gus might be single, but he had twins to raise and responsibilities in Conningworth. She wanted to be with him, and he, maybe, wanted to see more of her but...but their lives were complicated.

A simple solution for them to be together would be for her to find a job somewhere in the area. She could rent a flat in Conningworth, or a neighbouring village, so she could be close to Gus. But whether she could find a job, and whether her prospective employees wanted to hire her enough to go through the irritation of sponsoring her to stay in the UK was a big question mark.

The thing was, she still really wanted to work for Anders, to take up her job as an occupational therapist at Fort Johns Hospital. It was an opportunity she shouldn't pass up, a gold star on her resume. It was a way to gain experience in a field she truly loved. Staying around here, even if Gus wanted her to, would mean making a hell of a sacrifice. Did she love Gus – and yes, it was time to stop pretending she wasn't in love with the man! – enough to do that?

She did love him. No more doubts.

But if she gave up her dreams to be with him, wasn't she in danger of sliding into the same situation she'd just managed to extricate herself from? With Layla, it was all about her – Sutton had chosen to study at the University of

Cape Town because Layla didn't want her at Stellenbosch University, only forty minutes away. She'd initially wanted to travel for a year, but Layla talked her into only going for six months. She'd wanted to stay at home with her mum while she studied, but Layla insisted on her sharing a flat, which meant she needed to earn her portion of the rent, food and utilities. She'd allowed herself to be pushed around by Layla, so scared she'd lose her friendship if she didn't kowtow to her demands. She'd lost sight of her dreams, desires, values. Was she in danger of doing the same with Gus? Of being less, doing less, remoulding herself and her life to make sure the person she loved was happy? Was she exchanging one unbalanced relationship for another?

And Sutton couldn't forget that Gus came as a package deal. Being in his life would mean taking on the twins, something she still wasn't keen to do, not if she didn't have to, and not full-time. Was she allowed to feel that way? Could she love Gus and not want to be a full-time stepmum yet? She loved the twins and was sure she'd get there one day, but she wasn't there yet. Could one exist without the other? Sutton didn't know…and she was scared to find out.

Another tear rolled from the corner of her eye, and Sutton impatiently brushed it away. She was tired and overly emotional. She could also be overreacting. Gus telling her to return to Conningworth could be just him being nice, and she might be reading too much into him sliding a train ticket into her rucksack pocket. He liked her, and enjoyed her in bed, but he was a grown man and she doubted he'd ask any woman to stick around after just knowing her a month. She was misinterpreting his offer to spend Christmas with them. She was setting herself up to experience more heartbreak.

Just calm the hell down, Alsop. Take it minute by minute, day by day. Stop projecting and stop expecting. Your heart can only take so much kicking around and it would need time – ten years, twenty? – to recover.

She glanced at her watch. An hour to go. *Pull yourself together, woman!* And it would also be super-great if you could stop crying before you reach Kendal.

Sutton wrestled her rucksack off the train, stomping her feet as the wind whistled down the platform. The train was packed, and the platform heaved with people, all trying to get home for Christmas. Where was home? What did the concept mean? Did it mean less to some than it did to others?

Annoyed with herself – she always got too philosophical when she was upset – she looked around, unable to see Gus. Her heart sank as she hauled her pack onto her shoulder. She was about to slide her other arm under the strap when she felt the weight removed. Turning slowly, she looked up into his gorgeous but frowning face and tried to smile. 'Hi.'

'You look like shit,' he told her, touching the tip of his

bare finger to her cheek. Awesome, *just* what she needed to hear.

'I feel like shit,' she admitted. 'Go on, I know you want to say I told you so. Here's your chance.'

'I told you so.' He snapped out the words and Sutton sighed. Then she caught the sympathy in his intense eyes and realised he was upset at her being upset.

Sutton, needing to be close to him, to soak up his strength, because her legs felt like noodles and her head was about to split open, rested her forehead on his chest and placed her arms around his waist. 'I'm going to be pathetic and just rest here a minute,' she told him.

His free hand cupped the back of her head. 'Rest away,' he told her. After twenty seconds of his fingers gently massaging her scalp, his rumbly voice rolled over her. 'Did you give her the boot?' he demanded.

She gulped at the enormity of her actions. But funnily enough, she didn't doubt she'd done the right thing. 'I did.'

'Good,' Gus told her. 'I didn't know if you would.'

She pulled back to look at him, leaving one hand on his chest. Did he really think she was so weak? That she'd allow Layla to keep treating her badly? 'I might be a bit of a pushover, Gus, but I reached my limit.'

He nodded and hauled her rucksack over his shoulder. Sutton followed him through the station building, sucking in needle-sharp air. She'd kill for a cup of coffee laced with whisky. 'I'm sorry to pull you away from your Christmas Eve festivities,' she told him, hurrying to keep up with his long strides. 'How was the carol service on the green?'

'Cold,' Gus replied.

'Are the twins mad with excitement?'

'Mm. If I have to stop what I am doing or saying again because they're positive they heard the jingle of sleighbells, I might lose my shit. Moira and Will and Eli are on twin duty,' he said, nodding to his car. He opened the boot and threw her rucksack in it before yanking open her door. She climbed in and turned to look at him, standing in the space between the door and her. 'Get in, Rudolph.'

She glared at him and touched her red nose. She knew she looked a mess, he didn't need to point it out. 'Funny. But I've had a very hard day,' she told him.

His expression softened. 'I know you have. And I think you look cute with piggy eyes and a blotchy face.'

Dear God, he wasn't helping! Her bottom lip wobbled, and she stared at his booted feet, silently ordering herself not to cry. She might be dehydrated from all the tears she'd shed today, so she couldn't possibly shed any more. But, damn, there went one, then another.

She heard Gus curse and his arms encircled her. 'Sutt, don't cry. I can't handle your tears.'

'Deal with it,' Sutton muttered. 'And if you can think of a way to make me stop, then I'm happy to hear it.'

He pulled back and his sexy, lovely mouth curled up into a smile. 'Is that a challenge? You know I can't resist a challenge, Sutt.' Not giving her a chance to speak, he placed his mouth on hers, his tongue sliding over her dry lips. She squeaked, surprised, and Gus used the opportunity to slide his tongue past her teeth and into her mouth. His tongue touched hers and she was lost, found, restored.

Sutton looped her arms around his neck. Being kissed by Gus was all she needed, the only sustenance she required. He cradled her cold face in his warm hands as he kissed her, thoroughly, deeply. With intensity, and a little desperation. It had only been a few hours since she'd seen him last, but she'd missed him. No matter where she was, whether she was away from him for a day or a week, she'd miss him, miss the spark of lust, the warmth of their connection, the feeling of safety.

Gus pulled back and rested his forehead against hers. 'Merry Christmas, Sutt. I'm glad you're spending it with us.'

She kissed the side of his mouth and left her lips there. She didn't know where they'd go from here, whether there was anywhere to go, but she was glad to be with him, here. She lifted her head and noticed the first fluffy snowflakes drifting down. One or two landed on Gus's dark head. 'It's starting to snow,' she told him.

Gus pulled back, put his hands on his hips and scowled at the sky. 'Shit, snow means tobogganing down Conningworth Hill in the morning.' He closed her door and walked around the front of the car to climb in behind the steering wheel.

'Felix's idea?' she asked him as they pulled on their seatbelts.

'His and Eli's,' Gus told her, grinning. 'I'm not sure who begged the loudest.'

Sutton stood at the bottom of Conningworth Hill and brushed snow off her butt and her legs. It was Christmas morning, and so far it had been perfect, apart from the twins waking up at five-thirty and refusing to go back to sleep. At five-forty-five they barrelled into her attic bedroom and demanded she join them in Gus's bed to open their Christmas stockings. When she gently refused, because she wasn't part of their little family, the twins went away and returned with Gus, carrying their stockings. Gus, dressed in a long-sleeved T-shirt and pyjama bottoms and looking wide awake, handed her a cup of coffee, slid into bed with her and gently kissed her lips, wishing her a soft 'Merry Christmas'. His long thigh pressed against hers under the covers, and between admiring Rosie's sparkly hairbands and Felix's Matchbox cars, he sent her soft smiles. Like she was part of their little family, a piece of their puzzle.

She wasn't. She couldn't be.

Sutton stomped her feet and watched Gus run up the hill, holding Rosie under one arm and dragging the sledge. He called out a challenge to Eli, who was waiting at the top of the hill with Felix, who was bouncing with impatience. Will, sensibly, was back at the hall, helping Moira prepare their Christmas lunch. After letting the kids open their presents – the only adult present was Gus's photo frame from her – Gus had managed to convince them to eat a little breakfast, promising that if they did, he'd take them tobogganing before they went to the hall for lunch.

Sutton rubbed her growling stomach. Gus had offered her something to eat when they got home last night but she wasn't interested in food. Safe and warm, and helped by a coffee liberally laced with whiskey, she fell asleep on the couch in front of the fire and woke up in her bed in her guest room. Were they still hiding their relationship from the kids? Did they *have* a relationship? Would they go back to sneaking around, her slipping into his room when the kids were asleep, stealing panty-elastic-melting kisses when the twins weren't around? But then why did he and the twins invade her small double bed to open their stockings this morning?

God, it was all so *confusing*.

Eli and Felix won the race down the hill, and Sutton grinned when Gus accused them of cheating by starting early. Eli, his bright blue eyes sparkling, called him a sore loser and told him Mr Christmas wasn't setting a good example for the twins. Gus, making sure the twins weren't looking, lifted his middle finger at his old friend.

Gus told the kids to go back to the house with Eli and they ran ahead of him, excited by the promise of opening another batch of presents when they got to the hall. Rosie was convinced her elf was waiting for her at Moira's house, and Felix still hoped he'd get at least one of the many animals he'd asked for.

They'd ploughed through a heap of presents this morning, and she'd filled two rubbish bags of wrapping paper when they were done. There were big presents and small, silly presents, books and chocolates. Mr Christmas wasn't stingy when it came to spoiling his kids and Sutton felt her eyes burn. She and her siblings had never experienced the joy of being faced with a heap of presents under a massive tree. She was glad for the twins, but she couldn't help feeling a little bad and sad –for her siblings, and for herself.

Gus came up to her and touched her cheek. 'You're looking a little wistful,' he remarked. 'What are you thinking about?'

'Just how lucky your kids are to have Mr Christmas as their dad,' she told him, tucking her gloved hands under her armpits. 'They've had the best morning, Gus.'

'I think so,' he said, looking at the well-wrapped figures walking on either side of Eli. He gestured to the bench under the beech tree, its slats covered with snow. 'Let's sit.'

She winced and looked back at the house. She was desperate for a huge cup of coffee, and maybe a mince pie. Or six. 'It's freezing, Gus, I need coffee.'

He walked over to the bench, brushed off the snow and pulled her down next to him. He took her hand and placed it on his thigh, his hand on hers. 'Thanks for the photo of the kids, Sutt, I love it.'

She smiled at the obvious pleasure in his voice. 'Sure. It's a great photo.'

'It would be better if you were in it,' he told her. Oh, what a lovely thing to say! Before she could respond, he half turned to face her. 'About me being Mr Christmas, I'm chucking it in.'

'Chucking what in?' she asked, confused.

'Organising the Christmas market, and anything else to do with Christmas. I'm also putting the Christmas shop on the market.'

She frowned, completely surprised. 'That's...*wow*. When did you decide this? And why?'

'Recently – and because I don't want to run it, or own it, anymore. It was Kate's dream, not mine. Christmas was her obsession, not mine. It's time to let her, and the past, go.'

She squeezed his hard thigh. So she wasn't the only one who'd been through the emotional meat-grinder this Christmas.

'She did what she did, but I don't need to keep punishing her, and myself, and living in the past. Kate's memory will live on, I will make sure it lives on, for the twins, but I don't need to keep up the charade of being Mr Christmas or running the Christmas shop.'

No, he didn't. She was so glad he'd realised that. Sutton wondered how she would fit into his new life but was too scared to ask him. She didn't want to spoil what had been a wonderful day by talking about their future, and whether they could have one. She didn't think they could, not yet anyway. She needed to go home, and apply for her visa so she could take the London job; she'd regret it if she didn't. She loved him, she loved the twins, but she owed it to herself to take the wonderful opportunity she'd been offered. She'd sacrificed so much – this was her turn, her time.

Then again, love like this, a connection like they had, was rare and amazing and she didn't know if she'd experience it again. Would she walk away from all they could be for a career move?

Oh, God, she didn't know what to do!

He smiled and bent his head to kiss the side of her mouth. 'Breathe, Sutt.'

Sutton hauled in some air, felt it burn and nodded. She blinked rapidly and turned her head away to look at the imposing house, smoke billowing from its chimney. They'd have drinks in the green room, the room with the Reynolds painting on the wall, and then they'd eat in the dining room, sitting at the sixteen-seater table, joined by various friends of Moira's and Gus's. Roaring fires would ensure they didn't end up with frostbite as they ate their turkey…

'Sutton…'

She turned back to Gus and frowned at the set of keys dangling off his finger. It was the same set of house keys he'd handed her the day he employed her as his nanny. He hadn't removed the colourful wire giraffe she'd slid onto the keyring to liven it up a bit. A tiny torch also hung from the key ring. He flicked it on, then off. It emitted quite a powerful beam for an itty-bitty thing. 'Take this.'

He pushed the keys into her hand and closed her fingers over them. She licked her lips, trying to find moisture in her mouth. 'Why are you giving me a set of house keys, Gus?' she asked.

'Because I want you to think of my house as yours, and the torch is so you can always find your way back to me.'

Her eyes slammed into his. She understood the individual words but couldn't work out their context. 'Um...sorry?'

He rested his arm on the back of the bench but lifted his hand to her face. His knuckles drifted over her cheekbone. 'You have the most expressive face, Sutt, I can read every emotion in your eyes. You're sitting there wondering what you have to give up, aren't you?'

She tried to swallow the lump in her throat. 'I want to take this job, Gus, but I want to be with you too.'

'So, take the job, and be with me,' he told her. 'It's not like you'll be in Cape Town and I'll be here, Sutton. We'll be a few hours, not a continent, apart.'

When he put it like that... 'I might not be able to make it here every weekend, sometimes it might be during the week,' she told him. 'I have no idea what my schedule will be like, Gus.'

'Sutt, as long as we are *on* your schedule, I'm okay with whatever time you can give us.' He caught her wince and tipped his head to the side. 'Something I said made you feel uncomfortable. What is it?'

Sutton considered ignoring his question but then remembered grownups talked, they didn't avoid difficult subjects. She put her hands between her knees, wrinkled her nose and rocked back and forth. 'I love your kids, Gus, I do. But, God, how do I say this?'

'Say what, Sutton?'

The words gushed out of her, as if saying them fast would make less of an impact. 'I need to tell you I'm not ready to be their mum, Gus, I'm not ready to be *a* mum. I mean, I'm not saying I'll never be, I'm just not ready *now*.'

He didn't look even a little bit surprised. 'I know you're not, Sutton. And I don't need someone to help me raise them, I think I'm doing okay on my own.'

'Yes, of course you are,' she assured him, feeling like this conversation was getting away from her. 'It's just that...*crap*.'

'But you're not ready to be their mum,' he stated. 'Sutton, it's *fine*.'

'It is?' she asked, pulling a tissue from her coat pocket to wipe her drippy nose.

'Can you be their friend, Sutton? Can you be another person who loves them?' he asked.

How could he doubt that? 'I can, I do and I am!' she cried.

'Then that's more than enough, Sutt. You're enough. Exactly as you are, you're enough,' he told her, his serious eyes not leaving her face. He bent his head to kiss her mouth, then pulled back to look into her eyes. 'Can I confess something?'

She already knew his Christmas related secret, so she smiled. 'You thought I was hot the moment you saw me? Do you secretly love my singing? You really want to learn how to do the 'Pink Shoelaces' dance?'

'I did think you were hot, your singing causes cats to howl, and I'd rather die than learn that dance,' he replied, happiness turning his eyes lighter and brighter. He looked at her mouth, his gaze rueful. 'No, my confession is that you've turned my life upside down and inside out. I think I'm falling for you, Sutt.'

Sutton smiled at him, hope and happiness blooming. She lifted her fingers to touch his jaw. 'I *know* I've fallen for you, Gus.' She smiled against his lips. 'Merry Christmas, Mr Christmas. Thanks for rescuing me that night.'

'You're the one who rescued me, Sutt.' He stood up, pulled her to her feet and gathered her close. His mouth covered hers, and she sank into him as he kissed her, warming up every part of her. She felt his hand on her butt, pulling her into his hard shaft and she allowed happiness to roll over her. Then Rosie's series of quick hellos, courtesy of an ultra-loud bullhorn, caused them to spring apart.

'Merry Christmas, Daddy and Sutton!'

Gus spun around. 'What the *fuck*?'

Sutton looked past him to see Felix and Rosie standing on the back patio, with what looked like brand-new bullhorns in their hands. 'Daddy, I can't find my elf or my unicorn!' Rosie yelled into the megaphone, and Sutton lifted her hand to her ear. 'Santa forgot!'

'Bloody Eli and Will,' Gus muttered, scowling. 'Why the hell would they give them megaphones for Christmas?'

'To torture you?' she asked, grinning.

'I'm going to kill them, very slowly,' he promised. 'But first, I'm going to let the twins eat crazy amounts of sugar today and get them on a sugar high. Then I'll ask the boys to babysit tonight so I can take you to bed.'

'So, now I'm a means of retribution?' Sutton asked, laughing.

'No, Sutt, you're pretty much my everything,' Gus assured her.

Man, she loved this man. She stood on her tiptoes to kiss him but was slammed back onto her heels by Rosie's bullhorn screeching. 'Daddy, are you listening to me?' Rosie yelled.

'He also forgot to send me an octopus!' Felix bellowed.

Sutton wrapped her arm around Gus's waist, smiling as they walked up to Conningworth Hall. As far as she was concerned, and for the first time, she'd received everything she wanted, and more, for Christmas this year.

Acknowledgments

My lovely readers, thank you for spending time with my unruly crew. I had so much fun writing this book, and I only have my dream job because of people like you! I am endlessly grateful, and I hope you love Sutton and Gus, and the inhabitants of Conningworth, as much as I do.

It takes a village to raise a book...I am grateful to my writing partner Katherine Garbera, who makes sure I meet my word count and thus, my deadlines. She's also always lovely and encouraging and is a great source of new music and great playlists. Music and coffee, I couldn't write without either of them. To Charlotte and Aje at One More Chapter, thank you for allowing me to run with the story and for being so supportive. I do so love the end product!

To my author friends, Karen Booth, Reese Ryan and Joanne Rock, thanks for being the wonderful, talented goddesses you are.

Vaughan, Rourke and Tess, I like you lots and love you more. I think I'll keep you. ;)

ONE MORE CHAPTER

YOUR NUMBER ONE STOP

FOR PAGETURNING BOOKS

The author and One More Chapter would like to thank everyone who contributed to the publication of this story...

Analytics
Emma Harvey
Maria Osa

Audio
Fionnuala Barrett
Ciara Briggs

Contracts
Georgina Hoffman
Florence Shepherd

Design
Lucy Bennett
Fiona Greenway
Holly Macdonald
Liane Payne
Dean Russell

Digital Sales
Laura Daley
Lydia Grainge
Georgina Ugen

Editorial
Arsalan Isa
Charlotte Ledger
Jennie Rothwell
Tony Russell
Caroline Scott-Bowden
Kimberley Young

International Sales
Bethan Moore

Marketing & Publicity
Chloe Cummings
Emma Petfield

Operations
Melissa Okusanya
Hannah Stamp

Production
Emily Chan
Denis Manson
Francesca Tuzzeo

Rights
Lana Beckwith
Rachel McCarron
Agnes Rigou
Hany Sheikh
Mohamed
Zoe Shine
Aisling Smyth

The HarperCollins Distribution Team

The HarperCollins Finance & Royalties Team

The HarperCollins Legal Team

The HarperCollins Technology Team

Trade Marketing
Ben Hurd

UK Sales
Yazmeen Akhtar
Laura Carpenter
Isabel Coburn
Jay Cochrane
Tom Dunstan
Gemma Rayner
Erin White
Harriet Williams
Leah Woods

And every other essential link in the chain from delivery drivers to booksellers to librarians and beyond!

ONE MORE CHAPTER

YOUR NUMBER ONE STOP
FOR PAGETURNING BOOKS

One More Chapter is an
award-winning global
division of HarperCollins.

Sign up to our newsletter to get our
latest eBook deals and stay up to date
with our weekly Book Club!
<u>Subscribe here.</u>

Meet the team at
<u>www.onemorechapter.com</u>

Follow us!

🐦 <u>@OneMoreChapter_</u>
Ⓕ <u>@OneMoreChapter</u>
📷 <u>@onemorechapterhc</u>

Do you write unputdownable fiction?
We love to hear from new voices.
Find out how to submit your novel at
<u>www.onemorechapter.com/submissions</u>